For Myles Gallagher and Benjamin Eid

Responsible Distractions

A Novel

Abraham Timler

© 2022 Abraham Timler

All rights reserved. No part of this book may be reproduced, stored in a retrieval system, or transmitted in any form or by any means without the prior written permission of the publisher.

Responsible Distractions is a work of fiction. All characters appearing in this book are products of the author's imagination. Any resemblance to persons living or dead is entirely coincidental.

Book design by Sarah E. Holroyd, www.sleepingcatbooks.com
Cover design by Tamian Wood, www.BeyondDesignBooks.com

ISBN (print): 979-8-9850884-0-3
ISBN (e-book): 979-8-9850884-1-0

To Santana

THANK YOU FOR CALLING TO ME ON THE RAINY STREETS THE
other night. It was a relief to see you again, this time searching
for the church, knowing this was also my first meeting for alcohol treatment and that when we found the building we'd walk in
together. I should've been less anxious than when we first met in
the prison cell we shared overnight—was it really only two weeks
ago? And less anxious than when you saw me last week at my
arraignment.

Inside, how we were quickly pointed to the basement by the
Wednesday gospel-service regulars who realized why we were
there by our confused faces and gym attire—my pink running
sweats and your bronze shoulders exposed by halter top, clearly
too sporty for the worship service gathering in the sanctuary at
the first graceful notes of a hymn.

At next week's meeting, we'll keep our hair high in ponytails
and dress as formally as we did for last week's arraignments. And I
know you showed up to my arraignment because you were already
there for your boyfriend's earlier that morning, but again, thank
you. You were the only one there for me, save for my attorney.
And speaking of Tom, I know he's also defending your boyfriend's
higher-stakes drug charges, but if it wasn't for him getting us out,
who else could we have counted on?

As we sat down in a circle with our fellow patients in the
church basement I half expected to recall being arrested and put
in jail, but instead I thought about the nights I spent working
as a waitress in Phoenix during high school. I was reminded of

the military recruits we served dinners to on the nights before they shipped out to basic training. On Monday evenings recruits came over from the hotel across the street where the enlistment-processing station lodged them. The recruits ordered from a stripped-down menu of à la carte items and paid with meal vouchers. None of us were excited to serve them because they never tipped. The hostess would seat them in a separate room away from the candles and jazz of the main dining area. And similar to how we viewed the recruits, those churchgoers gave us pitying glances, likely happy they didn't have to face our similar reckoning. And like the church basement, the floor of the separate room where we served the recruits was scratched tile. Drinks weren't an option.

At the meeting I found it difficult to look up at the other members; their visible defeat compounded mine—slumped shoulders and absent gazes. Did you notice the guy across from me with the long hair and thorny tattoos growing down to his wrists? Or how about his shirt with the outline of a rifle? It's all I could think about when the counselor discussed trigger points.

"What triggers your binges? What thoughts, what friends, and at what times and in what places might you be tempted to relapse?"

I wanted to interrupt and let the counselor know that neither you nor I have an alcohol dependency. I'm only attending as a condition of release. Tom clarified this after my arraignment, interpreting the court proceedings for me because I'd blanked under the intimidation of the judge and how officially my name titled the court records: DISTRICT OF COLUMBIA Vs NICOLE RINSHAW. There was no better place than under the shadow of Tom's shoulders as he entered a plea of not guilty on my behalf on all counts of trespassing, destruction of property, second-degree assault, reckless endangerment, drunk and disorderly conduct, and driving under the influence. Tom accounted for both my employment as a contract auditor and for my lack of criminal record before requesting a date for a plea-bargain settlement.

"There's more than enough mitigating circumstances to work something out with the prosecutor's office," Tom had assured me.

To Santana 3

Then the counselor moved the group along to read their letters aloud. I was glad the counselor only had you and me pledge to who we might write ours. "Give yourself time to think about someone close enough who would be bettered by your sobriety. You're not required to send your letter. I'd rather you tell us as much as possible without filtering for their sake. Your letters can be an apology, a confession, or anything that allows you to sense from their perspective how your addiction has hurt those who most care for you."

Your choice to write your mom is perfect, and I think I'll do the same. There's so much to tell our moms, low as these days may be.

In the meantime, I'm writing you.

I won't be reading aloud any letters addressed to either you or my mom. I'll have something else written out and ready to go when it's my turn next week. Maybe I'll write to my younger brother, Dustin, who, partying college away on vodka, construed my drunk-driving charges as a chance to keep drinking by giving up driving in a city like Washington where a vehicle isn't necessary. I want to make clear that my charges are deserved judgment against alcohol; I'll detail an exaggerated history of alcohol abuse if admitting so shows the recovery progress intended from sharing aloud.

I look forward to traveling more than drinking anyway. All the shopping, nightclubs, gambling, and smoking weed are no longer worth the self-destruction, and while none of it required venturing beyond my limits of risk, their angrier replacements of booze and competing with other girls made for other dark places from which travel is a refreshing light. I can't remember ever not looking forward to my next trip.

Staying on the move is justified by the travel required by my job. I'm a contract auditor, as you'll remember, working for a firm specializing in third-party accounting of large government-awarded contracts. More specifically, I graduated with a political-science degree from the University of Arizona and also earned a paralegal certificate from Georgetown's one-year graduate program.

Thank goodness my arraignment's conditions of release didn't restrict me to the DC area because I'm scheduled to work down in Norfolk next week. I'd be fired if my boss, Edith, caught wind of my arrest. As long as I show up for work and my roommate, who also works there, doesn't voice her suspicions I can count on another month of pay before convictions put my job at risk.

You can see I've worried this outcome further along since our night in jail when I was too shaken to look ahead to the consequences.

And you work as a cocktail waitress? Or, as you explained your arrest, should I say *worked* now that the nightclub where you waitressed was raided? It's crazy they swept the whole place. However my memory of our night in jail might vary, you were dressed the lovely part of bottle-service stewardess, passing the unrestful night in that red dress. Complementing your dress, whose contents, undiscovered during your booking, included a vape pen, you offered me a drag. You'd said it was one of your "Vegas dresses," brought over from working the casino floors during the years leading up to leaving your desert hometown for Washington. Are you my age? I'll have to find out later. And you mentioned a two-year-old daughter back in Vegas?

Las Vegas is an annual corralling point I share with college friends. Once a year we book a weekend on the Strip and gamble too much. We also drink too much and cheer on whoever attempts to scale a pyramid or dives in the floodlit waters of the canals and fountains. We're due for Vegas again in a few weeks, but you're the expert, having grown up and worked there. Tell me more: Are you returning to Vegas once your charges are expected to clear? If you're there on the same weekend, let's meet for a few drinks. How about at the Bellagio? You can tell me more about your casino days. The late evenings holding gaze of the casino floors in backless red dresses, hovering drinks between poker tables.

My friends are planning this year's Vegas weekend at the Mirage despite my insistence on Mandalay Bay. We'll end up at Mandalay anyway, on the sixty-third-floor rooftop bar providing the best view, from pyramid to brewing volcano, of the full the-

To Santana 5

matic sweep of the glowing casinos along the Strip. We'll open the weekend at the buffet on the main floor, which is more than our annual launching point; it's an anchor point that yields a geographical essence between us and the city, dissolving the time between our previous visits.

I like to think of anchor points as identities I personalize for the cities I visit most; they're the essential experience I repeat for each city, such as shopping at the Mall of America whenever work brings me through Minneapolis. For each visit I have a picture of me leaning along the handrails of the mall's highest walkways overlooking the mechanical canopy of the theme park's Ferris wheel and roller coasters. It's a ritual by which I can step back through each visit to nearly a decade ago when Dustin and I first visited Minnesota on a snowy road trip.

When in Chicago I waste no time riding the commuter rails toward the imposing skyline. My coworkers and I will stop in for rounds at the bars beneath the Marina Towers, then gather with our pints on the balconies overlooking the canal and wave down to the tour boats gliding below. Then alone, I'm content to walk downtown, gazing at the rows of towers overcoming the clouds.

In New York, between meetings with clients at the MetLife building, I nap on the cool lawns of Central Park, sunning beneath the Frisbees sailing overhead and the laughter of children within sight of their nanny's picnic spread. I like to close my eyes to the towers looming above and descend through the cycle of seasons framed by each visit. The warming springtime blending into browning autumns until repeating like beads on a necklace. I can have New York's seasons all in mind at once, green and brown and white, until waking in the park or in our rehab sessions. By returning to the reality of the buildings and our meetings, my New York visits spread back across their time-drawn thread. This is when time's sinking passage is most noticeable. As the trips start adding up so haunts the years stretching back along the places I've gone. Time is an offsetting sadness seeping through sleep, busyness, and drinking.

In Tucson, standing at my mom's grave, I can reach all the way back to the brink of memory.

It must take this return to an unbothered toddler's half-awareness, to the years before experiential memory kicks in, to achieve the state of mind our counselor envisions when she ends our session by declaring, "Remember, there is no past." I know she means to empower us over our addictions, but what has already occurred is the entirety of our current selves. We're still the ceaseless and inescapable receiving of the present.

I remember walking you back to the metro stop when our session was over and asking what brought you to rehab, beyond just fulfilling your conditions of release.

"Probably my mom passing away," you answered. "It's been all downhill since then."

"When did she—"

"A year ago."

"Did you know it was coming?"

"No. Her neighbor called after finding her unresponsive on the couch. Heart attack."

My own mother's death might very well be why I'm also here, though this possibility didn't register until you shared your own emptied reality. My brother and I did what we could to tend the bedside of her last years. More memories follow, but mostly there remains an emptiness that I've staggered back and forth trying to fill. All the way to rehab.

I could go on about Vegas or travel or time, but our moms are why I'm writing you. Of our few commonalities shared during our night in jail—that we are Westerners, natives of Arizona and Nevada, and hoping to return from the grayer East sooner than later—it's the lasting loss of my mom that prevents me from regaining sure footing.

So, thank you, again.

Walking the streets home, the few passing faces diffuse across my moment-to-moment meditations, walking by, never to be seen again. But you have turned and walked right in and taken a seat in one of the too-few rooms of myself where the better part of my reality scatters its thin fortunes. Kick off your heels, loosen your hair, and have a seat. I'm looking forward to seeing you again.

To Santana

7

~

Our meeting with Tom in the visitation room the morning after getting locked up is a scene I chronically relive, at first to weigh the stakes of my arrest, but more and more I've started grading myself in anticipation of further meetings with him. For starters, it was good instinct to call Brad, my childhood friend who's now an insurance attorney in Phoenix, asking whether he knew any fellow lawyers in Washington. Not only did our lawyer arrive, a former law classmate of Brad's, but the more striking result was how he walked in and took immediate charge.

I once heard a morning radio show host urging his male audience to make the most of their first impressions with women because we decide within thirty seconds whether or not we *like* them. I can attest this is true by reliving the raw attraction of Tom marching through the doorway.

His first words promised better days. Having to call a lawyer was the lowest point, he assured us, likely noticing my wrecked appearance. The imprint of gravel darkened my white blouse, which was also missing a few buttons. Needless to say my makeup had worn off. So much for my chance at a good first impression. He was certainly right that he wouldn't see me looking this low again. My hair had been a mess. I faltered to answer why I was arrested. I didn't know where to begin.

"Nicole, were you told why you were under arrest?" Tom asked a second time.

"Not before I was handcuffed and tossed into the back seat of their patrol car."

"So how did the cops go about arresting you? Their guns drawn? They take you to the ground?" Tom asked, probably more an observation of my unruly appearance.

"I was pinned to the ground by security guards while the police handcuffed me." I choked over my words to the point that Tom, to save my embarrassment, shifted focus to asking your name.

"Santana," you said. "I was waitressing at a nightclub when the police stormed in."

"So, a raid? Everybody was rounded up?"

"All the bartenders, waitresses, bouncers, and everybody in the VIP room."

"Have they questioned you?"

"No."

"Busts like last night's always have a few targeted arrests in mind, then they release everybody else after questioning. If they aren't targeting you they'll want to know how well you know their targets. And if you were witness to reasons for their arrest?"

"A witness?"

"Investigators will want to know anything about drugs, prostitution, guns. Anything you saw."

"Coke is all I saw."

"Using or dealing?"

"When it was late enough the owner would invite friends into the VIP room, and there was sometimes coke."

"And you waitressed there too?" Tom returned his attention to me.

"No, sorry. We were just assigned to the same cell last night. My arrest was for wrecking my car while trying to sneak it off the impound lot where it was towed."

"So auto theft?"

"Well, it was my car, so maybe trespassing? I was pretty drunk." I lowered my eyes.

"Were you breathalyzed?"

I nodded.

"If you agree to hire me I can request the police report and get a good idea of what charges to expect at arraignment."

"An arraignment?" I sounded so dumb.

"When released you'll receive notice to appear in court. Expect to appear sometime this coming week. And expect a bail requirement before release. Call me. I can arrange posting your bail. I'll need to confirm the date of your arraignment anyway."

"Bail?"

"Expect five or ten thousand."

"Will I need bail?" you asked

TO SANTANA   9

"In your case it sounds like they're after bigger fish. If you're questioned I'm available to sit through questioning with you. They'll want your firsthand account of who was using or selling drugs or anything else illicit. After questioning I don't think you'll need me."

"But I might have to testify?"

"You could eventually be subpoenaed depending on what you know."

"I don't want to testify. My boyfriend was there last night. Arrested."

"Investigators don't let you pick and choose who you can testify against. It's everybody or nobody."

"I should probably tell you the owner is my boyfriend. I don't want to help put him away. We have a two-year-old."

"Was your boyfriend trafficking cocaine? Anything?"

"No. Can I have him call you about it?"

"If I represent your boyfriend, I'll have to immediately excuse myself in order to stop discussing this case with you. It's a conflict of interest to discuss what could be a future client's case with a potential witness."

"Martez is his name, if he calls."

"Either way, both of you call me on your release, hopefully later today. When you call, I'll also have information for a weekly meeting I'd like you to start attending this week. It's a rehab program which'll put us all in better standing with the court should either of you be charged with anything drug or alcohol related."

Tom excused himself before my weight of worries could reach him. Would my employer have to find out? Or worse, a criminal record? With Tom, at least, I can shelter my worries, and maybe that's the attraction?

~

When you asked me what brought me to Washington, I wasn't sure how much longer my arrest would allow me to work the contract-auditing position that'd brought me here. Tom assured me that my arrest wasn't anything my employer was required to know about unless it became a reason for why I couldn't show up. After this past week of relentless worry, heightened whenever Edith called me into her office, Tom's word is still holding true. My night in jail took place over the weekend, and my arraignment only cost two unnoticed hours the following Monday.

When Edith summoned me again into her office it was with Tara, my roommate. I had been able to deflect Tara's questions about where my car was, but I couldn't count on sneaking anything past Edith.

"I need you two down at the Norfolk port tomorrow," Edith said on behalf of the bearded guy seated in her office.

"For work?" Tara asked.

"Of course."

"For an on-site audit, actually," the man said. He introduced himself as Sam, the chief mate for an oil tanker contracted by the navy for at-sea-refueling support.

Can you two get down there tomorrow?" Edith asked.

Tara, without her own car, looked my way.

"I don't have a vehicle at the moment."

"Repairs?"

"Tow yard."

"If you can't get it back today, rent a car."

"I can drive 'em," Sam said, saving me the risk of talking around my suspended license. "I'm going there anyway."

Another bullet dodged: I would've been forced to resign right there in Edith's office if my arraignment's conditions of release forbade travel from the Washington area, a restriction Tom thankfully fought off during Monday's arraignment. And if travel were restricted, so much for moving back to Arizona.

"Do you own a pair of pants?" Edith turned her attention to Tara's tiger-orange sundress. "Dresses and skirts aren't appropriate for boarding a ship."

"We're sailing tomorrow?"

"The USNS *Kanawha* is in port for repairs," Sam said. "You're boarding tomorrow because the hard copies of timesheets and overtime hours requiring audit are all onboard."

"You'll be matching the past two weeks of sailors' hours worked to what was charged via their manning contract as over-time," Edith explained before returning to Tara's attire. "You don't own a single pair of work pants or jeans? I won't have you scaling ladders or visiting the engine room in a dress."

"Borrow a pair of mine," I offered.

"Both of you will wear pants. Sam can explain the rest."

"The oil tanker you'll be boarding collided with a navy destroyer during an at-sea refueling. To get ahead of the coast guard's investigation into whether insufficient crew manning contributed to the collision we need third-party accounting of the man hours billed to the navy contract."

It was early the next morning, while Tara and I waited before sun-rise for Sam to pick us up on the doorstep of our upstairs apartment in the Capitol Hill neighborhood, when I texted you that business in Norfolk would keep me away from that evening's rehab meeting.

The August morning burned bright and clear, the industrial port perspiring oil and salt.

"We'll work through lunch," I told Tara. "Take photos of what I point out. Write down what the crew tells us."

Across the baking lot Sam marched us to the pier's security checkpoint.

"You look so young in your IDs," gushed the enlisted navy guard. "This cain't be you."

"You saying I look old?" Tara flirted back.

"Oh, you ain't too old," his Georgia accent assured—or was that Alabama lulling us through the gate? Either way, no similar sweet tea was served for Sam's ID. As he finished signing us in, the guard, setting aside his energy drink, clicked his boot heels and stood upright with his rifle strapped over his shoulder.

Approaching the oil tanker, cables moored its six hundred-foot length against the long pier carrying us a safe dozen feet above the harbor waters, which were as green and madly entrapped as the few glass beer bottles ensnared in barrier nets sectioning each ship from the choppier main channel. The water's only escape was humidity, which, by the raw power of the sun, was felt to a saturating stickiness on crossing the ship's steep gangway to firmer footing aboard the main deck.

"Divers." Sam pointed to a commotion of bubbles breaking the surface of the water near the hull. "See?"

"Yes," I said, though not until we fully crossed the gangway did I register the bubbles as from the divers.

"Underwater welders touching up cracks along the hull caused by the collision."

Sam knew the crew of the *Kanawha*, introducing us to the chief engineer and captain as "the auditors" and "here to help with the investigation."

"You two ever sail?" the chief engineer already knew the answer, as he, along with his crew, looked us over, our jeans free of oil stains, our boots unscuffed, and Tara hesitant to be handed a hard hat in light of her newly highlighted hair.

"No sir."

"Ships are a new world for them," Sam answered.

"Well, you're at the right place for ships. Norfolk is the world's busiest naval station," the chief engineer said, his big voice multiplied in echoes off the metallic walls of the cavernous storage bay as he led us aboard. "You up for a tour?"

"We need to see the damage to the ship," I said, "but first, may we review the timesheets?"

The captain escorted us up several levels to an administrative office where we picked up a file. From there we were walked up another deck to the officer's mess and, before leaving us to our work, we were offered coffee, donuts, and a dining table on which to spread out the paperwork.

"Like, so different," Tara said, sliding open the trim curtains of the circular window near our table.

"What, wearing pants for once?"

"That, too, but I actually meant the ships." The view impressed her, from the carriers to more auxiliary ships to smaller destroyers along the dozen piers.

Tara tried pulling our table closer to the window, but it wouldn't budge.

"It's welded to the deck," I noticed.

"The deck?"

"The floor. Just about everything in here is either welded or bolted down." I looked around. The salad bar, the deep freezers along the wall, the coffee makers atop the counters.

"Why?"

"Tara, we're on a ship. Hold still, and you'll feel the slight sway of the water."

"So that's the feeling." She took a seat beside me. "I just figured I was due for settling myself with an addie."

From her purse Tara picked out one of several prescription bottles.

"Adderall? You brought your meds onto a ship? If they're not prescribed to you it's the same risk as sneaking pot onto a flight."

"The Ambien I got from my mom. But no worries, the Klonopin and the rest are all prescribed to me. How else are you going to focus?"

"Coffee."

Truth is, and maybe you can relate, I badly needed a dose of Tara's Xanax. What kept me from asking was Tom's warning of a possible court-ordered drug test.

Through the morning my mind drifted with worry as I stared out at the harbor view. My impounded car, suspended license, the pending charges, and maybe even prison—it was all too much and made it hard to focus on the paperwork or working with Tara or this new experience aboard a moored ship. My mind yielded to all the time I had spent with Tom. In only a few days I had allowed myself to depend on him completely. With you I have the solace of sharing most anything, such as needing our moms more than ever, but with Tom I live from one discussion to the next, always about my case, of course, and who knew just how much a defendant depends on their defense attorney? Or how vital a defense attorney's assurance, their bedside manner, so to speak, is to their client's well-being?

Tom lets me be scared. He lets me vent. He walks me through what's next and takes my side through it all. Together we faced the judge as the charges were made official last Monday. Afterward he put the worst of my prison worries into a tolerable perspective, promising me the worst won't come to pass when it's time for "our say."

For the assault charge he says there's more than enough mitigating factors to work out a favorable deal, namely by emphasizing how I was brought against my will into a hostile situation and how difficult will it be to hide a lack of driving privileges in a city where we mostly use the metro.

Do you remember our counselor repeating how faith and love are only theoretical until demonstrated? How many of Tom's attributes were similarly theoretical until I needed him? Thoughtful, strategic, protective?

Your boyfriend is fortunate to also have Tom's legal services; I meant to ask, how is Martez's case going?

"Nicole." Tara brought my attention back from the window. "What's with you?"

The sailors strayed into the officer's mess for coffee refills, each trying to come up with a catchy greeting.

"You're not part of the crew."

"Not yet," Tara indulged.

Soon enough the lunch hour came, and as sailors placed their trays on nearby tables we took the captain's invite to sit at his.

"How long does it take to cross the Atlantic?" Tara asked.

"On this last deployment it took eight days to return from Spain."

"What were you in Spain for?"

"We were assigned to escort a carrier strike group from the Med."

"The Med?"

"The Mediterranean."

Before Tara could connect their Atlantic crossing to last week's at-sea collision, the topic turned to us—where were we from and how did we end up in Washington? But conversation will always stale when fascination holds more to the other person, us girls in this case, than to the substance of dialogue.

To occupy us after lunch, the captain assigned Sam to take us down to the main deck to show us the ship's external damage. Over the railing of the sunny main deck and on the shaded waters alongside the hull floated a maintenance barge on which reinforced scaffolding elevated to the area of the structural damage above the waterline. In a small harbor boat a pair of laborers painted over the impact's periphery of steel-scraped gray coating. Sam explained the destroyer's impact as a refueling operation gone wrong.

"The destroyer pulled alongside our oiler at about fifteen knots, and once those refueling lines are connected between the ships both must sail in perfect parallel or the gap between them will close in a matter of seconds and, as you can see from the damage, one of us will be walking away with bruises."

The destroyer's side impact had caved in the outside walls of several storerooms, but we couldn't get clear pictures until one of us could climb down the scaffolding, where several coast-guard inspectors were assessing the damage.

The chief mate volunteered me to pair up with him and go onto the scaffolding because Tara wasn't wearing proper boots.

"Steel toe. Not Uggs," he joked as he helped me over the railing.

Gaining step on the barge's highest level of scaffolding added to its top-heaviness and further rocked the barge.

As the chief mate began scaling down the scaffolding the painter's boat struck the barge, and the top platform yanked liked a carpet from beneath my footing. I couldn't reach the scaffolding's framing poles, so to avoid a thirty-foot drop to the base of the barge, I leapt out over the water.

Midair was nice. Unreal and too real. My peripheral vision swept together my view of the harbor into a postcard—two destroyers resting away the afternoon along the next pier over, cranes loading both with pallets of energy drinks, pelicans grooming on the dock posts, and the distant tree line across the harbor.

And the waters, when they splashed over, how nice they were, warm and close, so I sank and forgot. But drowning? I don't know. The watery darkness deepened—why wasn't I floating back up?

No, I didn't want to drown, as though the decision must be forced until my survival instincts kicked in. Still, kicking and upward strokes required a surprising amount of will. I didn't want to face these unrestful weeks of work and court, rehab and wishing.

Wishing and kicking . . . a sudden light surged underwater. Outward from the light's pure source an expanse of the ship's massive hull gleamed—welders. I remembered, as I fought against the glowing green waters. A rope landed on the surface. Sam pulled me to the barge while the inspectors and crew watched.

Sam pulled me onto the barge, drenched and dazed, and through the pierced opening in the hull, seated me in the storeroom. Tara arrived with a blanket, wrapping my shoulders and calming me down. The commotion of falling nearly thirty feet was enough to keep me huddled in silence, but more importantly this was the first moment I internalized the quiet transition from the overruling shock to the recognition of my arrest, my night in jail with you, the following arraignment, and rehab. Which is why I didn't mind the nearly hour it took Tara to retrieve my overnight bag of dry clothes from Sam's pickup. Until she returned I eased into a welcoming numbness, unconcerned by how to later explain myself to Edith or by the deck officers borrowing my (suspended) driver's license to make copies for their mishap reports. Finally, alone in the sweltering storeroom, the night of my arrest internalized into coherent chronology: the singe of vodka on my breath when waking in the back seat to my car being towed; the pale, guiding streetlights of the tow lot when racing my parked car at the closing gates; the guards' forceful strength when they yanked me from the driver's seat and held me on the gravel until the police arrived; the cold hardness of the handcuffs; the equivalent restraint of both the police cruiser and cell doors slamming shut; your perfume filling our cell; Tom calming us down.

Tara handed over my duffle bag. "Find somewhere to change clothes. The crew asked us out tonight."

"We leaving now?"

"Soon. I guess they were supposed to celebrate their return at the oceanfront hotels until the captain cancelled because of the crash. So they're all heading up to party at a beach house on the Chesapeake. Apparently some of the sailors have timeshares there."

Knowing Tara it was too late to protest; she'd already accepted the invite on my behalf.

"Wasn't the plan to get back to Washington tonight? We promised Edith."

If relaying to you the details of my arrest isn't a realization of how much last weekend was a subjection to everybody else in their strict domains of police cruisers, jail cells, and courtrooms, today is a subjection to their ships and soon their parties.

While I showered in a below-deck locker room, Tara slipped into one of her sundresses. She was touching up her makeup over one of the sinks when I stepped from the stalls and changed into a pair of jeans and a collared polo.

"They have an extra room for us to crash." Tara handed me her hairbrush. "And the lobby has an open bar. Besides, it's Friday, and the sea mate says he'll drive us to Washington tomorrow."

"Chief mate."

"He told me to call him Sam."

Sam was waiting for us at his pickup. The guest room, he clarified, in case I preferred skipping the party for an early rest, would be available across the inlet from the beach house at his own house where we needed to stop by anyway and pick up his wife who was cooking for the party. I agreed; offering me a way out of the party and admitting a wife clarified his motives for inviting us: He could've left Tara and me at a hotel and let us figure out our way back, but I guess he wanted to make up for my fall by getting us back to Washington.

Starting over the first of several bridges on our way from Norfolk, Sam talked about working his way up the deck-officer ranks on container ships crossing the Pacific. When he took the position of chief mate aboard a freighter delivering crude oil from the Gulf's rigs, he was only twenty-six (my age now); it was hard to believe he was still in his twenties.

A tunnel from Norfolk crossed us into Hampton, and from there the interstate caught Highway 17, a four-lane shot bypassing the sprawls of Richmond and Washington following north along the Chesapeake Bay into Maryland. The pines swayed taller once over the York River and away from the cities. From the radio the rural imagery of country music mirrored the passing scenery of stars and stripes painted on mailboxes, porches with rocking chairs facing the eventual sunset, and crosses atop churches and grouped in threes along the roadside. After a few more farming counties Sam turned up a highway that narrowed over the bridge sweeping us into Maryland high above the Potomac River.

"You going to jump again from here?" Sam joked when he noticed me studying the waters below, as colorless in the late-afternoon sun as the burnt roads and shapeless emissions from the power plant along the shore.

"Where did you even find the rope you threw me?"

"Had to untie it from the barge. One devil of a knot while you were drowning."

"I'm always drowning."

"How do you know if you're, like, really drowning?" Tara asked.

"If it's any indication I saw ghostly lights flashing in the water."

"Welders." Sam laughed.

Sam lived close to the water, his house on the shores of a calmer inlet pocketed off the greater Chesapeake. His property was the sort of treasure-heaped escape worthy of the hopeful retirement estates endlessly crowed over by our older coworkers. The garage housed a dirt bike, Jet Ski, a sports car tucked beneath a tarp, and vintage arcade machines. And the pier out back gave dry footing to his fiberglass-hooded motorboat tied at the pier's end thirty feet from shore.

Sam's sweetheart of a wife, Becky, greeted us in the kitchen. She asked Tara and I if we needed a glass of anything or a place to put up our feet.

"Thank you, but we'll rest later."

"You sure? Sam, can you check the cages? Water's almost boiling."

The crab-trapping cages were sunken to the mushy bottom below Sam's pier. Sam pulled up both cages by ropes staked to the boardwalk. The first was empty; the second held seven scurrying crabs.

"They hate being out of the water. They don't function away from it." Sam flipped open the lid and used tongs to toss the first crab back in. "A female. Can't keep the females. It's illegal. I'll show you the difference."

The second he gripped carefully. "These are the famed Maryland blue crabs. On their bellies the females have a spitting image of the capitol dome. And the males—see," he picked one up after tossing the second female, "they have an abdominal imprint almost replicating the Washington Monument."

"They *do* match!" Tara gushed

"Yes, you could stand across the Potomac and hold them up against both landmarks and not miss a beat along the Washington skyline," I said.

"Or maybe they foretell their territory since blue crabs are the real natives here." Sam dropped four Washington Monuments in a plastic bucket. "My parents remember blue crabs being a lot larger and more plentiful than now." Sam pointed across the inlet. "That's their house with the porch on the water. Last winter the ice was so thick Becky and I walked clear across."

The timeshare complex was further up the waters of inlet where the clearing of the Chesapeake could be seen. Sam's was the last pier down before the inlet ended as a bedding of thick and high saltmarsh grass where herons scavenged and over which the lowering sun withdrew. Willows swayed along the waters like the hems of dresses slow dancing in the breeze.

Another postcard: "This is nice."

"It's all answered prayers, my house and all."

It was hard to believe someone only a few years older than Tara and me could arrive home to so much.

"It's too late to take the boat out now, but if you can get yourself here some other weekend you'll give Becky some much needed fishing company while I'm sailing the oiler."

"Yes, well, not anytime soon," I said. I wasn't about to let anyone else find out how restricted to DC I am without a car or active driver's license. Not to mention having to our rehab meetings and court appearances.

Becky called from the back porch: "You got 'em?"

"Coming right up." Sam handed me the tongs. "Check the last crab."

"Another capitol dome. A female." The crab slipped from my grasp and landed on the pier, scuttling sideways over the edge.

"Tomorrow she'll be back." Sam tossed the empty cages into the water. "For now it's back to a crabby life of eating and laying eggs."

"What do they munch on anyway?" Tara asked.

"Whatever they get their claws on."

We walked to the porch where the back door accessed the kitchen, and Becky took our bucket to overturn crabs into a giant boiling pot.

After cooking the plan was to leave me early to bed while they attended the party.

"You don't need anything? Maybe a Xanax?" Tara asked.

"Do you have Excedrin PM?"

"You sure it's OK to leave you here?" She handed me a bottle from her purse.

"I'm wondering more about you."

"Me?"

"Drinking with a bunch of sailors."

"And drinking like a sailor!"

Becky, ready in a dress, took the moment Sam went upstairs to change out of his oily coveralls to show me to the spare bedroom.

"The kitty thinks this is her room," she said, driving the tabby from the bed, "and won't be one bit pleased when I make space for you."

"She's welcome to stay." I motioned the kitty back into the room.

Becky was showing me the house's best overlook of the waters from a window of the guest room when Sam called time to go, holding a bottle of vodka, which I would later smell on Tara's breath when she returned from the party and collapsed alongside me at 2AM.

It was too late to call Tom. I tried calling you—if Martez had a court date maybe I could guess mine? My legal troubles are all that's on mind once the clamor of the day wanes. But I also wanted to ask you about arrangements for hanging out in Las Vegas in a few weeks.

I killed the lights and stood at the window, gazing into the backyard leading to the pier, the pier extending over the calm water, the mingled voices of the party skipping across the Chesapeake's calm surface as ghostly as the shimmering lights.

~

I texted you from the air as soon as my phone regained signal on descent into Las Vegas. Beneath the wings flared the casinos along the desert floor, a dusty rug transforming to magic carpet by dusk, the many-colored resurrection of sundown in the desert. In your case, welcome back to all you've missed of your hometown.

See u tmrrw, you texted back. Taxiing toward the terminal I could see, sloping from the darkening sky to the runway, the wingtip lights of incoming passenger jets spaced in linear landing order. I thought about walking the straight shot of Las Vegas Boulevard's fountain mists and blazing marquees to the old downtown where my first night would be cheaper spent, but Dustin texted me to find him in the airport, hoping to share a cab.

"You didn't just drive from Arizona?" I asked when I found him in a bar with two margarita glasses between him and a brunette, the dim light showing blonde in his long hair.

"Mom's life insurance finally cleared. I'm planning on buying a new car here in Vegas this weekend," he said to me, breaking off conversation with the brunette.

"I didn't want to buy her another glass if I wasn't going to see her again," Dustin said in the cab. "She was leaving in another hour on a one-way to Hawaii."

"I dream of doing the same," our driver said.

"Her only plan was to get a lei around her neck and mai tai in her hand."

"How 'bout I leave you to the same treatment," the driver said, turning onto the interstate, "at the California Casino where our Island visitors stay? Hawaii's Ninth Island, as it's known."

More texts awaited response, but none from you. I watched from the back seat as the famed procession of casino towers slid by—the Mandalay, MGM, Cosmopolitan, Bellagio, Caesar's, Mirage—before bothering to answer, in the sudden industrial darkness past the gold bar of the Trump Tower, a message from my dad. In the month since my DUI, my dad was back to keeping tabs on me; he wanted the details of where Dustin and I were planning to stay. I hadn't hidden my detour through Vegas when telling him of the trip to Arizona. His reaction wasn't against relapsing; instead he warned of my grandma's last years of frequenting the tribal casinos on the outskirts of Tucson.

Another message, this one a picture sent to Dustin and me from Brad, the childhood friend who suggested Tom, seated beneath Fremont Street's blurring lightshow—*Hurry here*. Beside him was Carly, a fellow lawyer who brought along her sister and roommate, holding up a neon drink with multiple straws with, of all people, Tom. Save for him, none of them know I'm going through rehab. Of course, I dread them finding out, especially Brad and his likely lack of surprise. He's seen me drink too many times before. Especially in Vegas.

All week Tom's texts were teased with poolside photos of pink drinks and poker cards spanned across felt tables. I remember him mentioning his trip to Vegas coinciding with your visit, which I coincided with my own, because who am I fooling? I wanted to see Tom, and if nothing worked out at least I'm getting the Vegas weekend I'd looked forward to before the DUI, before needing Tom, before seeing him sharing drinks with Carly, before fooling only myself. Comparing his "work" explanation to your explanation of why Tom's here, yes, Martez running several nightclubs in Vegas can justify casework here, especially given a possible connection to the legal troubles of his Maryland nightclub, but according to the missing piece of information provided by you, Martez's co-ownership of the Bellagio's headliner club overlooking the fountains includes a top-floor suite where, as his defense attorney, Tom has an open invitation to spend the week.

Once our taxi eased to a stop beneath the California Casino's fiery ruby marquee the driver unloaded our luggage while a pair of tuxedoed security guards rolled out an older, probably homeless, wheelchair-bound man cursing threats. "Where else d'you expect me to go?" He lobbed beer cans into the street as the guards radioed the police. After checking into our room and touching up my makeup, Dustin and I rushed back out to see the cursing vagrant being lifted by his wheelchair into the back of a police van, its flashing lights drowned out in the bright runoff of Fremont Street's electric glow.

We found everybody lounging around the coffee tables outside the Golden Nugget, their bronze tans radiating in the waning evening heat beneath Fremont's soaring awning of hourly lightshows. On crowding ourselves at their table of numerous empty beer bottles and margarita glasses, more drinks materialized from waitresses running orders from inside the casino, the glitter of their cocktail dresses briefly suspending the attention demanded by Tom's presence. The sparkle of their rings, from pinky to thumb, as they handed out the next round recalled your stories of working the casinos, of the job fairs attended between your college classes, where getting hired for looking nineteen was assured by actually being nineteen. And the shifts of running trays of drinks, too, at the Bellagio, classes be damned, and lovelier than any waitress tonight. I wonder how much the pay averages, because couldn't you clear enough cash here? Was Martez really worth your risky move to Washington? With him possibly going to jail I wish you'd consider returning home. Of course, tomorrow it'll be easier to bring it up.

Another distraction on top of distraction, a dynamic that no better sums up one Vegas moment to the next, was the lightshow that began pulsing on the awning stretching the length of Fremont Street's wide casino walkway. As the electric spectrum of racing colors flushed our faces, the pausing crowds raised their phones to watch and record. Then all of us, except for Tom and Carly who

found as much illumination in each other, paid passing attention to the racket of a bachelor party staggering obnoxiously by.
I checked again for a text from you and wondered if you remembered me guessing the steepest dollar amount you ever swiped on
a customer's credit card. You remarked that it was probably for a
bachelor party spending thousands on bottle service. I'll admit
that even in that moment, surrounded by longstanding friends
and with many sights to hurry my mind away, you were a welcome
pilgrimage for my thoughts.

As for my friends, it was too convenient to assume that Brad
and Tom would hit it off. Yes, they're both lawyers, but Brad han-
dles insurance cases, and Tom defends his firm's felony cases.
Both sat on either end of the table, immersed in their respective
girls. Brad's ongoing phone call, it turned out, was to a girlfriend
he'd made over the summer. He hadn't yet broken away to greet
Dustin and me. By the time Carly stood from Tom's side and led
him into the crowds of Fremont Street without wishing us goodbye, Brad was finishing his call. "I love you very much," he said
before turning to us. But it was Carly's roommate, Erin, who beat
him to it, accusing more than asking: "How do you know Tom?"

"Nicole knows Tom through her dad," Brad answered.

"They've worked cases together," I lied.

"Have you spoken with Tom since he attached himself to
Carly?"

"Not really," it bothered me to hear.

"Not really?"

"Erin, cut it out already," Carly's drunk sister Connie said.
"Tom treats Carly well."

"Carly's only keeping Tom around."

"Keeping him around—what does that mean?"

"Every time we turn around Tom's buying Carly another gift.
She's having him lavish her knowing full well she can keep all
the necklaces and piercings even if she doesn't see him again after
Vegas."

"That's his problem to figure out. Tom's smart enough," the
drunk sister said, looking over to Brad and me, "right?"

"Tom always knows what he's doing," I said.

However, no answer could dissuade the public argument between Erin and the drunk sister. Emboldened by the alcohol and applause of Fremont Street's instant spectators, they chorused back and forth as to whether Tom was indeed spending too much on Carly.

In the boisterous moment I could've enjoyed a front-row seat had I not looked away from their argument for Tom, hoping to spot his white sport coat among Fremont Street's foot traffic, even if it was Carly and not me he was leading away.

My first night's sleep in Vegas was aided by the margarita I'd unburdened from the drunk sister, steadying her high-heeled balance as she argued with Erin. I downed her full glass and went to bed earlier than the rest, though late by my East Coast clock, looking forward to our plans to meet in the morning.

Finding my drowsy steps downstairs the next morning, I followed a chorus of bells to the gaming floor to order coffee from the Hawaiian-shirted servers running drinks to the slots occupied by the Island clientele. Outside, on a morning walk, the desert heat was instantly familiar from my Arizona upbringing as a hallucinogenic force. The sidewalks led back to a Fremont Street that was hollow and silent of last night's energy. Empty margarita glasses were gathered at the heels of vagrants as curb-level depositories for spare change. The awning's synchronized lights were pale outlines, as was the enchantment of the frontiers, islands, and other escapes themed by the casino marquees, which in honest sunlight stressed the sun-cracked plastering of buildings from which equally dispelling souls drifted between the gaming floors as yawning voids. When I circled back to the hotel room, stalled briefly by a few dollars lost in the samurai-themed slot machines, Dustin was on his laptop, scrolling through used cars. He wanted gas efficiency but also room for hauling his climbing gear to Joshua Tree. He found several Subaru Outbacks listed on the north side of Vegas but couldn't settle on anything, so I headed back downstairs, thinking through the math of whether my portion of Mom's life insurance could pay off the rest of my student loans.

I found Brad at the blackjack tables. The last time we gambled together, roulette cost Brad over six hundred dollars at the Bellagio. This time around he restrained his bets. The crop-topped dealer never lifted her eyes between shuffling. She probably guessed Brad and I were another boring couple, more likely the married type given our relaxed getup—jeans and T-shirts.

Having grown up together we like to joke about our married vibe. In fact, our moms, best friends and nurses at the same hospital, were the first to joke about us making a sensible match, and their humor, if not hopes, haven't been wrong when it comes to the practicalities. Brad is a comfortable three years older, wants kids, and his profession fits my auditing experience, but we've never taken the idea seriously.

Naturally, I understand Brad enthusing about his new girlfriend, and that's when our dealer raised her eyes. Brother and sister? It was a better guess and went well with me asking Brad if he could drive me to the address you provided for lunch.

"Who are you meeting? You're welcome to join Dustin and me for lunch." He pointed to the six-dollar T-bone special advertised in bold across the sagging banners above the carpeted thoroughfares of the gaming floor.

"I have plans with Santana. You'll meet her later."

"Oh." Brad suddenly didn't care. "Long as it's not Tom."

"Tom?"

Brad shook his head. "He's changed so much. And anyway, I didn't drive here. I flew."

"Wasn't the plan for you to drive Dustin and me back to Arizona?" I remarked.

"Dustin's serious about buying that car."

"Then I guess I can't ask anybody for a ride yet."

Brad and I might match, but I think we both understand we could never be romantic. Whereas taking with Tom the risky parallels you're taking with Martez is, for better or likely worse, what I wanted before putting college and work first. If a man, good or bad, is the default too many of us girls choose anyway, it feels like the responsibilities I've taken with education and work are also distractions, albeit responsible distractions, from the irresponsible distraction of Tom. Why not learn the hard way while I have a foundation of education and work to fall back on? But who knows what's left to fall back on once the courts finish with me? Mom's life insurance will have to go toward the legal bills before student loans. In court I'll have Tom at my side. If only he wasn't disappearing into crowds with Carly.

I hailed a cab to your dad's dusty address. Riding away from the casinos, the streets appeared as familiar as another Tucson or Phoenix neighborhood, passing adobe homes hunched low over fences along frying roadways that aimed into the dry distance of far desert. On foot from the cab, the baking, unpaved roadside lifted hot through the soles of my slingbacks. Your dad's front door was wide open and approaching near enough for a look inside explained your refusal to consider temporarily crashing at his place should you return. Sand blew thin across the floor. Black trash bags were taped as curtains over the windows. Between the futon and the only light of a TV a stack of pizza boxes served as a coffee table topped with empty cans of Miller Lite.

"Come in," you said after my knock.

"Hello," I said, because you weren't anywhere near the open doorway.

Finally, to the drip of a mini fridge in the corner, paced soft footsteps across the tiles.

They were toddler's steps, and they brought the startle of recognizing you in the little girl returning my surprise. She has your deep-brown eyes and raven hair and butterscotch skin. A lovely girl – the both of you.

"Cupcake, have you met my dear friend?"

In one graceful motion you picked her up from behind.

"Bianca, please, why don't we say hi to my dear friend Nicole? Why don't we show Nicole how we dressed you up today? Your yellow flower dress and matching shoes."

Bianca's little hand felt for a loose ribbon dangling from her ponytail before shyly burying her face in your neck.

"So this is Bianca."

"Hi there," I greeted.

Bianca lifted her head to exchange eye contact.

"So, lunch?" You handed me Bianca's car seat.

"Yes. I've already turned down my shot at six-dollar steaks."

"I'm guessing you were with all guys if the brunch consensus was six-dollar steaks?"

"The girls were still getting their beauty sleep."

"But last night the guys treated you to somewhere fancy?"

"Last night was more about drama than anything else. Centering around Tom."

"Tom was with you?"

"Not exactly with *me*."

"Maybe we'll see him in Martez's sky suite?"

"We're going to the sky suite for lunch?"

"We'll order up lunch from the Bellagio floor and bill it to the suite. It's where I agreed to drop off Bianca with her aunt. Any amount of time I get with Bianca has to be mediated through Martez's family's custody of her."

"And this belongs to Martez too?" I asked of the Cadillac Escalade you unlocked.

"Yes. And like my time with Bianca, his family isn't happy he's letting me borrow one of their rides."

The Escalade's coal finish shone with not a wisp of blown dust hazing its perfect reflection. And the interior was cool to the touch on buckling Bianca in the back seat.

Taking the driver's seat, you rolled back the tinted sunroof. "I missed the sun, the desert."

"And the palm trees along every street," I added.

And these streets without curbs like ancient paths unburied, the mountains providing distant direction, and beyond, the sunlight so wide across the sky; this is the open West I also miss.

"And how much easier it is to keep a tan."

"You have friends you could always return to?" I hinted.

"Yes. I didn't realize how much I missed my girls until reliving the old times with them a few nights ago. After our third bar came this sinking realization of knowing how much I'd miss home once

I'm gone again. I woke up sad until Bianca got me out of bed. Didn't you, Cupcake? Asking how we'd wear our hair today when you saw my hair still styled from last night."

"And, of course, you miss Bianca?"

"I know you're wondering how I could leave my baby, and of course I want to be a good mommy and raise her, but before I ever bothered following Martez out East his family sued for full custody to prevent me from suing Martez for child support, which I didn't even plan to do. I couldn't afford to fight in court, so when Martez invited me to follow him out East I went in hopes that my time working in his club would go well enough to convince him to eventually move Bianca with us to Washington."

"Given how much work it takes to raise a baby, isn't it easier for them to let Martez agree to pay whatever you need?"

"For as much child support as I can sue for they don't want to risk my foot in the door of their bank accounts. Martez is involved in the ownership of several clubs along with the one he opened in Washington."

"Can I ask how they won full custody?"

"Their lawyer used my two convictions for marijuana possession from a few years ago to discredit me as a junky unfit to be a parent."

"Martez wouldn't defend you?"

"He refused to admit that our baby was hijacked until I moved with him to Washington."

"You don't think he's just using you to help out at his new club?"

"Part of following Martez East was to get away from financially supporting my dad. He's such a lost soul! His drug felonies keep him unemployed, and you saw his place. It's a rat's nest of somebody who can't function. If I were to return I couldn't let Bianca visit often, much less raise her there if I'm ever allowed to raise her. My dad's indigent."

I gazed out the window. What was there to say? Hearing *indigent* fixed a cold formality to your no-win circumstances that left me at a loss to help you think through other ways forward. The world outside was sunny with the promise of neon nights under the shadow of the approaching casino landmarks. I wanted to tell you that the constants of school, work, relationships, and having a baby are a matter of taking the good with the bad. Or, to put it another way, the highs are worth riding out the lows. But not when it comes to losing our moms. What's there to say when it's been all downhill since?

"The Bellagio will lighten us up," you finally said.

"Bianca." I turned to her baby seat. "Do you know the Bellagio?"

"Cupcake, remember the singing fountains?"

"Chockyet," she babbled.

"Yes, the chocolate fountain. We'll stop by again. Nicole, can you hand back her juicy cup?"

By the time Bianca finished her cup you were rounding the Escalade beneath the overhang of the Bellagio's side entrance. From the doors of the Escalade and into those of the shopping promenade, both opened by valets, I strolled the aqua carpet beside you and Bianca in her stroller, keeping stride of your confident ease past the designer storefronts.

"There's the salon where I'd go with my fellow servers to get our nails done before we went on shift."

"Have they all remained cocktail waitresses?"

"Most. It's good money, especially if you're handling bottle service on the weekends. They don't see any reason to chance the corporate nine-to-five life. Last night was fun hearing how little has changed. They want me to save them from their boyfriend dramas. Even my dad said that if I'd stayed I would've worked my way into a better shift by now. On our busier nights I'd get tipped a ten or twenty merely because someone liked my hair or dress. I do miss those nights. Dressing up to take on the casino floor with my fellow servers."

I hadn't seen the chocolate fountain before, the world's tallest, as its plaque certified. It was more fun seeing Bianca's entranced silence and beaming eyes following the flows of dark, milk, and white chocolates pouring thickly from a canopy of tilted glass bowls and mixing below into the fewer larger bowls at our knees.

Bianca squirmed from her stroller when you announced it was time to move on. I picked up the pacifier she spat out as you lifted her from the carpet. Fussing over your shoulder she grabbed a fistful of decorative vegetation, only letting go and quieting to your promises of candy in the sky suite.

The sky suite, the Escalade, and most of all Bianca—your life, in the course of our drive over, added up at a pace as hyper-real as the casino floor's flashing slots, heartless roulette spins, and hovering trays of drinks. Words and letters glowed in all directions: JACKPOT, HIGH LIMIT, BUFFET.

"The Hyde! This is the club where I was waitressing when I met Martez. He's one of the owners." You pointed to the double-doored entrance along the lengthy wall leading to the atrium of the Bellagio's marble-floored check-in lobby. Overhead were sculptures of stained-glass flowers leading to the elevators. You had Bianca happily press the highest-numbered button, and up we went. Letting off at the top floor Bianca yanked on her ear, fussing at the pressure drop until you unlocked the door of the sky suite.

Instead of Martez's mom waiting inside, it was Tom in the kitchen, already off to a day of drinking, evidenced by a few empty shot bottles of Irish whiskeys topping the counter to a gift basket of chocolates that Bianca zipped toward across the zebra carpeting.

While the three of us sorted out the dialing up of lunch orders from the casino floor, you started in on asking Tom about Martez, about the charges he faced, and how many months the courts might take, a subject I didn't want to lead into open discussion of my case. But Tom and I hadn't ever discussed anything besides my case, and I worried whether that left any room for informal space between us when the moments found us alone, such as after lunch when you announced "nappy time for Cupcake" and wiped the chocolate from Bianca's face before ushering her into one of the bedrooms. Hearing the bedroom curtains lowered shut, the doorway went dark, and out mingled the whisperings of your lullaby shepherding Bianca to sleep.

"You see this view?"

I joined Tom at the windows overlooking the desert, from the sun-filled urban valley of Vegas to the surrounding valley's jagged ridgelines lifting and dipping along the nearly perceptible convex of the world. But it was Tom's presence, not the sunny view or alcohol on his breath, that warmly overwhelmed me. To see him dissolved the mist cloaking my mind's image of him.

"Vegas look a lot like home?" Tom handed me a shot of vodka.

"Yep. Mountains and desert, just like Arizona."

"Nicole, check this out." Tom withdrew into the other bedroom. I followed into the darkness.

"Here." He shut the door and flipped on a projector. "Best view is to look up from the bed."

The ceiling was a scroll of stars. Galaxy to galaxy—hundreds, thousands. The panorama of the starry beyond quickened our shared awareness from the bed, where fused hand in hand, we watched the interstellar deep roll by. The universe of Tom; I breathed easy, lifted and adrift, never cold. More than finally seeing Tom, his presence was my escape in the stars.

When I awoke the ceiling animation had shut off, and the dark room was only the seashore resonance of Tom breathing asleep. Your voice had woken me. Your tone not the tenderness meant for Bianca but that of a determined back and forth with someone whose side of the dialogue wasn't carrying as sharply. Rousing from the bed to leave you to your business, Tom, also awaking, wanted to come along to meet back up with my guy friends. But your business was sort of his too, because before I thought better of remaining hidden, I opened the door to interrupt you arguing in Spanish with Martez's mother. Tom told me who it was once he caught up with me at the elevators and joined the ride down to Bellagio's chiming casino floor of oxygen-fattened air and overhanging gardens and chandeliers.

"So where did Brad and your brother say they were?"

"A few casinos over." I held up Dustin's text: *checking into mirage.*

"I got death stares from Santana and Martez's mom when I came out of the bedroom," Tom said.

"So did I." I gratefully put a hand on my purse, which, left by the sky suite's entrance, made for a quick exit. What I could guess of your surprise was filled in by the questions sustained in the lookover Dustin, and especially Brad, gave Tom and me when finding them with my luggage at the Mirage's check-in desk.

"Brad, the tip?" Dustin prompted Brad's attention back to the concierge.

After Brad tipped her, the ponytailed concierge quickly went back to work on her computer.

"How much did you tip her?" Tom asked in the elevator when Brad punched us up to the top floors.

"Sixty."

Sixty dollars upgraded us to a corner room where the higher views accounted for the nearby Caesar's Palace, the Venetian across the street, and more impressively, the famous Volcano brewing red below.

"You think we should've stayed with Santana?" I whispered to Tom, worrying about you.

"She can handle herself fine." Tom likely didn't want to think about the conflict we'd left you to handle. He turned from the window to ask what this evening's plan was, interrupting the exchange Brad was having with Dustin through the bathroom door, beneath which we caught the first whiff of a joint.

Brad looked over: *he's your brother.*

"I just didn't think this would happen," I said.

"This is the best stuff I could find, and none of you want any?" Dustin burst from the bathroom. "I don't want a repeat of last night's drama, so let's see if we can find a different pack of girls to hang with."

Smoke billowed white from the bathroom.

"I'll have a hit," Tom said.

"Please, guys, blow it outside," Brad said, gesturing to the window from which I was anticipating a view of the volcano's eruption. Bystanders congregated along the railing of the emerald lagoon surrounding the volcano with palms and waterfalls.

"Wouldn't it be a great time for my eagle screech?"

Dustin nudged open the window and shrieked a terror so sharp that faces waiting for the volcano looked up in hilarious alarm. Dustin and I laughed, leaping on the beds and egging on further screeches. More faces hesitated to search for our place in the sky, slowing the sidewalk traffic. Brad, annoyed but amused, passed out glasses of vodka-infused orange juice before counting down to chug when the lava burst from the volcano.

"So, where for dinner?" Dustin asked.

"The buffet at Mandalay. We had it last time, remember?"

"I'm too hungry to remember."

"Suddenly hungry and no memory . . . I wonder what could've caused that?" I gestured an imaginary joint to my lips.

After we dressed up and the guys drank another round while I redid my makeup, we ordered a cab from the Mirage to Mandalay Bay at the other end of the busy Strip.

Along the ride over other palaces and so-named Grands and foreign skylines of passing casinos blurred into the merry-go-round of our vodka-boosted world.

"My ex is here," Dustin said. "She brags all over social media whenever she spends the weekend partying in Vegas."

"Maybe we can run around with her crowd tonight?" Tom said.

"Santana can get us into the Hyde," I said.

"Or, here we go." Dustin directed our attention to four girls walking in high heels beneath the misted palms of the veranda's long sidewalk winding toward the Mandalay's sparkling marquee.

Approaching from behind, their sleek dresses of cherry and violet, Dustin lowered the back-seat window and shrieked his eagle screech. They startled into a barrage of vulgarities, drowned out by our idiotic laughing. Brad grinned in the front seat as he pointed our driver beside the casino's revolving glass doors. Rounding the sidewalk beneath the marquee, the girls regained sight of the cab in time to catch Brad lingering behind to pay our driver. The four of them swore like Tara whenever she loses it, leaving Brad to labor through their profanity as they followed him through the doors where from the cooler inside we watched, laughing.

"Yes, they're assholes," Brad said.

"Does anyone happen to know a good spot for birdwatching?" Dustin followed.

"You're the screamer," they accused.

For dinner we drank too much, and afterward we rode the sixty-three floors up to the Mandalay's rooftop lounge to watch nightfall over Vegas, unsure of where we were.

"On top of the world," Dustin said in the much needed fresh air of the viewing deck's open patio, looking over the casinos blazing down the Strip and extending his arms in triumphant view of Egypt's pyramids, medieval castle spires, New York's skyline, and the Eiffel Tower, all glowing at our feet.

The evening view over the city was what the girls Dustin had screeched at had dressed up for. When we saw them again, Tom and Dustin waved them over to the ledge, making friendly amends with a pledge of drinks on us. A tray of foggy blue shots hovered our way. Shooting together, our throats were a column of fire as the heated spirits descended like a swallowed torch.

One of the girls slipped, caught the ledge, and bumped several shot glasses over the side. We all watched the glasses disappear into the dizzying distance above the palm trees, which drew the bouncers over.

"Did you just toss a glass over the ledge?" asked a pair of bouncers.

Our hesitant answers got us hurried out of the rooftop lounge. Looking back at the bouncers watching us in cross-armed intimidation on the casino floor, I wondered how long our nonsense would last. We took the train from Mandalay Bay past the Luxor. Dustin flipped himself upside down and hung from the overhead handrails, feet pressed against the ceiling, striking alarm into the cart of trapped passengers. Tom and I laughed, but Brad, avoiding association, blended into the seats of unnerved passengers pressing in dismissive distance against the side windows.

"Brad, take pictures!"

As Brad ignored Dustin, his girlfriend called just as the tram doors slid open at the Excalibur. The swell of outside heat traded space with the load of passengers eager to leave Dustin hanging like a bat. We lost Brad over the bridged intersection in the New York casino as he answered a phone call and took off alone into the Times Square-replicated alleys of bars and gift shops. It was then, failing to relocate Brad, that we began sobering up with the unexpected loneliness of knowing the paradise of casinos continuing back along Las Vegas Boulevard, one to the dazzling next, wasn't enough. Seeing the Bellagio again I looked above its fountains to guess which of the higher floor windows Tom and I had shared a few hours ago. And with Dustin and Brad looking for anyone besides our half-drunk selves, this was my chance to convince him to go back up there.

I tried by detouring the three of us into the Bellagio, where if nothing else we might see you again. We stopped at a high table in the crowded food court tucked from view of the casino floor as a sort of cheap dining triage. Our loss was Brad, and we weren't the only ones down a friend. At the next table over sat a trio of guys sorting through similar withdrawals:

"I already let him know where we are," one said.

"So he's ignoring us?" Another asked.

"It's like we don't exist."

"We didn't ask to."

"We do when we go asking and waiting for him."

Listening, Dustin went pale. "I'm mourning this loss of Brad," he said. "And my ex wants to know where she can find us."

"Tell her to meet us at the Hyde," I said.

That was when I texted you.

The feature DJ was hours from taking stage, but the line of sport jackets and black dresses waiting outside the Hyde extended onto the gaming floor by the time you emerged with a bouncer to escort us inside. There you led Tom and me across the dance floor to the railing of the shallow balcony overlooking the Bellagio's lake of fountains singing Sinatra and misting the glow of the famous casino signs and marquees across the dark waters.

"This was your view every shift?"

"I was too busy to appreciate it," you said and motioned to the passing bottle-service delivery of four girls synchronized in scarlet, barebacked dresses. They raised bottles of vodka like lanterns illuminated over flashlights across the dancefloor's laser lights—girls once like you but decidedly not you by the sternness of their abstracted gazes.

"You look great, by the way, just as dazzling."

"Guess who helped them look especially lovely this evening? After Martez's mom picked up Bianca I called a few of them upstairs for hair and makeup."

"Good work," Tom complimented.

"Where's the rest of your group?"

"We lost Brad," I said, "and my brother's hiding somewhere."

"Not exactly hiding." Tom spotted Dustin grinding with a server atop one of the lounge tables. "He's been off the rails all evening."

"And tomorrow he's looking to buy a car off a desert lot."

"Maybe I could get Martez to sell him low on one of his? If he can't beat this case he'll have no use for it."

How began your involvement with Martez? And what exactly are his legal troubles? I wanted a chance to ask you this since our first meeting the night Tom picked us up from jail.

"No, Kelley, this isn't him," you said when our server praised Tom over the sky suite, assuming he was Martez.

"Sorry about that," you said after she'd left.

"She doesn't know the sky suite belongs to Martez?"

"She knows the owners share it, and even though I never hid from the rumors of who Bianca's dad is none of the servers know Martez as Martez because he never uses his real name."

"We could've let her believe I was the owner," Tom joked.

"If you want to be Martez, start with sizable investments in nightclubs in LA and Washington. And have us call you names like Chris or Louis until we gradually learn your real name by catching it on our airline tickets to Florida and Colombia. It wasn't until I was pregnant with Bianca that he told me his real name, and he didn't use it again until I asked for financial help with my mom's funeral and noticed 'Martez' credited to the deposit. Now I see his name all over the court records."

"Can I ask what he ended up getting charged with?"

"We shouldn't talk about it here." You leaned along the railing, deferring to Tom.

"A slew of drug-trafficking counts," Tom added.

"All because a dealer he barely knows plans to testify that Martez knowingly allowed cocaine trafficking at his Washington club. As part of a plea deal the dealers ratted him to undercover investigators who raided the place, arresting a bunch of us on that night we met in jail," you finished as you were recognized by yet another red dress and led away toward the dance floor's dark commotion, leaving Tom and me to the slower fountain songs. My question lingered, best unanswered by Tom.

"I don't know how Santana does it with so much on her shoulders. Her baby, her dad. Finding dependable work," I said.

"You too," Tom said.

"I can't think of anyone else I'd rather have defending me."

"You probably don't need the alcohol rehab."

"I haven't drank until pretty much this weekend."

"With me." He raised his glass. "That's irony, right? Drinking with the guy who booked you into alcohol treatment?"

"Without my downfall we wouldn't be sharing this view." I took the risk of resting my hand on the cuff of his sleeve.

Tom looked away to the fountains as their jets synchronized with the opening chords of the next song.

"And if I hadn't ended up in rehab or court I wouldn't be here," I said, trying to engage his sentiment.

In the lull between us the assurance of standing beside him would have to do. Any chance beside Tom welled within me a contentment lasting long after we stood before the judge together or laid beneath our sky full of stars.

"Tom, do you know this song?"

"I've heard it before. 'Dark Day On?'"

"'Danke Schoen,' which is German for *thank you*. This is the original Wayne Newton recording. Thank you for all the joy and pain." I hummed along to the fountains. "Second balcony was the place we'd meet, second seat . . . you were sweet . . . Danke schoen,

darling, danke schoen . . . Thank you for walks down Vegas lanes,
I can see us go on a plane, let us fly away . . . for all time."

"Those aren't the exact lyrics."

"I'm sure Wayne Newton improvised when he sang here in
Vegas."

Tom was suddenly beyond being humored, unlike you, allowing for any laugh, which occurred to me as I turned back, searching for you under the laser lights. Instead we spotted Dustin
approaching with drinks as the rest of our night receded as the
lyrics rang over the water.

Looking back to retell these softer moments, I wish I'd have
been pushier, even to the point of killing my chances with Tom.
Let's go somewhere, I should've pressed, back to our stars.

The rest of our night, like our walkway back to the Mirage,
was more forgettable than forgotten. In the room we continued
drinking judging by the disarray we woke up to. Pants and over-
coats over lampshades. Flipped chairs. The pair of queen mat-
tresses crooked atop their box springs. The only upright furniture
was the corner table, presumably due to the alcohol it served alter
to. Half-full bottles of vodka and whiskey—way too much to be
sanely consumed by . . . was it three of us? On the other side of the
room, where Tom caught a few hours of sleep before leaving for
an early flight back to the East Coast, Brad stood awake with the
same annoyed expression he wore before ditching us last night,
surveying the room for damages.

"You wrecked the place," Brad said, his credit card on the line.
The mess likely helped him choose his girlfriend over us.

Dustin urged Brad and me along to a Subaru Outback test
drive he'd arranged. Realizing that car shopping was our first
chance for a ride to Phoenix, the three of us went from dead asleep
to dead awake and back to cruising the Strip in a taxi. In bare
sunlight the bleak undertones and pale casinos marked in far-off
thought the unrestful sight of another year gone, our destroyed
hotel room fit for protesting the long wait for next year's shared
sake of having Vegas to look forward to. Past the Strip the desert emptiness laid the morning bare, the casinos dwindling in

both size and regularity along the hot streets. From the half-scale, classical Four Queens and Plaza themes of Fremont Street until nothing more than a few slots in gas stations, we zoomed into the desert outskirts.

Brad and I remained a step behind when the owner, a silver-bearded, cowboy-booted fellow stepped from the cave of his dark garage to shake Dustin's hand. We both stayed back during Dustin's test drive with the owner. Brad called his girlfriend until Dustin texted us. He was buying the Subaru and didn't know how long he'd be sorting out the sale with the owner at a bank. Brad and I decided to roam the desert range. Keeping straight course toward a palm tree isolated tall above the bushy terrain, we noticed on closer inspection that it was actually a cell tower, disguised for uninterrupted desert view above the faint traffic of a service road.

"So, I have a theory," Brad said. "Three of us can handle Vegas fine. No trashed rooms. No getting kicked out of the Mandalay Bay. But factor in a fourth, and one of us goes off the rails."

"Dustin?"

"And now he's left us stranded in the desert."

"Kind've like finding a casino in the absolute middle of nowhere." I pointed through the uneven topography of cactus to a sign bordered with bulbs. The casino was one of the dozen Station casinos scattered throughout metro Vegas with the industrious recurrence of the diesel-refueling stops along the service roads. Its air-conditioned interior was a letdown of worn carpet, vacant slots, bald bartenders, and antlered chandeliers of such dim lighting my eyes weren't adjusted by the time I found the nearest bar, a straw-thatched cantina selling one-dollar crushed margaritas by clear plastic cup. I ordered strawberry, leaving the tab open for however long Dustin's car sale took.

"Did you get a chance to meet Santana?" I kept myself from asking Brad about Tom.

"I don't think I did."

By the way, when I say that rehab and all my troubles were worth getting to know Tom, I mean it for you too. I wondered, in the letdown of soon leaving Las Vegas, when I'd see you again.

By the time Dustin picked us up from the Station Casino it was still early enough to make it to Phoenix by dark. Riding in his new Subaru we crossed into Arizona and stopped for a late lunch in Kingman before cutting south from northern Arizona's pine-topped high deserts down the rockier highways. Too tired and late to continue on to Tucson, Brad let us crash at his place.

Not knowing when I will see you or Tom again was to feel each second of the sleepless night ticking restlessly by. Long into the night I could hear Brad on the phone with his girlfriend, unaware of me awake and thinking of you.

Nearly a year has passed since my mom's passing. Eleven months to the day on this morning after leaving Vegas. "It doesn't get any easier," you've told me. I open my eyes to the fresh morning light on the walls of Brad's living room. There's no peace blanketing her loss. Coping is splitting a bottle of chardonnay with Tara, relief our Vegas weekend. It's a matter of escaping and forgetting, admittedly on irresponsible terms. Who knows if my drinking's turn for the worse came sooner with Mom gone, but you best know a bottle carries me through these nights when I can't call her. In the emptiness without her, expanding beyond the reach of any supporting walls, I'm no more than a pair of unbalanced steps. I miss her so much.

"I miss you," I chant in whispers.

And I need you, too, when we're lockstep, together reflecting on our moms—those are the certain steps forward.

Brad emerged from his room, his brief goodbye apologizing for the early deposition he was due for downtown. When Dustin rustled from the floor we set out for my first return to Tucson since Mom's funeral. Along the way the late-morning sights were a familiar fostering of Arizona missed more now that I was back again. The forearm tattoos on Circle K cashiers ringing up coffee refills, the mirage of jet exhaust across the passing Sky Harbor tarmac, the overhead entanglements of interstate exchanges on exiting southward from Phoenix, the fast-lane spacing of semitrucks beneath the slower-motion traffic of directionless clouds, the signs for reservation lands and exits west for San Diego, the halfway point of Picacho Peak solidifying into the distance—sights closing in on a careful reliving of our old home waiting empty.

Mom knew she was dying. She never looked away from the countdown that met her gaze at its eternal point beyond anything Dustin and I could see. Whenever we were overwhelmed by the decline of her health she softly bid us hope for life soon without her. On the interstate, I was reminded of her urging to finally drive the Pacific Coast Highway.

I'll still miss you.

I know.

Every day when I can't call you anymore.

I hear it's beautiful. San Diego on past San Francisco. See the redwoods for me. All the places we've wanted to visit since you were a little girl flipping through your picture books. A road trip might help move you beyond the loss.

I'll need some time.

"The world won't stop after I'm gone," she would remind us, too often from bed, eyes covered under a damp cloth.

But the world did stop, fittingly enough and brief as it did, momentarily joining me in falling apart the morning after Mom passed away. After an all-nighter of Dustin's calls updating Mom's unresponsiveness, from the ambulance ride to her removal from life support, I headed off to the airport for the earliest flight to Arizona, and while waiting for the metro, I didn't notice in my grief how entirely deserted the platforms were until the first rail-cars arrived just as empty of their morning rush, as though Washington was clearing way for my departure.

Had I paid any attention to the headlines of the newspapers underfoot, nearly all of Washington's workforce was home due to a budget impasse that you'll remember resulted in the federal government shutting down last October. A day, an illness, that for six years we knew was chasing her down had finally arrived, railcar after empty railcar. My mom lasted three months past your mom's sudden passing.

I often wonder how much harsher the unexpectedness of your mom's death must feel. And I can't vouch for whether holding privy to the warnings of my mom's passing better carry me through our darkest nights. Then again, I can't imagine missing my chance at goodbye. Whenever you especially regret missing out on that final Christmas or hug or hour with your mom, please hear it from me how hushed my last goodbyes fall in the silence without her. Even having told her in so many ways, more goodbyes commiserate along with the hope she can hear me in the many unrestful nights that I solve with sleeping pills. The bottle of which, I realized as Dustin exited the interstate, was back in Washington.

"Think there's any Excedrin PM leftover in Mom's bathroom?"

"She left way more than just the over-the-counters. Her prescriptions haven't been touched."

The undeveloped road Dustin exited onto straddled the county line for several miles of cotton fields before cutting across rockier cactus-guarded terrain. Before joining the busier state highway from the north, a lone gas station approached as still as its picture of desert solitude expanding toward the mountains. This particular Circle K, where Dustin stopped to refuel, was the last personal landmark I'd seen of Tucson as the home I'd had with Mom in Arizona. This location being where I bought vodka throughout the week spent arranging her funeral. It was too much to hear the funeral director open our appointment with "You'll have to call the hospital to have the body released." In the laminated pages of the funeral director's master binder were price ranges for obituary submissions, caskets, headstones, embalming, and renting the chapel. "It's not uncommon for the Tucson crowds to just wear jeans and untucked button-downs to our services."

Walking the cemetery lawn for burial plots, the sunny and clear Arizona sky returned no answers to questions so heavy with loss: *So, this is it? Life without Mom? Do I really believe in Heaven?*

Nothing that day came without plunging realization.

After Dustin refueled (and I didn't find Excedrin PM but did buy vodka again) we turned onto the last leg of highway, widening into the grid of Tucson's commercial arteries. Beyond the curbside burger and taco drive-thrus were business parks of mesquite-shaded offices where Dustin and I spent many turns chauffeuring Mom's doctor-shopping for painkillers. As prescriptions for the Oxy doses Mom counted on were increasingly restricted across the state, eventually it was back and forth between the same doctor and pharmacy, the county's "last duo," as Mom put it, "giving strong drink to the perishing." The semiretired doctor relocated offices every few months from one northside plaza to the next, but the pharmacy stayed put, down the aisle of a grocery store, which Dustin also drove by.

Finally, the old home, intensely recognized, and how empty on our return to find no celebration or welcoming, a homeport with no one waving from the sun-bleached pier of the driveway. With only Dustin living here, stale rooms were expected, but I was unable to brace myself for finding Mom's bedroom exactly as it was since the day Dustin called the ambulance: the bedspread folded diagonally back, exposing the side of the bed where she slept within reach of her Bible atop the dresser, the gentle hollow of her bedridden imprint now vanished. Hanging in her closet were blouses, sundresses, and skirts I wasn't ready to donate. On the wall I straightened portraits of Dustin and me, at two and five years old, grinning above the mirror facing the bed. Black trash bags were taped across the windows to keep at bay the many sunny afternoons she napped through. Other than every few weeks loosening the taped trash bags from the windows and sliding open the glass to billow in the dry evening breeze, Dustin kept her bedroom nearly untouched and unvisited, including by Mom's church friends who, for months after, dropped by with meals and to help clean the rest of the house. Pairs of socks, dress shoes, and diamond earrings remained boxed beneath the bed or stowed in drawers as Mom still deemed them necessary. I like to believe that what I couldn't find of her diamond-link bracelet was instead borrowed for the night by her.

Her bedroom's only definitive difference was the missing combination lock from the red metal toolbox where she kept her arsenal of medications. Until her passing Mom summoned Dustin in the mornings to unlock the day's dosages by a combination only he knew; she didn't trust herself against overdosing if the pain became too much.

"Goodness, Dustin, so many pills left." I counted the translucent-orange prescription bottles.

"She left over twenty Oxy scrips."

"If the street value is a dollar a milligram that's forty dollars a dose."

"Forty bucks by roughly fifty pills a bottle is two grand. Rounding up the number of bottles to twenty makes it forty. She saved up what she could for events like my graduation."

Mom also talked about taking one last trip to her native West Virginia. In recent years she was on closer terms with most of her extended West Virginia family, in large part due to our cousin Brandon moving in with her and Dustin while he worked at a tribal casino outside Tucson during my college years. When he moved out to work the bigger casinos in Las Vegas, his own mom, unable to reach him, filed a missing-persons report, which prompted police to request a search of our house for signs of Brandon's whereabouts. Mom, in the spirit of ordering us to get rid of "whatever you have in the house," asked me to hide her prescription toolbox in my dorm room. We didn't have weed in the house, I promised, and besides, I told her, storing someone else's prescriptions on campus was certainly riskier than hiding weed. Her helpless protest helped me understand how truly dependent she was on the doctors and pharmacy pickups. I agreed but instead kept the toolbox in the trunk of my Mazda for the night, which I parked off campus. A week later Brandon turned up; he had been crashing with a girlfriend in Pennsylvania, not far from Easton, where our dad lived and where about the only relevant similarity to Tucson was the street value of Oxy.

Along with Oxycontin Mom saved up bottles of the following prescriptions:

Doxycycline: antibiotic

Gabapentin: anticonvulsant

Ciproflaxacin: antibiotic, also for treating anthrax

Klonopin: for treating seizures and panic disorders

Tramadol: moderate pain reliever, often for post-surgery discomfort

Zolpidem: sedative for treating insomnia

"Zolpidem is Ambien; it'll do the job of Excedrin PM," Dustin said.

"Do you ever see Mom in your sleep?" I asked, but he just shook his head, refusing to go there. I asked him because I'd yet to receive the assurance of my mom like you have for yours, shining across your dreams. Mine visits no one, and for an impatient while it was disappointing to hear of your mom appearing to you with regularity in the weeks after. "She looked so young," you'd said, "and so beautiful"—exactly what I had hoped for my mom, radiating the ultimate light from where she's free of pain and smiling in relief—"I'd nap after work in the hopes of seeing my mom again."

I'm glad for you to especially be graced by her shining presence given the shock of her sudden summoning to an unknown all-knowingness apart from us, together so dearly needing our moms.

To credit my mom's deeper silence to her burial in Tucson, I promise you that nowhere else is a retreat from winter more of a relief from the weary competition that is our working lives out East. Where better than Tucson to sun your outstretched limbs and let your thoughts distill clear as the desert sky? I wish you were here to take it slow with me for a few days of the minutes giving way to hours and for a few nights of counting in your sleep the overnight freight trains thundering beneath the night's roll call of stars. Where better to recover than beneath the palms and cactus? For this I'm glad Mom chose to rest in Tucson over the muddy grounds of her West Virginia upbringing.

"Visiting is part of the grieving process," she'd said.

After Dustin intensively tended her last months, she wanted to give him a clear and present place of mourning. "I suddenly have all this free time," Dustin noticed after her passing, "but it took a few weeks before it hit me why."

I'll visit her later today.

It's in the absences where her loss most coldly confronts us, here at her last address, in this bedroom, among the last of her living presence, where she couldn't be further, save for in my prayers where her absence burns most unbearably.

Throughout the seven years of her sickness leading to her eventual passing, I prayed whenever her health worried to mind, which was nearly every day. And I brought to Washington the more methodical formality of every Sunday marching my prayers through a list on a notecard that when the next week's was inked I'd save with the rest in a Christmas-cookie tin. The ritual, when it started in Arizona, was a sunny after-church walk of praying through each listed request along the desert trails and sandy washes crossing the back brush of Mom's subdivision. *Mom's health*, as always scribbled, I listed atop every week's notecard. The earliest notecard dated back several Decembers ago when the Christmas tin of home-baked cookies was gifted to us from West Virginia around the same time I first recognized Mom's alarming decline into prescription dependence. The ritual, when it ended in Washington, was a lonely wait on a metro platform for empty railcars. My prayers had failed.

Leaving my latest prayer card in my purse during the week of Mom's funeral, I showed Dustin: "I prayed for her seven years, and look how it all ended?"

His response still surprises me: "Would she have lived those seven more years without your prayers?"

Nevertheless, I haven't kept up with prayer, not until my arrest, and I can't bear Mom's absence at the top.

To pray for someone is to build upon them hope. Praying as much as I prayed for Mom built a definitive tower of that hope. The higher I built her name, the further, like a flashing signal, I hoped to alert God's cooperation on her behalf. To no longer have Mom's name to lift in prayer is a loss that in mourning is the tower fallen, that in coping is bearing abandonment for living.

Vodka: for treating hopelessness

At some point I plan to walk the same desert trails, but first I'll drive to the cemetery. What to expect at my mom's grave—will I cry? You've cried much more than me. Your cycle of immediate grieving didn't match mine. Shortly after my mom died you confided your months of crying and napping. I wondered how many tears it took to uphold the duty of mourning, as though Mom's life meant more the more tears I wiped away. It's wishful to assign meaning in the shadow of so much meaning suspended during the aftermath of my endeavored tears and mostly never napping and certainly never catching the blessed glimpses you had.

On the day of Mom's funeral, I cried with an unmindful abandon of any daughterly duty to do so.

I skipped the breakfast cooked up by Brandon, in town for the funeral, and went right into dressing. Black stockings, black low-heeled slingbacks, and of course the black dress, which altogether isn't a difficult difference from the dress codes of the hotel bars we've waitressed. For the black cardigan I fastened only the top button and pulled the sleeves to my elbows to balance the knee length of my dress. I worked through my makeup, glossing my lips and nails plum, and lastly fastened over my tied-back hair a netted black veil, like nothing I'd worn before, cast enough shade to avoid retouching the mascara I was too upset and unsteady-handed to carefully reapply. Instead I brushed on a thicker liquid foundation where I'd wiped away tears.

Now, driving these same foothills of gated neighborhoods leveling to Tucson's flatter commercial terrain of auto shops and nameless plazas, I'm reminded how Mom's friends and fellow churchgoers were already seated and facing her casket in the chapel. Nearing our front-row seats, I wanted to shut the casket, so garish was the sight of her embalmed features that threatened the delicacy of her memories I wanted to nurture through the morning. Mom hadn't looked anything like herself. I wiped away more tears in the restroom. What a worthless bother tending to my makeup again, but more frustrating was the expectation of those expecting me. I sobbed quietly through the hymns, the brief sermon from her Baptist pastor, and through the carrying of her casket into the hearse.

Now I turned from Oracle Road beneath the arched entrance of Evergreen Cemetery and noticed how potholed and graveled over the single-lane vehicle paths were, as though kept crumbling to keep the speeds as calm as that day the hearse drove us to the other side of the cemetery. Mom's grave was toward the far border, a few rows from the dense barrier of oleander hedging that dampened the rustle of interstate traffic and concealed view of the roadside's yesteryear hotels along Miracle Mile. Only the distant rim of blue mountains peered over the hedging's pink-and-white flowering.

As Mom's casket had lowered into the ground, autumn's first gusts blew oleander petals atop her casket before the first shovel of dirt was tossed over, a sight of such fitting sentiment that from wherever autumn gusted was as good a direction as any to start asking "why?" I still carry that sinking sense of *why* when I wonder too long why Mom left us. The answer is instead this harsh emptiness that overcomes me, never the crying that in its sentiment, and with everybody there, and in the raw wake of her passing, flowed so easily on the day of her funeral.

I parked and approached her grave, stepping into the void of becoming its silence and stillness as I crossed the cemetery lawn, the sun in the grass as tranquil as I hoped she rested. No emotion welled from kneeling at her gravestone, not even sadness or loss, which by their familiarity were at least comprehensible.

Around me stood gravestones engraved with scriptures, military ranks, running shoes, toy airplanes, anything to lovingly mark its life lost:

Roads? Where We're Going We Don't Need Roads
The Dead In Christ Shall Rise First
Somewhere Over The Rainbow
Wind underfoot, Free to find, What lies beyond
Mom's engraving:
There's a land that is fairer than day
And by faith we can see it afar

For the Father waits over the way
To prepare us a dwelling place there

In the weeks after I'd returned from Mom's funeral to Washington, crying put me to sleep or more often saddled me through an early morning before the distractions of the day freed my mind. Soon enough my tears were a reaction too self-aware to mourn. It was an easy release compared to the emotional paralysis of hearing nothing at the cold touch of her gravestone, nothing through the wall separating the living and the dead.

To Mom

WE MISS YOU SO DEARLY AND SO MANY TIMES A DAY. AND DUSTIN and I wait for you. We wait insofar as fate envisions you also waiting for us.

Remember us as kids in the back seat with the atlas open, you driving us to church or practice or Flagstaff, looking forward to the days when we'd drive ourselves? As the back seat was our wait to drive, so were the back rows of our high school classrooms our wait for college, and college likewise our wait for a career. I'm still holding down the job I left Arizona for in your last years of diminishing health. Work is a wait for my own family and the inevitable rest. Pray for us.

You'll be glad to know that Dustin is still on track to finish college this December. I've continued the dialogue you were unable to finish with him, asking the necessary questions about what's next after his time at the University of Arizona (work or more school?), praising his better plans and urging him to follow up on job searches and applications to grad programs.

I'm not sure whether he stays in Tucson or continues school up the road in Phoenix. Either way, I think up abstract connections to you, like how the I-10 traffic rumbles by his apartment nearest to you at the Miracle Mile exit. This is what I think of when I'm lost as to how you might still be with us. I do look for you, the presence of your past, and wonder on colder nights whether you and Dustin can hear the same passing traffic. And if you see the same lightning storms and anticipate the purple skies from opposite directions. Or is it really us looking up, waiting, while you gaze down over our storms?

Pray for us.

Many restless nights I've spent looking up from bed. A cold night in southern Arizona is a colder night here in DC. Across the dimmer skies of the East the scarcer lightning is blanketed by cloud cover as urban-gray as the cities sprawling the seaboard below, no less dreary with each autumn I spend here, restless for sleep or the next trip. My friend Santana warned as much when speaking of her own mom's passing. She says it doesn't get any easier. We know each other from spending the night together in jail, if that's any indication of how she might as well be speaking to any which unfortunate way the days have proceeded since your passing.

~

I was arrested for drunk driving several months ago. My arrest is a night I relived this morning as rains hastened the sidewalk traffic past downtown's federal buildings. I walked to the district courthouse to plead guilty, letting my mind escape anywhere else, even to the brain-dead meetings of today's interrupted work routine. Then I stepped in from the rain to the courthouse reality of the security guards wanting my purse, phone, and my few steps through their metal scanners. I followed along with a hollow obedience serving also as helpless anticipation to whatever the judge and lawyer would soon agree to.

I'm sorry to come to you on such disappointing terms. Lately I've taken my worries to Santana, but this morning, if my troubles aren't already enough for the both of us, her attentions are tied up by her boyfriend's grand-jury hearing held today in this same courthouse. I can't ask her to divide her attentions like I'm paying my lawyer, Tom, to do, who at the moment is also representing her boyfriend. Tom had me promise to arrive early and text him once inside the building. Searching through the schedule of posted courtroom assignments for my hearing is a reliving of the numb Monday of my first arraignment after the Friday night that I was jailed for trespassing, destruction of property, second-degree assault, reckless endangerment, drunk and disorderly conduct, and DUI. In the few months since, the uncertainties were expensively sorted out between Tom and the prosecutors. Only one charge, the DUI, would stick as long as I plead guilty and agreed to the following: a six-month driving license suspension, four thousand dollars in fines, and completion of an alcohol-treatment program, of which the biweekly rehab meetings are already underway, fitting harmlessly around my work hours. Overall a highly forgiving deal. There would be no jail time, and the hiring and firing powers of my employer can be kept clueless. My boss will have no idea as long as I'm at work.

The passing few months have taken their anxious toll of waiting, and this last and longest hour passed most tensely as I waited on the benches along the wide central hallway's stony repetition of numbered courtroom entrances. From their double doors marched armed guards escorting prisoners. Fear skipped past the janitors pushing mop buckets and found dwelling in those, like me, who never planned on testing their fates in court. Waiting, fear, and so much loneliness.

Though Dad was on his way, driving the darker morning hours down from Pennsylvania, it was the reassurance of your presence that I most needed today. If you're curious as to how Dad's doing, I'll let you know if I see him on happier terms.

Given today's circumstances, don't expect Dad's presence to provide me any more of a familiar comfort than either the judge or prosecutor. I say this because Dad doesn't sound any less upset since I first told him of my arrest, again dressing down my irresponsibility and untrustworthiness over the phone last night. So whose sympathies am I left with when Santana's sudden appearance in the hallway yields only "hello?" I needed more from her today, to stop and talk me through this! Today her sympathies were tied to Martez. After hearing so much about him from Santana, this was the first time I was seeing him, as he passed by to the courtroom, stride for stride with Tom, both handsome in suits and ties. Watching their march inside the courtroom until the doors closed behind Santana, somehow I felt left out of the last place I ever wanted to go.

"You know them?"

"Hey, Dad." I stood.

"Who was that? The girl I saw you talking with?" Dad's own suit and tie matched the formality of his abruptness.

"Oh, Santana?" I peered to the doors she now stood behind. "We know each other from church."

"You're going to church again?"

"Church in the sense that's where our alcohol-treatment program takes place."

"So she's here for whatever arrest entered her into the program alongside you?"

"Yes." I didn't feel like explaining Martez until Dad shifted his attention to where "the lawyer" was. After an hour of waiting and Dad asking three more times where my lawyer was, Tom found us in the hallway.

"Sorry. Sometimes these hearings run over."

"Is that good or bad?" Dad asked.

"Bad. In your case, be very glad they didn't find drugs on you that night," Tom said to me, lowering his voice. "Gun and drug charges compound everything."

Through the double doors of our assigned courtroom the case before mine hadn't quite finished. We waited, the three of us, seated in the back, receding into the suspenseful stillness of the courtroom ready for the decision from Judge Sheila Parks. Hanging by the silent moments of her thumbing through paperwork before finally the scrawl of her signature whispered over us, it occurred to me how there are few greater displays of power than for the controlling force to have all the time to react. To the handcuffed man standing before her the judge impassively granted the conditions of his plea deal. Six years for cocaine distribution. Armed guards lead him away.

I was next, my case called aloud: NICOLE RINSHAW Vs THE DISTRICT OF COLUMBIA. The judge peered over her reading glasses as I followed Tom forward. A surge of recognition passed between the judge and me. With eye contact she kept us standing.

"How do you plead to the offense of driving under the influence?"

"Guilty, ma'am."

"Let it be noted that the defendant has entered a plea of guilty to the offense of driving under the influence. You may be seated."

Once seated the judge asked: "What was the State expected to prove had this case gone to trial?"

"Your Honor," the prosecutor stood, "in the very early hours of July twentieth the defendant was arrested at the impound lot of Capital Towing and Recovery Services located in the northwest corridor of Washington. It was determined by breathalyzer that the defendant was intoxicated, registering a blood-alcohol concentration of point one two. Authorities obtained witness statements identifying the defendant as the driver of the vehicle, which was deliberately accelerated into the impound gates. Witnesses also identified her as the aggressor of the ensuing physical altercation against the employees of Capital Towing. Their statements can be found in the interviews section of the summary investigation that has been submitted to the court. The defendant was then booked on charges of trespassing, destruction of property, reckless endangerment, second-degree assault, drunk and disorderly conduct, and DUI."

"And the State is seeking to dispose all charges except for drunk driving?"

"Yes, Your Honor, as written in consensus with the defendant's legal representation and submitted for consideration to the court."

As the judge studied the report, Tom leaned over and whispered, "The judge might question why the prosecution is offering to drop those charges rather than have them pled down to misdemeanors."

"What do you mean by *offering* to drop those charges?"

"Do you remember our last meeting when I went over the terms of a nonbinding plea agreement? A nonbinding agreement gives the judge discretion to reject the plea agreement."

"So it's only a recommendation?"

"The judge won't want to toughen the sentence without the other charges included. If she doesn't like the deal she can reject it and leave it to both sides to rework another agreement that adds back some of the dropped charges."

That sounded horrible. The risk of prison time and losing my job was as squarely back on the table as the copies of exhibits stacked before me on the defense counsel's table. They weren't encouraging exhibits. They included breathalyzer results, the police report, and photos of the sliding gate's mangled fencing and the black eye I'd given one of the impound-lot employees. I'm sure the photos were prompting the judge to doubt the logic of my plea deal.

"Why were these charges dropped?" The judge named each charge and brought back to life the night I had managed to contain, seizing me with the unsettling confrontation of its dark reliving.

"Your Honor," Tom began, "were this case to go to trial on all six charges the circumstances which can be presented to a jury will likely find my client not guilty on those charges offered as dropped. As to the count of trespassing . . ."

The sweltering July evening began with cocktails. Dinner was lined up for a second date at one of Dupont Circle's well-reviewed Italian restaurants. My impulse to wait at the bar rather than a table for two looked worse now. My wait increased by a second drink, and by the third I knew my date wasn't showing. He'd stood me up. Access turns to excess. Under dim bar lighting I steadied my disappointment to the pace of another drink, slowly exhaling to keep my loss of balance at bay. But at bay I drowned anyway, in alcohol. Self-destruction is always the most compelling justification. Without ordering a meal my tab still topped forty dollars. The signed credit card statement made for another relevant exhibit.

Reliving Dupont's streets I wished I'd wandered in the rain for as long as it took the night to sober over. Instead I found my car, only later learning that it was illegally parked and that in sleeping off a hangover in the back seat you don't have to actually operate your vehicle to face DUI charges. Though the impound lot's surveillance footage demonstrated their tow truck in control of the vehicle through the gate, it was me visibly unawake in the back, later failing the breathalyzer.

"... my client was illegally, dangerously, and against her will towed onto the restricted premises of Capital Towing's impound lot. The tow driver was negligent in checking for vehicle occupants before towing and as a result the seizure of my client's vehicle was illegal and dangerous."

The judge nodded, still studying the report. "I'm reading the trespassing charge was pressed by police rather than the impound lot."

"That is correct, Your Honor. Capital Towing did not pursue trespassing charges. This would expose their driver to a revoking of his towing license and expose their business to further conduct inquiries once it could be established that my client's unwanted presence was achieved by methods of forced detainment."

"And to the charges of destruction of property and reckless endangerment which Capital Towing did pursue?"

It was darker when I awoke in the back seat. The only light was the floodlight above the graveled entrance. A fenced gate slid open at the growl of loaded tow trucks, and a hefty figure stood at the guard shack waving by each arrival, tapping a button mounted to the exterior of the adjacent guard shack. I counted four tow trucks unhitching vehicles in my row of cars before plotting my getaway. When the gate reopened for the next tow truck, my plan was to follow one out. I crawled to the front seat and turned over the ignition, confident the smaller Mazda engine wouldn't catch attention over the diesel power of the next tow truck. Keeping the headlights off, I nudged the car forward and aligned its approach at the gate. As the truck neared the gate I studied the slow, chain-driven tempo with which the gate slid open, anticipating that if closing at the same rate I could easily follow a tow truck through. That was unless, as he did when I gunned the engine, the ox-shouldered security guard stepped into my path. I veered away from the opening and struck the gate's closing edge, tearing it violently from its sliding rails as its fencing clung to the front fender and was dragged through the gravel until halting behind the tow truck's red haze of brake lights.

"Your Honor, my client reacted as anyone would to unexplained confinement in an unknown location in the middle of the night. The damage to the gate was a risk assumed by towing employees who very forcefully attempted to further contain my client to their impound lot."

"And to the charges of assault and drunk and disorderly conduct?"

The fencing mashed against my car proved a useless barrier against the guard who launched the entire chain-link frame aside. He was colossal, and with my door already jarred open, he reached for my shoulder. As he leaned in I whacked his face with my small umbrella, stunning him backward, giving me room to step outside where I got in one more hit before being slammed to the gravel by both the guard and the driver who had hurried over from his idling tow truck. A mellow downswing of alcohol replaced anger as the active ingredient driving my very unladylike aggression toward the situation: a knee in my upper back grinding my torso against the gravel. The commotion garnered yells from a witness arriving for their towed car. They called the police as my car, having been left in first gear, gently coasted into the rear of the idling tow truck. Soon enough red and blue lights flashed all around.

"Your Honor, my client's alarmed reaction was strictly in self-defense against Capital Towing staff who escalated the confrontation to a physical matter. Security footage shows the security guard approaching my client's vehicle and forcing open her car door. And my client's aggressive instincts proved not uncalled for given the police confiscation of a loaded revolver from the guard along with a hunting knife from the driver."

"Your Honor," the prosecutor objected, "the gun cannot be cited as justification for the defendant resorting to violent altercation. The guard was permitted a gun as a matter of employment."

"A necessary duty," Tom responded, "that also requires adherence to a full uniform while in possession of a loaded weapon. The guard was stripped down to a dark undershirt when intimidating my client. If the lack of uniform was reason enough for the police to confiscate the gun then why isn't the same reason enough for my client to believe she was in enough danger to react with force?"

"Did you know the security guard had a gun?" the judge asked me.

"No, I did not know, ma'am."

"The court won't pay consideration to the gun."

Tom and the prosecutor nodded. Then, while the judge mulled over further pages, Tom again leaned over. "She's heard enough from both sides. Any second and she's ready to decide."

It wouldn't matter if the judge's report laid out the events more severely than I worried because my memory was condemning enough. Slugging the guard in the face was the most reoccurring memory from that night. I'm grateful that I didn't get in more blows and that he seemed fine enough to retaliate and later argue with the police, but it was all awful, this standing before the judge, beside lawyers, and with Dad looking on, knowing more than anything my matter-of-fact awfulness. The failure of myself. When the judge finally stilled her papers and looked up, blurred anticipation surged into focus.

"Have you heard what the prosecutor said would be the State's evidence?"

"Yes, ma'am."

"Is that what happened?"

"Yes, ma'am."

"Are you entering a plea of guilty to the charge of driving while intoxicated because you are in fact guilty?"

"Yes, ma'am."

She turned to Tom: "Before I accept your client's guilty plea, have you consulted with your client and found any advantages should this case proceed to trial?"

"Yes, Your Honor. I have consulted with Nicole, and together we do not believe a trial will offer any certain advantages."

"Do you and your client believe that this guilty plea is the best outcome for your client?"

"Yes, Your Honor."

"As do I," she said and signed. "Were this case to go to trial on all counts the many avenues of defense would not likely result in a more just outcome or an outcome that is worth the court's facilitation of a trial. Nicole Rinshaw, for your conviction of driving while intoxicated, upon your plea of guilty it is the sentence of the court to suspend your driving privileges for six months. You are fined twelve hundred dollars payable to the court and three thousand dollars in restitution for facility damages to Capital Towing and Recovery Services. You are also ordered to complete alcohol treatment, which I understand you're already attending a program endorsed by the court."

So, finally over, sighing when signed, I followed Tom from the courtroom, mindful to exhale again. The indifference of strangers brushing past was oddly welcoming. Dad joined us in the hallway, and with neither of us saying more than a round of congratulations, I looked gratefully to Tom while he and Dad set their gazes down the corridors of receding strangers.

"Will you see your friend again?" Dad pried for when my next meeting for alcohol treatment was. "Sandra or something?"

"Santana? Tomorrow."

Out in the streets the rains had stopped, and the foot traffic swelled along the sidewalks. As the three of us dodged the sidewalk puddles along 7th Street I felt what should have also been Dad's relief: the city effectively hid my mistakes and addictions. Nobody walking past or back in Pennsylvania, where Dad would drive, had any indication that I'd just plead guilty.

"And what about attending Sunday church like I raised you?"

"I should."

"And no drinks before then or after? And no more fighting tow lot guards."

"Of course."

"I'll call you when I get back to Easton, once I navigate Maryland's tolls," Dad said, departing into a parking garage.

Once Dad's car exited onto the street we exchanged a wave, and seeing the navy-blue-and-yellow Pennsylvania plate as he drove away, I was glad that back in nosier Easton nobody knew what he didn't want them to. The same was fortunately true of the office. Weeks ago, once today's hearing was set, I excused myself on account of having "an appointment." There was nothing for

Edith to be suspicious about as long as I made an appearance this afternoon.

"So now what? Back to the office?" I asked Tom, relieved to have the storms of my legal troubles clearing between us.

"Not before I treat myself to a drink. After a long morning in court I give myself a break at the bar on the walk back to the office."

"Are you inviting a known rehab patient out for a drink?" I flirted.

"I saw you drink plenty in Vegas." He smiled.

"I did promise myself, if we got through this I'd find out more about you. It's only fair since you've had to learn enough about me."

"Did Brad have much to say?"

"He promised you were a great lawyer."

"Would you agree?"

"I'd say you're good enough to deserve the first round on me."

The long breath we'd spent the morning holding together deserved to also be exhaled together. I ordered us a pitcher of Yuengling once we were seated in the sports bar not far from my office building. For the first time since my arrest, and maybe in years, I was able to appreciate breathing worry free, savoring this drink, and soon retreating to a refocused routine of work.

"You don't usually finish your cases over drinks with clients?" I joked.

"I celebrate in peace because most of my clients are off to jail after pleading guilty."

"Like Martez?"

"His case'll take a few more months to resolve. But yes."

"Santana said they denied his bail."

"The prosecutors are suspicious of his ties to Colombia."

"His vacations? Santana thinks it's unfair to consider Martez a flight risk."

"She's right. He's an American citizen. Born in LA. But I guess because he's ethnically Colombian and regularly vacations in Barranquilla, prosecutors fought against his pretrial release."

Hardly ever did I talk boys with you, and when it comes to my interest in Tom I know you'd quickly point out the ethics: He's my lawyer, doing what he's paid to do. But in defending me, how could his presence not welcome to mind his closeness?

"So, where are you from?"

"Chicago."

"You always want to be a lawyer?"

"Like most everybody that ends up in Washington, I once fancied myself a congressman."

"Maybe someday? A future rep from Illinois?"

"I worked on a senator's staff for my first job in Washington. Unless you're a lobbyist the more stable career is on the periphery. There's more than enough DUIs, drug arrests, and contract fraud to make a high living."

"Besides defending Washington's finest, what else are you up to?"

"Church. Maybe a weekend trip to Chicago."

"What about working out? Or music festivals? Or baseball games? Anything besides wearing a tie and advocating for your clients?"

"You're probably right. I deserve a break."

"Does stargazing sound restful enough?" I recalled our time in Vegas.

"Still the mem-ry stays for al-ways," he recalled the lyrics we'd heard sung by the Bellagio fountains.

"You remember." I smiled as my regrets of not being pushier with him that night also returned to mind. "Do you keep in touch with your clients?"

"Only if they call me with more business."

"How often do you treat yourself here?"

"I'm usually here for the Friday happy hours."

"Well, if I happen to see you here again, would you say I owe you another drink?"

"Sure. Anytime you happen to find me in here, we'll catch up."

Finding Tom at the bar only worked once. The next week I learned of his parents' careers as Chicago teachers, his college days as a scholarship baseball player, and his summer spent touring Europe prior to law school. Before we could share further happy hours, the reality check that ensued wasn't him growing sullen with me and disappearing to another bar. It was worse. We were interrupted at the sports bar by Tara, my coworker and roommate.

Given what I've told you of her partying, it's no surprise Tara was starting her weekend already on her third stop of a bar crawl when she wandered in a few blocks from our office with some coworkers. Recognizing me, she helped herself to our pitcher and Tom's attentions for the rest of the evening.

My lawyer, I kept myself from specifying after Tom introduced himself as *a lawyer.* But Tom being my lawyer fed right into the professional ethics that justified focusing his evening on Tara, which I had to know would be the case because my looks can't compete with hers. It was why I soon left—so I wouldn't have to see myself lose.

$\sim$

In the following weeks that I didn't see Tom, Tara did. I'm sure. Hearing Tara in her bedroom on her phone, I was sure she was talking to him. And when it was only me in the apartment a few evenings a week, I was sure she was out dining with Tom in one of Washington's many fine restaurants. I wouldn't risk her pretending nothing had changed by asking. My suspicion only confirmed Tom as a focus of my disappointment over not having what I speculated Tara did, a speculation confirmed when early on a Friday in our cubicle she invited me to join her and Tom at a Virginia Tech football game that night in Blacksburg.

"Tom?" I was surprised to be included.

"Your church friend. We're seeing each other."

Tara was too empty headed to reflect on whether I really attended church, and Tom had thankfully kept our confidentiality intact.

"All three of us?"

"My sorority's going all out. It's going to be a wild time. The more the merrier."

"I'll go, I guess."

If legal confidentiality was the only privilege shared between Tom and me, why so easily agree to play their third wheel? Short answer: I didn't want to spend the weekend alone. Of all places to fill an unpromising weekend, I weighed spending the evening at a church concert given by a Baptist college choir touring the region. Santana had noticed the posters in the church hallways during our latest session for alcohol treatment, and we agreed it sounded like an easy start to our weekend. But she lost interest as the week moved along, and I hated the idea of spending a concert worrying whether a whole choir would notice me alone in the back.

So, across the river in Arlington with Tara an hour later, we loaded Tom's black Mercedes with overnight bags and a beer-filled cooler, aiming to be on campus for several hours of tailgating before tonight's kickoff. Blacksburg was a several-hour drive into the Appalachia region and upstream of your hometown. You'll remember last year I was there in Rainelle visiting Aunt Cindy over the weekend before you passed away. I drove down on a similarly chilly Friday, getting in a call to you, our very last words, before losing signal through the rising forest of the shadowlands parting for sunlight along the river clearings, the low-angled sunset silhouetting the standing armies of mountain pines and spruce. You slipped into a coma sometime during my Sunday drive back. Crossing back into Virginia along the New River, I remember the cliffs overlooking the phantoms of river fog mirrored above the sleepy waters. The AM dial aired Marty Robbins. Along Interstate 81 toward Washington, I remember leaves hastening from the last of summer's glossy green confidence to autumn's cider-yellow, wine-red, ember-orange quilt draped far across Appalachia. Come Tuesday you left us. Dustin had picked me up from the Tucson airport, humming the tune played over the hospital intercom in final requiem of your passing. Forgetting Tom and Tara, church and the rest of my worries, the weekend's utmost importance was this: the first anniversary of your October passing.

"Thursday-night kickoffs are a really big deal at Tech," Tara promised once Tom had his Mercedes topping eighty.

"Today's Friday." Tom eased off the accelerator.

Riding in the back seat, I was audience to the natural familiarity they'd grown for each other. In her protest of Tom exiting the interstate at signs for Shenandoah Nat'l Park to experience "the peak of the seasonal colors" along Skyline Drive, Tara knew where he was from: "Um, excuse me, didn't the seasons change for you in *Chicago*? Stay on the interstate. Skyline Drive will take forever."

"But it's supposed to be the best weekend for autumn colors. If Skyline swerves too much pretend it's the Long Island Ice Teas you'll be drinking later." Tom knew her favorite drink.

"Cut into my tailgating, and I'll start drinking right here in the car. I'll drink until you refer me to treatment." Tara knew the nature of his lawyering well enough to keep me hoping Tom hadn't mentioned me as his client.

"I'll keep two hands on the wheel, and we'll fly along the mountain ridge." He knew how to talk past her by involving me: "Look, my right hand, the dominate one, it's like the hand of fate, acting on its own predestined accord, independent of my awareness. And my left?" Tom gestured to the back seat.

"The left hand acts according to free will?" I played along.

"Exactly, requiring conscious effort."

"Predestination is right-handed?"

"Yes, Tara, and which hand always takes the lead?" On the armrest between them he placed his right hand over her left.

"I got my fill of religion in Catholic school," Tara dismissed. "If it's all predestined, what's the point?"

"The point of having to participate in reality where our only response to reality is free will," I added.

"We're forced to participate in reality anyway, so . . ."

"So, why must we be cornered with both the inevitability of predestination and the moral responsibility of free will?" I asked.

"Adderall helps." Tara waved a prescription bottle from her purse.

"Addies? Now?" Tom squeezed her hand.

"Nope. Not before tailgating. I promised my sisters I'd bring them a bottle."

"No wonder they miss you."

"They're paying me."

"Adderall: For when you drive Skyline," I said.

"I want back on the interstate," Tara said, rolling up her window.

The mountain road lifted into dismal cloud cover, and through the drizzle and thinning hems of leaves, the yellowing and browning of valleys between parallel ridges were, on view beyond Tara's window, comparatively muted by her bright-red frown. In another thirty miles Tom turned down from the mountains to the interstate town of New Market and boarded I-81 to Blacksburg. To the west bulkier Appalachian ranges straddled the border of your West Virginia, its rocky rhythm of mountain terrain ongoing to the Ohio River.

I'll always know your stories of growing up in West Virginia. Never leaving me, they flicker in my mind as headlines whenever a map or highway sign or silent drive awakens their telling.

Miners rescued.

Father Michael screens theater's newest releases.

Missing horse, unknown rider last seen late on highway.

The way you told them; the hope of someday seeing a younger you, it is you over the mountains . . .

When we reached Blacksburg Tara looked up from the past hundred miles of using her phone to excitedly narrate the sidewalks of faces and frequent hangouts that until last autumn had absorbed her last semesters.

"I always saw him at the gym," she pointed, "and in that corner deli we always used student coupons after computer-drafting exams." Tara announced her former sorority house as its four pillars advanced into view of its forested enclave of surrounding student duplexes. Behind the sorority house the rumble of live music deepened as Tom eased the Mercedes to a stop. Grasping Tom's bicep Tara lead him around to the back porch. Behind them I dragged the cooler through the chilly air that in a rush of wind filled the gutters and swept the streets with brown leaves. Around to the back lawns, encircled by more student housing, crowds of college kids loitered, skipping afternoon classes and leaving underfoot the litter of red cups across the grassy clearing where at either end two bands competed within percussive echo of each other.

"So . . . college." Tom inhaled from the slight overlook of the back porch.

"Such a lovely campus!" Tara said.

Kegs flowed and ping-pong balls landed in red cups patterned across flimsy folding tables. Above the music bustled the chorus of drinking the afternoon away. I opened our cooler to present our contribution.

"You brought old-guy beer," said a dark-haired girl who, alongside other pretty house sisters, ambushed Tara with hugs.

"Stella beer?" I gave Tom, who bought it, an annoyed glance while Tara shared a porch-thumping group hug.

"Tom's a lawyer, and Nicole works with me in DC."

"Your boss?" They shook my hand.

"Kinda," I answered for Tara, my darker office attire of a long skirt and buttoned blouse contrasting their ripped jeans and baggy sweaters tilted and cropped to expose shoulder and midriff.

"Nicole, this is Erin and Lindsay."

The dark-haired girl introduced herself as Jenny.

"Is Tara a good employee?" she asked.

"Nicole isn't seriously my boss," Tara answered before motioning us inside.

"Who're they?" whispered a trio of girls ladling cider over the stove.

"They work with me," Tara minimally introduced.

"Okie dokie hokie," came the similarly dismissive greeting from the taller one who, by her scrutiny of the doorways, I pegged as queen bee. In her eyes simmered suspicion, whether of our business-casual getups or dismissing us as already lost to the wrong side of a difficult house history between her and Tara. Her suspicions weren't wrong, as Tom and I realized when joining Tara and her porch friends back in their room.

"Like, how cool is my mom?" Tara shut the door and held up a prescription bottle. "She gave me this last weekend."

"Thanks for helping us study," Jenny told the pills while holding the bottle up to a lamp.

"Addies?" Tom tried the vocabulary of his own drug-defense cases.

"And?" Tara exchanged the pills for the stash of weed Jenny kept inside an eyeless Mr. Potato Head on the top of her dresser. Tara next checked the dresser drawers: "This is where I kept my pipes."

Jenny had a lighter, and Tara joined in by sliding open a window and letting in the outstretched fingertips of several bare branches.

I vacated the room before a joint made its way around to me and hurried back through the kitchen, Queen Bee serving cider to what looked like her visiting parents. Tara did mention it was homecoming on the drive down.

Back on the porch I downed a beer, and on chucking the can onto the trampled grass, Tom appeared. He convinced me to join him through the crowds to the neighboring frat house where one of the bands held stage. The cordoned-off grass behind the porch was packed with students who, for admission, purchased a plastic cup that allowed endless refills from first-year pledges manning a lineup of kegs stacked against the support beams. Tom was high; in his stoned daffiness he didn't grasp this fundraising arrangement when the assurance of his hand on the small of my back guided me through the crowd to fill Tara's DuckTales mug. Lost as to why the pledges refused him a fill, Tom handed me the mug: "A pretty girl like yourself stands better odds of free service." As it stood the pledges had many attractive options—the surprise of Virginia Tech's brainy campus was the volume of pretty faces, one after the other, chatting nothing across the lawns, stopping to pose for selfies, then fading into the shifting masses.

Sharing two fills of her DuckTales mug we walked back to the sorority house to find the porch crowd growing and advancing denser into the kitchen and hallway, down which stood a line

To Mom

waiting for the bathroom. In the bedroom Tara was plopped face-down on the big pink-pillowed bed next to Jenny. After Tara gave off a bored moan, rolled over, and pointed to the dresser, Jenny knew what to do—she opened the bottom drawer and found the cocaine. Meanwhile, house sisters passed around pipes, their long glittering hair and polished nails sparkling through the calm ambience of the smoke clouding from the windows and doorway. The fallen darkness instead wanted in, turning the windows black. When enough smoke drifted down the hall Queen Bee marched over to where I stood at the doorway, and seeing Tom stuffing a pipe, slammed the door. "Can we shut this!"

I stepped back into the hallway, reminded by the last glimpse of Jenny's left-open bottom dresser drawer, my long-ago argument to you once: bottom drawers can be left open because the point of closing a drawer is to grant access to any lower drawers. The memory resonated as a funny comment to tell the room, but their door was closed in my face; and stoned and drunk, they would dictate the laughs.

What else do you line up and huff? Wisely back on the cold porch, I fought back a fit of guilt. Friends and boredom leading to alcohol, alcohol leading to . . . why did I continue to corner myself into trouble?

The arrest, alcohol treatment, pleading guilty, crushing on my lawyer, partying with him on campus is, I'm ashamed, all I've amounted to in the broken year since our parting. My guilt waned to self-conscious isolation among the crowds outside the closed door. Through the hallways and kitchen there was no shoulder space to casually drift from room to room, unknown beneath the burning amber light fixtures swaying above. Joining the social pulse was a matter of finding deafening conversation to hide my lonely appearance of disengagement. I was coming up empty every which way. There wasn't space to intrude into any of the established dialogues; the only one not occupied was Queen Bee ladling more cider. Looking my way, she dismissed me standing off to myself with another beer. Other interactions were a matter of soliciting interest that fed the interaction on itself, and once over, like the latest meal, came the need to reengage a new face. And across the broader course of years, conversation extended as friendship to you, to Dustin, and to whoever else school and work might sustain for me. Finding someone is difficult.

Tara, Jenny, and the rest emerged as a lovely beckoning of the football game soon to kick off. The crowds parted for their color-coordinated unity of sweaters, skirts, and leggings, the Virginia Tech orange and maroon also coloring their bows and scarves. I followed their parade outside and joined the greater masses lagging toward the stadium. Across the lawns, cutting wide as fairways between the student duplexes, lulled the drunken porches and live music in anticipation for the football game whose floodlights shone through the barrier of narrow forest dividing the stadium from our approach. As the stadium neared into brighter view through the tree line, the surprise of a familiar voice turned me around.

"Nicole," Tara said, catching up, "let's hurry!"

Her left hand reached for warm surrender in the grasp of my right.

Picking up the pace we dodged the few fire pits smoldering with the last of the pregame grilling and reached the head of a short trail through the woods.

"You have to help me finish this." Tara halted in the shadows. She held a bottle of cinnamon whiskey into a stray light piercing the trees. I could see one fourth of the bottle remained before the light shifted over Tara, and in her eyes gaped a startling nothingness—she was high.

Finishing the bottle together, I hurled it through the trees. We picked up the pace again, on toward the clearing of light, and as Lane Stadium towered into view once through to the other side of the woods, its floodlights illuminated like a halo the heavy descent of mountain mist.

"I need your ticket," Tara announced as we joined the long lines of students filing through the gates.

"Where's yours?"

"One works for both of us. See?" She pointed ahead. "You go first, then hand me yours through the gate."

There was a delay in the ticketing system, the student ahead of us turned to explain, so that after registering admittance it took another few minutes for the database to block repeat tickets.

"It's why the student section always overfills."

The trick worked. Through the gates we raced by concession stands of richly brewing smells of popcorn, hot dogs, and roasted peanuts, and from beneath the rising bleachers Tara rushed ahead into a tunnel exiting to the student section whose stands filled high with Hokie orange-and-maroon hats and jackets.

"Tara, Tara!" I caught up to her, hoping to get her seated.

Her answer was to again jet away. In her eyes an alarmed absence peered over the cliff's edge of consciousness, unresponsive to voice and touch, the uncertainty stormy like the darkness of a lighthouse extinguished.

To those who saw her turn up the steps and bisect their rows of bleachers, she was the pretty girl I followed under the lights. Guided upward by her blonde highlights, damp in the mist, felt like stepping out on the bright stage. All the way up there were no empty seats. At the highest row we found Tom saving room for us. The scoreless first quarter was half over, and Virginia Tech's offense marched the ball toward our end of the field. Unaware of the game's progress, Tara swayed in Tom's arms, free to lose her balance before she took a seat away from view of the glowing field.

"Look, look!" I wanted her to stand higher with the rest of us. "We're about to score!" When on the next play the Hokies ran in the touchdown Tara grabbed my hand and, sprinting off, lead me under the raised archways of celebrating arms. Tom raced after us through cheers so loud that calling for us remained as unheard over the thundering bleachers.

Tara and I darted ahead, losing Tom as we reached the open steps, leaving him to guess which lower row we cut back into. But peering down each row on descent of the rattling bleachers Tom found us, and ambushing us from behind, wrapped his arms around Tara before she worked her way out and rushed off with a thrilled laugh. I was happy, too, leading Tom on this delirious chase.

Tara and I rushed our feather-footed way row by row downward, each time looking back to see Tom racing after us. I was drawn into the trance of the moment promised as real in our later memories, those someday, long-ago days of our sandy hair flung back to look at the times boys raced after us.

We let Tom catch up in the tunnel. There Tara hunched over, a knee to the ground, her hair nearly reaching the pavement.

"Sick," Tara gasped.

"She needs to throw up," I said as Tom lifted her to her feet, his grip large beneath her arms as we shared the shouldering of her past the spilling-over trash cans and through the guy's bathroom to an open stall.

In the stall I eased her to her knees, and from her coat she handed me a wide orange ribbon with which I tied several handfuls of her thick hair into a ponytail that I kept from falling past her face as she threw up.

Tara leaned against me on our way out, the men standing in line resorting to vulgar jeers animated by raised beer cans.

Beyond the stadium gates and into the chillier darkness Tom and I walked her back.

"I'm gonna die now," Tara said, slowing her pace.

"Princess, almost back to the high castle," Tom urged.

"Don't." She let go of Tom's torso and slipped into the grass. We sat her away from the walkway at the base of a tree along the forest line and settled beside her. She leaned her head against Tom's shoulder, dazed and quiet in the stillness settling over us as the stadium roared in the distance. On the colorful video screen visible between the open corner of bleachers radiated another Hokie touchdown until the cameras panned over the waves of jumping, arms-raised cheering in energetic contrast to our calm beneath the trees. Tara dozed through the marching band's halftime show.

"Tom? Tom?"

But he, too, was drifting off.

Eventually, the footsteps of the first students exiting past us from the stadium prompted our way back. Returning through the woods, Tom and I balanced Tara, and when we were near enough she indicated her back porch where on the foreground of the lawn Jenny, along with a few other house sisters, were warming themselves around a bonfire.

As Tara's house sisters recognized her, she let go of me to be moved inside by all of them, Tom included, whose motion to come along I refused.

"Can I sleep in your car?" I asked, because whoever's strange bed we overcrowd would be an unwanted redo of cramming in Vegas rooms.

"You sure?" Tom was confused. "I mean, last time you slept in a car—"

"This time around I'm not drunk if I wake up towed."

Tom gave up the keys with an urgency to tend to Tara, and that was that: our evening together came and went with Tara between us.

For no other reason than a frustrated protest against ending the night alone, I tossed a stray camping chair over the bonfire and watched the light sharpening my shadow brighten with the rising flames as I walked away. In Tom's car I blasted the heater for twenty minutes, listening to the postgame call-in show on the radio, before killing the engine and climbing into the back seat to sleep.

In the morning, the three of us in the Mercedes, Tom and I outvoted Tara to begin the day by driving deeper into the Appalachians through West Virginia's more colorful falling leaves. Through foggy towns and burnt-colored valleys the roads meandered. Radio stations stripped to the basics of old country. We lost phone signal. I mostly thought about nothing. What did come to mind filtered numbly through the alcohol from last night. Yesterday wasn't worth dwelling on, especially if its disappointments overflowing into today were doubly felt once apart from Tom.

You'll agree it's another belated lesson to stay away, as though I haven't already learned the hard way: I'm past the age of ending up where the drugs and drunkenness are. And I've wasted the anniversary of your passing.

Northward along the narrow highway we passed the birthplace of Pearl Buck, the gigantic Green Bank telescope, and Snowshoe ski resort—sights nearly unknown to the much more populated eastern side of the Appalachian ridges straddling the Virginia state line, a remoteness beckoning my last time in West Virginia when I visited your hometown over the weekend before you passed away. I drove down on a similarly chilly Friday, getting in a call to you, our very last words before you later slipped into a comma.

In telling you this, of your last waking day, I'm not sure if I'm recounting to you events you can relive at will or if you're only left with the days you've known. Hopefully you know us even now, and when you picture us let it be a present and true summoning. From where you wait, let there be so much more.

Since you've gone away a West Virginia highway in autumn is reason for the closer remembrance that falling leaves become of you.

～

It was only a few weeks later before I was back in West Virginia, this time for our great-grandma's cold and rainy hundredth birthday in Charleston, downriver and from the foot of the mountains where we'll spend the night before in your hometown of Rainelle. Dustin joined me, flying into DC earlier this week for the fall break of his last semester. You'll be proud to know he'll graduate this December; he's weighing options for graduate school, fresh off applying for a few. He spends the week losing himself in the Smithsonian buildings along the National Mall while I occupy the office. By Friday we've convinced Dad, visiting from Pennsylvania, to give us a lift to the Rainelle exit where Aunt Melva plans take us in and send us off to Charleston the next day.

So, through your West Virginia we detour to visit those in your family who never left. By cooperation of its rivers and mountain ranges, as though impassable barriers for too many siblings, cousins, aunts, and uncles, there's no shortage of Appalachian terrain to contain the greater mass of West Virginia's homegrown.

I'm counting on the weekend to serve release for my ever-present thoughts of you, always cooped up in the cubicle with me and my dead-ended preoccupations: *Why isn't the positive outcome of my DUI case more of a relief? And why does it have to be my idiot roommate getting between my slim hopes for Tom, as though I didn't already know I had no shot as his client or otherwise?* There's nobody else to ask these questions.

It's hard enough talking about you with Dad or Dustin. For Dustin your passing is a loss to which he hasn't given much word. You and I both know that it's characteristic of Dustin to contemplate rather than talk about something. He knows I'm always available if he needs to call. Silence is the best I can offer seeing just how relieved he is to not have to come up with more observations or learnings at the inevitable mentioning of your passing. "I hope Mom dying isn't for us to *learn* something," is the most he's said.

As for Dad he's more given to hearing his pastor's promises of heaven, but when does the afterlife ever turn around to my tapping on its shoulder and answer to whom its home to? My faith hangs in large part on however you might be. Which at simplest heart leaves me with relentless uncertainty.

At my alcohol-treatment program, the Christian counselors appreciate knowing that you died a churchgoing believer, but I'm at a faithless loss when they promise your life renewed with the Lord. To say I'm "at a loss" is putting it too vaguely; rather, with their repeated assurance of Heaven, at some point I lose step of following their faith, and left without any hope of standing with you as before, that's the loss and uncertainty that leaves me grieving alone.

I was again at a loss once Dad, driving us from Washington, wasted no time referencing the recent anniversary of your passing.

"Dad, we knew she eventually had to leave us." I rested my head against the window.

"Words can't describe the loss."

"Not yet anyway," Dustin dismissed.

"Remember Heaven," Dad said, "where there will be no more death or sorrow or crying or pain."

It's easier to picture your next life much like this one, as though the next comes and goes like an exam, and even if you hadn't scored so well on this last one, it's now out of mind because you're occupied with the next. I can't reach you, and the next life is how I reason why you cannot reach back. Yes, another life free from pain and worry and loss too. There's painfully no way to know. I'm far less sure what to make of those who were once here than those still here.

Dad tempered his pitch for the afterlife once losing Dustin to a nap that put him out cold where past the DC Beltway, I-66 West abruptly sideswipes I-81 as the first of the mountains close in. Between long-hauling Appalachian ranges, blue along either side of I-81, the interstate lays low for gaps shallow and wide enough to deploy nimbler state highways over the mountains west. Even in sparing no expense to cut away hillsides and bridge the many gulches and hollows, there are no straight shots through West Virginia. It isn't for another hundred miles, after I-64 links up and overlaps its truck traffic from Norfolk before diverting west at Lexington, that the width and volume of an interstate finally tests the taller ranges making passage into your home state. As the highway elevation climbs the pines heighten and shadow into thicker forest, and the traces of earlier snow whiten the rocky slopes.

Dustin awoke a few miles from the state border. Lowering his window to snap a picture of the West Virginia welcome sign, the thinner native air cooled our faces and wisped its mountain-fresh breath through our hair. The most elevated few miles of mountain crossing rose and fell, and rising again, cliffs verged against the interstate, their serrated facings braced with wire meshing to prevent erosion from loosening a boulder onto the rushing lanes. Reaching a point of gradual descent, the downhill views opened to a distance of pasturelands rolling beneath the darker skies.

Soft rains omened the forecast of flooding from clouds swiftly rearranging like furniture for our expected arrival. I like to think of West Virginia as a boarded-off, windowless room in the same house where Virginia and Maryland share coastal views as the

To Mom   77

breezier living rooms. Who knows what's forgotten in this back-room of yours over the years?

"Are you sure Aunt Melva's picking you up?"

"Yes. Or one of the cousins. I'll call once we pull off."

"They won't be waiting for you?"

"Rainelle isn't too far from the interstate."

"Believe it or not the first time I heard of Rainelle wasn't through your mom. A dentist I had in Pennsylvania did her residency there back in the seventies. Said she pulled more teeth in her year there than throughout the rest of her career. Loggers would walk in with tooth pain and pay for the twenty-five-dollar pull rather than the two-hundred-dollar filling."

"That reminds me," Dustin said, "whenever Mom took us to the orthodontist in Arizona she'd tell us that if she'd raised us in Rainelle she would've had to drive us all the way to Beckley for braces."

Off-ramping at the Highway 60 exit, Dad let us off at the Exxon.

It took more than paying for his refueling (me) and pumping his gas (Dustin) to send Dad off; we again had to assure him that Aunt Melva, or one of her boys, would be on their way. We lied to avoid having to convince Dad of Dustin's idea to hike the twelve or so winding miles left to Rainelle along the old James River and Kanawha turnpike.

"The turnpike," Dustin said, unfolding a county map, "was used in early America as the wilderness bypass linking the trading routes of the Atlantic-flowing James River to the interior Kanawha River flowing to the Ohio. Even if it's only a few miles of paved road, I want the raw experience of crossing the land on foot when coal mining was bringing the first foot traffic to West Virginia."

After buying bottled water we wrapped our raincoats over our backpacks and started out.

"What'd you think of Dad's insistence on Heaven?" Dustin asked.

"We all agree that Mom departed for a better place, but Dad won't realize that believing in Heaven doesn't fill the emptiness that her passing leaves."

"That's what I'm getting at: Dad offers little sympathy for how much we still need Mom. His response to her death is to only talk Heaven, Heaven, Heaven."

"He refuses to understand the difficulty of waking up to another day without her no matter how wonderfully we can picture her in Heaven. I wish I were as sure as Dad, but his confidence relies on denying the impossibility of really knowing. It gets to me that what happens after death can't be objectively known."

Our road followed from the Highway 60 exit and for a brief distance joined view of the heavier truck traffic back on I-64 before bending away and narrowing into a shadier single lane bordered with enough gravel on either side to make room for any infrequently oncoming vehicle. White clover flowers brushed our steps along the graveled shoulder. Rain scarcely fell, and no houses appeared for the first few miles. The unfenced fields made for level blacktop on our straight approach into the rise of thickly forested foothills.

"Philosophically speaking, you can't objectively know anything," Dustin said.

"But that's no case for or against Heaven."

"Do you believe in Heaven?"

"I want to preview Heaven."

"For where Mom is?"

"For us too."

The road lifted, aiming for a tree line that once crossed, the forest canopy of shedding leaves loomed as an ever-shifting sky unto itself. Roots of trees lay exposed in the muddy embankments rounding the course of the road to higher overlooks of richly patterned cropland.

I wish you could once again experience with us how beautiful West Virginia is. Miles of narrow road and slumping barns proceeding into immersive depths of further farmland rolling into forests, of birds singing their gossip in the trees. Above the hills stand mountains at centuries' attention, begetting creeks beneath our footing over the guard-railed bridges we crossed before joined by wire fencing and power lines emerging alongside the road.

"I've been thinking," Dustin said, "when we reach Rainelle, the town will offer an experience of Mom, not in the immediate sense but at least as an exhibit of her through memories Aunt Melva might share or through her sisterly resemblance and mannerisms."

"And we'll likewise give Aunt Melva similar exhibit should she see Mom in us?"

"Exactly. Either by our speech or laugh or personality—an unavoidable reminder of Mom."

The nearness of your hometown, that here you were raised, sunk in when a school bus stopped to release grade-schoolers at a posting of mailboxes.

"Think they could be related to us?" Dustin counted three pairs of earmuffs hurrying home over the gravel.

As we closed in on your town, the lawns of more frequently passing houses bordered nearer to the road, widening for unhindered cross traffic. Oncoming cars slowed to stare their guesses—who could we be? Soon a muddied pickup stopped alongside us.

Behind the wheel a silver beard spit black chew into a Mountain Dew can.

"You're not from 'round here," the man said.

"No sir." Dustin slowed his step. "Our Mom was."

"Who's she?"

"She left Rainelle before we were born," I answered.

He introduced himself as Barry, offering a lift.

"Our mom grew up Rosalynn Crowe," Dustin said.

"Crowe, Rosalynn," he reordered, "over a hun'erd of her kin scattered across the valley. Yes, I 'member a Rosalynn at some point." Your first name took him back several decades.

"We're staying with our aunt Melva if you might know where she lives?" Dustin asked.

"Melva? Where Ada Crowe lived before leaving for Charleston 'bout a decade ago?"

"Our grandma, Ada, yes sir," Dustin said.

"You really are long-lost Crowes." He waved us into the bed of his truck, but only Dustin jumped in.

"I graduated high school with your grandma," he said, realizing I needed more convincing. "She had two baby girls right after. Her eldest, Melva, still lives back against the creek. Anyone on that side of town got baptized there. I know right where to take you."

With only a mile or so left to town, I climbed in back. Past Rainelle's outskirts of churches neared its first residential lanes, their open ranks of houses tightening into confined lots of low fencing as the blinking red traffic lights of Main Street drew into view. Barry, narrating through the back window, knew that your "branch of the clan," the many unlike you who "didn't leave and stay gone," still huddled together, yard by yard, in the same corner of town they'd filled since the "saw mill's years of full operation," going well back before the seventies.

"You've always lived in Rainelle?" We asked.

"Never left. Town or people. Though these days the souls I best know are mos'ly gone to the cemetery."

At this dinnertime hour, no fresh light fell through the trees or over the brown hills rimming town, leaving Main Street as shadowed as a burrow. No signs were illuminated for business. The flower shop across from the funeral home, insurance and tax offices sharing the same storefront alongside the pillars of a law office, a photography studio, pawnshop, and power-tool rental had all followed the bank's lead to close shop before dark. The only lights of commerce burned at our backs, as signs for gas stations and burger drive-thrus, until Barry steered us down a residential lane before Main Street widened to Highway 60 leaving town.

"Found me two little Crowes looking for their nest," Barry hollered on recognizing Aunt Melva on her porch. Slowing his truck to let us hop out.

"We were hiking from the interstate."

"Ten years! It's been ten years." Aunt Melva hugged us.

Her boys crossed the lawn for handshakes, appearing the full decade older with beards, tattoos, smoke trailing Austin from the porch and Brandon heavier with a beer gut and lip fat with chew.

"I was hoping you'd show up in your car," Melva said to me as she waved thanks to Barry.

"Mom wants your plate numbers for playing the lottery," Brandon said with a laugh.

"I've already played Barry's plates."

From the porch Dustin and I were tossed cans of Miller Lite, consorting us with the over dozen others cramming the living room, drinking in front of the flat screen. We were greeted by their rowdy toast of beer cans raised to Aunt Melva's introduction of us as her nephew and niece.

"Looks like you're still as popular as Mom always bragged," Dustin said to Aunt Melva.

"Everyone knows this is the place to watch the game," Austin said.

"You picked an eventful night to return," Aunt Melva added.

"The West Virginia Mountaineers kick off at seven."

"Austin, d'you 'member what I asked for by kickoff?" Aunt Melva gave him a moment. "To tend the garden?"

"How? Rainin' all day."

"Here, we'll do it." Brandon enlisted me outside and handed me one of the shovels leaning against the railing of the porch before taking up one for himself. Aunt Melva followed us to the side of the house where over a square of lawn lay a blue tarp kept tight by cement blocks pinning down its corners.

"How'm I supposed to count on growing watermelons and tomatoes next spring without a little help winterizing my garden?" Aunt Melva pulled back a corner of tarp.

"Austin's already too baked and drunk to be worth any effort," Brandon said, motioning me to help him drag the tarp aside, exposing a plot of dark soil whose surface of spent plants and scattered weeds Aunt Melva wanted uprooted and buried for adding organic matter to the soil. While Brandon and I shoveled over the plants, behind us, toward the oak-groved creek falling black as the sky, a few more of their friends waited for kickoff around a bonfire shorter than the nearby stacks of branches and lumber waiting to be tossed in.

"So, how are you and Dustin?" Aunt Melva asked.

I compressed the last ten years into a few minutes, stressing the decline of your health and how deserted the days were without you. I touched on my work in Washington along with Dustin's options for graduate school, limiting either situation from sounding very accomplished or ambitious because from what I knew of your calls with Aunt Melva and from what I could see in Rainelle, I didn't want to offer her the chance to dwell on an achievement gap she might have sensed between her kids and yours. Austin's back still suffered from his army injuries to the point that it might never recover, and like your last years in Arizona, the painkiller prescriptions he relied on were increasingly restricted, even through his treatment at the VA Hospital in Beckley.

"Pain management is just Austin's excuse to smoke weed every day," Brandon said.

"Austin's back slowly gets better," Aunt Melva insisted. "He moves around in the yard easier and can handle sitting through classes for longer."

I didn't ask whether Austin had held full-time work or earned anything more than disability. As for Brandon, his newest gig was dealing cards at the casino where grandma gambled outside Charleston, working mostly weekends when their tables were busiest. Only slightly more than Austin did Brandon give thought to occupationally steadying his approaching thirties. As we shoveled, Brandon recounted his seasonal work in Vegas, dealing cards for the larger poker tournaments. When he mentioned working the MGM Grand tables last fall, I was reminded of why it was Brandon, rather than Aunt Melva, attending your funeral on behalf of the three of them: Brandon was a closer drive away. He was a big help coordinating floral and meal arrangements in Tucson during the week of your burial.

When we finished in the garden Aunt Melva invited me for a walk through the "new section of town," as she termed the extended street of housing added a few years after you fled. Six additional houses faced the creek from across the street before it turned up 13th Street and intersected Highway 60 between a row of apartments and a hotel of an equivalent two floors of rooms. Hard to believe Aunt Melva still owned and operated the "Hotelle," as glowed its sign above Highway 60.

"Between your uncle Jim's weeks of driving his big rig, he'll climb a ladder to clean out every fly and beetle that swarms off the creek and works their way to the lights inside the sign covering. You can tell if he's home by whether his truck is parked behind the hotel. Sometimes it's the lot's only vehicle. Hardly ever a night with no vacancies."

"On holidays, maybe?"

"No. Rainelle's getting too old to visit. It's more like everyone to bum off elsewhere to see the grandkids."

Aunt Melva also still operated the adjoining coin laundry: "Dryday the Thirteenth used to be the hotel's indoor pool, but after buying the property I figured we could get some steady customers between the hotel and apartments so I tiled the pool over and hauled in a row of washers and dryers. Convenient for washing the hotel bedsheets."

Overshadowing the pallor of appliances stood another row for quarters: arcade machines.

"Pac-Man, Space Invaders, Street Fighter. Pinball. How clever."

"When Jim spotted Pac-Man cheap in Philly he knew it was the perfect trap for customers waiting on their laundry with pockets of extra quarters."

On the walk back Aunt Melva rang several doorbells from more houses of distant relatives—no answer.

"Darla substitute teaches several days a week, sometimes sending the kids to me for the morning when their dad's busy delivering orders from the woodshop."

Leading me around their house to the woodshop's mulched doorstep, Aunt Melva recounted the story of Rob and her cousin Darla.

"They married and were living in Pennsylvania after she dropped out of college. Rob was a furniture craftsman, so after returning to Rainelle, he converted what used to be this storage shed for fishing pontoons into his woodshop with his saws and drills. And the raw lumber that goes into anything he builds— church pews to porch swings—is easily gotten from forests 'round the valleys. He runs a good business, with customers as far as

Pennsylvania and employs summer help from the high school boys. Rob tries arranging work for Austin, but his back bothers him, and I'm afraid his painkillers don't mix with working the machinery."

I recounted all this to you for my sake too. If you'd stayed and raised us in Rainelle would we know any better than what I now see of the place? Your hometown doesn't come across as much more than its silent hotel rooms and lasting back pain, along with hushed moments of digging up the garden with Brandon or walking the neighborhood with Aunt Melva. There's no knowing whether an upbringing in Rainelle is comparably enough, but life as not enough is an inexpressibly sinking feeling I'm confronted with when facing your grave. Were your years enough for you? Your years weren't long for me, and I wish you were here. Especially as I heard your voice in Melva's. By and by, let life be worth the wait, and the wait worth life.

Tell us we're more than enough for you.

As is, I'm overly renouncing Rainelle if I withhold mention of the festive commotion back at Aunt Melva's packed house. By the time the football game kicked off two distant cousins, Connie and Shelby, along with their four children between them, arrived from a church potluck with pot roast leftovers. Their children, all under age seven, rushed from room to brown-carpeted room, the smaller toddlers scrambling from lap to doting lap for the span of brief attention Austin's buddies and their girlfriends diverted from the football game. In every room of its airing the game cast a blue glow over the unison of cheers for every Mountaineers score. Puzzles framed on the wall rattled. Seven, ten, seventeen, twenty-four, the Mountaineers outpaced their opponent, momentum interrupted only by penalty flags met with fits of cursing.

West Virginia's eventual win moved the party outside, along with the beer coolers for seats around the bonfire. Dustin waved me over to his conversation with Brandon. They wanted a final vote for their sudden plan to reach Charleston tomorrow by way of boating the Kanawha River.

"It's the river where Mom and her friends rafted the summers away."

"Actually, our moms were raftin' the New River upstream," Brandon clarified, "before it flows into the Kanawha. Before it got all dammed up. We can unramp the boat past the electrical plant at the rapids about thirty or so miles upstream of Charleston. The river's moving so fast from all the rain runoff we'll be able to have Grandma meet us before dinner at the boat ramp near the capitol building."

I voted yes. As for who would drop us off at the boat ramp: "My mom."

And whether the boat would hold the three of us: "If anything, the more weight, the more stability on faster currents."

Or whether we had enough life jackets: "Of course."

Any preparations for tying the fishing boat down to the trailer and hitching the trailer to Brandon's truck would wait until morning because Austin, urged by the fifteen or twenty of us rowdy around the bonfire, latched the trailer to a tractor backing into the yard. We piled onto the trailer's empty flatbed, dragging the coolers aboard for seats, and gave the signal to go. Pulled onto the streets the tractor's diesel exhaust sputtered. Along the dark streets front doors opened to our neighborhood commotion. A big-bellied man stepped barefoot onto his grass and, waving the blue-and-gold West Virginia flag, Brandon tossed him a can of Miller Lite.

Into other yards we tossed our empty beer cans, I'm guessing because no mutual respect was lost, because later, passing a house that our whole trailer flipped off in booing chorus, a full beer can was heaved through a window. I'm guessing again, the cops were called. In another block a flashing police cruiser pulled behind us. The pullover was justifiable several times over, from the lack of headlights on the tractor and license plates on the trailer, to the open containers and questionable sobriety of the tractor's driver, not to mention the few riders passing around a blunt. The stoned were the first to sprint away, and with Austin and Brandon scattering half a step later, Dustin and I took off, too, right past the cop car, our shadows leaning away from the cruiser's spinning lights as we trailed Brandon and Austin all the way back to Aunt Melva's.

In the morning Brandon had the boat roped atop his pickup before he could ask Aunt Melva, frying us a breakfast of eggs, to drive us to the river.

Brandon did the driving to the river with the plan of handing over the keys to Aunt Melva once the three of us launched his boat. The forty drizzling miles took a long hour. Aunt Melva cautioned Brandon around the slick highway bends slowing us along with our splashing through the mountain runoffs gushing over the dips in the road. She also had Brandon pull over at the Hawks Nest overlook to inhale the high view of the Kanawha through Appalachia.

"Hawks Nest is the very top of West Virginia," she said walking us to the stone ledge where we stilled to the vast expanse of river spanning in both directions around the river bends, sweeping between slopes ascending from the river.

Sights of vastness sure to visit my quieter moments; silence brings a lot to see.

Quieter, quieter; the silence summons you, for better here and worse gone. Give us a moment atop your West Virginia, as told by you in days gone.

Downriver the narrowing of a bend resumed the distant lull of rapids. Along the flooded banks the boat ramps were submerged when we reached Kanawha Falls Park for launching our boat past the rapids of the old power plant. The rush of the river also drowned our voices as Brandon thought aloud through revising our boat launch to instead use the park's graveled entrance, dipping below the waterline.

"Are you sure you don't want to drive the rest of the way?" Aunt Melva beheld the rising river surging through the standing masses of oaks and sycamores holding ground in the flooded park.

"Too late to ask."

Brandon handed us our life jackets. We hugged Aunt Melva, and once we loaded into the boat we waved goodbye and began our swift float through the park. Using his oar Brandon pushed off the thick trunks until clear of the oncoming trees. Then ordering our oars riverside to guide us toward the more open waters, we crouched low as the choppy waters threw us side to side until the more headlong inner currents took steady course.

"Let the river do the work." Brandon yanked over the hood of his raincoat to keep dry the blunt he lit. The smoke dissolved without hint of its spirited scent in the steady rains.

Brandon offered us a toke.

I shook my head. "We're already surpassing our limits with nature today."

Brandon laughed. "How'd you guys like getting tossed around back there?"

"As violent as moshing," Dustin said.

Soaking through our jeans and boots, the rain fell colder than the river splashing into our boat when broadsiding the roiling foams of cross currents fleeing through the towns as torrents down the mountainsides. Spotting either side of the Kanawha the small towns of names like Falls View, Deepwater, Alloy, Mt Carbon, and Boomer weren't more than a few blocks of houses, churches, and schools leading up the leafy slopes towering high into the drizzle and clouds. Their buildings were cracked, mossed, vined, and molded over in long wait for gentrification as nature had in mind. Time faded to past seasons in the rain; Christmas wreaths hung above the garage doors of a fire station. The abandoned red-bricked factories were in such deteriorated fallout their operational days of shifts swapping at the ring of a bell, rail yards busy loading gross tonnage, and bricks of actual red were too long gone to picture. Drifting downriver was witnessing a region unable to keep up, as though the passing towns, in living out the last of their nine lives, were hardly worth a fresh coat of paint, so grimly did they turn black and white in memory as soon we drifted far enough or vanished behind one of the forested islands standing midriver.

The islands had to be fought around like the trees in the park until the swifter channels were found again, which was made difficult by the crosscurrents threatening to run us aground. Eventually rounding a wider bend, Brandon announced the towns of Smithers and Montgomery on either side of the bridge spanning into view.

"We also need to portage around a lock and dam once under the bridge. Portaging is like bodysurfing your boat over land," Brandon said, smiling back at Dustin.

"Like a punk concert," Dustin joked.

"We'll need to carry the boat along the riverbanks for a good half mile."

Beneath the bridge Brandon grounded us into the banks of Montgomery. Dragging our boat onto the stony ledge of land that in another few hours would swell over, we lightened the boat by capsizing its chilly accumulation of water.

Then along the puddled streets Brandon shouldered the bow, and Dustin and I shared the stern as we carried our boat past the roll call of Main Street businesses. Like Rainelle, half the storefronts beneath signs for insurance and cafés were boarded up. Montgomery's major economical distinction over Rainelle was the state technical college, housed in a row of three- and four-story buildings along the railroad tracks.

"The state's proposed closing the college," Brandon said.

"Then what?" Dustin asked. "I mean, for Montgomery?"

"Pills and booze, I guess. That or everyone leaves for a bigger city. Pittsburg or Cincinnati or wherever. Same loss of soul."

From a drive-thru we bought burgers right as the menus traded breakfast for lunch. The rest of town was porch after porch of reclining smokers watching us in the rain as impassively as the cats huddled beneath the porches. I half expected someone to know Brandon and wave us over; he was by now in my mind such a fixture of the rural area, doubling his hunting jacket and coveralls as rain gear.

At a cemetery gate we again emptied the collecting rain from our boat. Ahead was the dam. Red-lettered warning signs were chained across the river: NO BOATERS BEYOND THIS POINT DANGER TURBULENT WATER.

To Mom

Past the dam we laid the boat back in the river just downstream of the dense mists ghosting from the overflow. Brandon pointed out a coal-transfer plant along the opposite banks.

"Raw material arrives by train, gets piled into the mounds of black soot you see behind the fencing, and after processing, it gets scooped by crane onto the barges for tugging downriver. Coal barges are always my biggest boating worry, more than getting caught in the rapids."

Brandon didn't think the barges were operating today.

"When the river rises high enough the wake risks spilling into the streets."

Standing above rust-red barges moored beside tugs of dark pilothouse windows, the processing plant's fuming stacks brightly welded a commotion of fire against skies divided by ridges and darkened by rain. We lowered our oars center of stream and drifted. Headlights on the bordering highway sped past. The swiftness of the river assured us to Charleston by evening. Brandon remembered another dam to get around after the towns of Belle and Marmet. Until then we leaned back, the rain falling in marvelous uniformity around us, a drop-by-drop acupuncturing of the river's hurried surface.

"When's the last time you saw Grandma?" Brandon asked.

"Mom's funeral," I told him, "when we last saw you."

"Oh right, out in Arizona."

"So about a year ago."

"And here you are passing through my stomping grounds."

"More than just passing through," Dustin said. "We're finding what we came for."

"What's that?" Brandon asked.

"We didn't define it because we knew we'd know it when we found it."

"And what have you found?"

"West Virginia." Dustin swept his oar over the river.

"I get it," Brandon said. "The essential experience."

"A losing of ourselves to West Virginia until its very rivers flow through us."

"We ain't lost yet."

"Transcendentally lost."

Brandon grinned. "This is my transcendence," he said and patted the pocket of his coat where he kept another blunt.

We drifted; only the river spoke, bend after bend, until at once: NO BOATERS BEYOND THIS POINT . . .

We floated closer to the next lock and dam, before portaging alongside the railroad tracks. It was nearly evening when we settled back into the water. Nightfall's slow heralding was shrouded by the ever-grayer weather. Amber streetlights flickered on through the towns of Rand and Malden. Drifting past, the river straightened and widened like the parallel highways bracing for the final stretch into Charleston. I-64 joined along the west banks, its heavy truck traffic bellowing through the waning rainfall for a few adjacent miles before crossing above us at the slight curving of the last bend. At last the state capitol's gold dome came into view. Brandon removed his phone from a grocery sack rolled up for water tightness and, gazing at the dome, phoned Grandma.

"We're here," Brandon said. "Well, we can see Charleston anyway. Can you get the pickup to the boat ramps off exit ninety-eight?"

And so, our river journey ended at the crumbling cement launch ramp where Grandma stood, watching and waving when she caught sight of our approach past a number of private piers jutting from the shores of their wealthy estates.

You'll want to know that Grandma's hair is shorter. The hug she had for us lacked the enthused grip from when she held a smaller me. Or perhaps when she held you in Rainelle. It takes an instant of effort to remember that you're her child. These days Grandma moves slower; days I imagine she takes like leftovers. Or chores. Driving to her new residence after we helped Brandon tie over the boat, she had little interest in catching up, avoiding the usual preliminaries leading up to whether Dustin and I were dating anyone. I'm glad she didn't ask.

"Radio saying if this rain continues the Ohio will spill over," Grandma warned. "They say Huntington might flood the worst."

To Mom

It was difficult being reminded of you by Grandma's presence. When I speak to you it's a matter of missing you. Of searching for you, above and beyond for the above and beyond. It is a matter of you becoming in death the here and gone of the greater search preexisting your passing. If I could see you again—to find and be found. To close our eyes and have you here.

To look to others, Grandma, or Tom, the sight of him a fading fix for "knowing it when we found it." What we would find if we could know it when we found it, I would gladly take as finding you.

The next day our great-grandma's hundredth-birthday celebration took place along the river at a dance hall renovated inside a historic train station. I wish I could tell you more about her birthday. At one point the mayor presented her with a commemorative certificate, and a news camera captured it all, but what I mostly remember is the rain, rain, rain, day and night. Puddles grew into ponds across the farmlands. The river rippled through the streets and against the steps of the dance hall. Strings of pale lights draped from the rafters overhead and glimmered on the waters of the river cresting into the building. Dancing splashed on.

Standing at the edge of the dance floor was to watch the swirling freedom of Dustin gliding a sparkling gown here, another there. I finished a drink and waited for the next song before taking the dance floor, and finally—so what about the watery footwork, let me dance where shines a strong face on approach, a welcoming hand extended, yes—this splashing of life is a forgetting of its embers gone gray after losing you. Such are the tragedies inevitably disengaging us from these escapes of life. I let my partner sweep me into a rhythm around the floor that on circling was the ascent of a staircase spiraling vibrantly above the night. And such are the highs, hoped and tried, overcoming loss. But the distance between us has no bridge; you cannot return.

To Tom

AT CHURCH LAST NIGHT THE CONGREGATION VOTED ME AND twenty others into church membership before the pastors administered the next vote, which was to excommunicate you. A rough turn of events. The news of your "live-in girlfriend," as the pastors entailed your situation to the several hundred of us, stirred within me a flight-or-fight confrontation that I immediately began losing to anger and loneliness. I voted no, raising my hand when the pastors solicited the nays against their recommendation to kick you out. I was alone, fighting. The pews turned my way, to this new girl, their regard closing in like walls. So I didn't bother lifting my hand and guessing the next vote. This one to excommunicate a married couple who returned from graduate studies in Pennsylvania as confirmed Catholics. But isn't Catholic still Christian? Who knows if you ask them?

What I did painfully wonder was how much you might be hurt. Oddly by the very flock I was joining. And did the pastors know whether you and I were well acquainted? What did they make of my no-vote? That I might know circumstances they don't? Like, who exactly it is you live with? I knew it was Tara, as I should've known earlier. Or, to be honest with myself, I should've come to terms with it earlier.

She has you, and I have church. Yay or nay?

"Did you know Tom?" I was asked by one of the pastors' wives as we were dismissed from the pews.

"I guess I don't know," was my hollow answer that might as well have doubled as their response to their question of whether you're even a Christian. You should ask yourself what she asked me. And know that their answer was to vote you out. So why, last night, despite myself gaining the church life you've now lost, was the careful inner path of prayer and remorse that led me back into church replaced inside and out with exactly what I appeared on the sidewalks home—a lonely figure walking in the dark?

For the first time in weeks I paid attention to whether Tara was home when getting back to our apartment. Again, gone and easy to guess where—and not alone. You and her.

To believe or not; I guess you're free from the distinction mattering.

Voting against your excommunication made for a tense admission into church. A week after the congregation saw my hand as the only one raised against your excommunication, it was too much to hope they'd forgotten. Yesterday, as the dismissed morning service talkatively exited the sanctuary, the pastor who'd presided over your vote-out recognized me at the door and asked me to his glass walled-office in the upstairs hallway. It was like the study rooms from my university's library—anybody could look right in, such as the younger pastor he waved inside, and see us taking a serious seat on either side of his wide desk.

"How are you?" he started. "It's Nicole, if I recall?"

"Yes, and you're Pastor . . . ?"

"I'm Pastor Kraikmeyer."

He introduced the younger pastor, an intern whose name I can't remember, before shifting. "And how's church going for you so far?"

"Still settling in, I guess."

"I take it last week was your first member's meeting?"

"Yes."

"And how was it?"

"I didn't know what to expect," I answered, realizing this also applied to stepping into his office.

"So I imagine this was your first time present for a case of church discipline?"

"Yes."

"Was it a little overwhelming?"

"I didn't know what to expect," I answered again, striving for a breathable pace of exchange; the looming subject of you had me outnumbered. I looked up at the intern, standing, smiling in the uneasy setting where my mind could correctly place the unknown conversations between you and them.

"Formal church discipline is a practice our church leaders have slowly incorporated over the last decade in order to uphold standards expected of members. If we, as a church, speak to certain standards that we expect Christians to walk in a certain way then do absolutely nothing about enforcing those standards then our walk shows that our talk doesn't mean anything."

"Maybe last Sunday was a little overwhelming. I wouldn't've guessed someone's Catholic confirmation warranted *discipline*." Especially now that its definition paraphrased to mind: *using punishment to correct disobedience.*

"We average about one Catholic case per year, and we usually have a case like Tom's once per year. I can understand if last Sunday evening was a little overwhelming for you, especially if you knew Tom."

I nodded, aware of the foot traffic peering in from the hallway, pretending not to notice us. At some point he had to be direct with you, too, so it couldn't have been as hard for him to ask as it was for me to be questioned: "Did you happen to know Tom?"

He wanted me to cough up everything. Testing my obedience or transparency or whatever, I could tell he wanted to know whether you slept with me like you do Tara. My options were to downplay his suspicions ("not really") or guess my way through with flimsy half-truths ("only from court, we both work in law"), and I didn't know how deeply he suspected we were connected inasmuch as it's true I'd found this church through your referral to alcohol treatment, so I answered "Yes."

In the long, unexpected silence he caught himself smiling.

"Do you know why Tom was disciplined?"

"Yes."

I let the silence build into a staring contest.

"So, Nicole, do you have any questions about the scriptural basis I gave for why Tom should be excommunicated?"

"No," I said, because how was this conversation anything but a discovery for more info on you, from an angle possibly involving me?

"Well, I don't want to take up any more of your time," he dismissed me.

Noting the wall of glass again, I walked out paranoid of the walls acting as mirrors, the kind for a police lineup, as sharply one-way as his discussion with me, and for the second Sunday in a row his dooming scriptural basis weighed on my walk home.

I'd rather address my questions with you, such as the scriptures he surely reviewed with you as warning. Last Sunday he read aloud from Hebrews: *If we deliberately keep on sinning after we received the knowledge of the truth, no sacrifice for sins is left, but only a fearful expectation of judgment and of raging fire that will consume the enemies of God.*

From Second Peter: *These people are springs without water and mists driven by a storm. Blackest darkness is reserved for them.*

And from Jude: *They are wild waves of the sea, foaming up their shame; wandering stars for whom blackest darkness has been reserved forever.*

The first fate is fire, and the other two are darkness.

I'm inclined to believe in the hell of darkness: cold, distant, soundless.

On the night of your excommunication it hadn't been but a few hours before I stirred awake, and as I remained sleepless through the soulless hours, sinking worry persisted with an inner coldness as that of deep space's deep chill, in such a darkness where light was never spoken, to a place as isolated as that of existence reduced to a voiceless and deaf awareness exiled among the wanderings of the stars. This was the dramatic hell to which I flipped on my radio. I worried about you all night and through this past week.

Did you read the rest of Second Peter?

If they have escaped the corruption of the world by knowing our Lord and Savior Jesus Christ and are again entangled in it and are overcome, they are worse off at the end than they were at the beginning. It would have been better for them not to have known the way of righteousness, than to have known it and to turn their backs on the sacred command that was passed on to them.

Anyone fostering a faith in the Bible should understand how harsh its terms can be in its black-and-white confronting of gray reality. Or better yet, this adult reality, where there's no safe closure. Remember our moms holding our younger selves, even moments after disciplining us? The stakes are comparatively unforgiving now. So there's no sense in trying to talk everything out with your pastors if the case they've built against you scrutinizes me by association. How upsetting my return to church must begin by hiding, by intending to go unnoticed, as though minding time in somebody else's home, where of course we're welcomed to make ourselves comfortable. However you might define existence, consider where it effectively takes place: always in someone else's home—think the captain's ship, the judge's court, the pastor's church. Or consider tracing our most idyllic hopes of Love or Justice to the Bible and finding those dooming versus I've repeated above.

I'm a little alone in this. But only when alone does any space become our own. It's a harsh tradeoff.

I wish you could know me beyond the girl you found scared and jailed on that summer night I needed you to shepherd me through court. I feel like a straggler whose turn for your help has ended, and for you it's on to the usual matters while I fall back behind as though nothing but a new day has happened. It was such an inexplicably low point for me, all of it, the aftermath leading nervously to court to relive the night you played down for the judge who thankfully agreed that the DUI conviction served justice. I've since felt that the least I can do is offer you a sort of relaxation—a reassuring shoulder rub while you kick off your shoes and I listen for a while. In court I sensed the tense movement in your body while you stood facing the judge, defending me. I wish you'd let me thank you.

To Tom   97

I expected your secretary to keep me waiting while she buzzed your office, but she waved me past without checking. So there I stood in your doorway, silent until you glanced up, regarding me indifferently, as though I were more of the paperwork on your desk.

"Nicole, I meant to touch base with you once the treatment ended."

"I'm still going to the church."

"Your treatment with them ended months ago."

"It did, but I took the membership classes to officially join. I was there at the member's meeting when they voted me in."

"I hope you know I never intended for you take my referral to their alcohol-treatment program as a suggestion that you needed church."

"I know. Church is something I've been meaning to return to since my mom passed away. It's been too long since I took church seriously."

"You'll find the Baptists definitely take it seriously."

"Tom." I spoke your name to soften the landing. "I'm sorry. About getting voted out. And last Sunday one of their pastors was asking me questions about you, trying find out how well we knew each other."

Then you leaned back.

"I didn't mean to drag you into this."

"Can we talk over coffee?"

When we stepped into the cold, I tightened the belt of my puffer coat, beneath which I hadn't put much thought into picking today's color-muted business attire because the nature of seeing you always came on a whim. I'd rather you see me in my purple sundress that waited for spring at the end of my garment rack. But this was the wrong season, and doesn't anything we plan risk falling apart? Nevertheless, who comes to mind when I'm reaching past my sundresses for the heavier sweaters and leggings? And there you were—so glad was I to walk alongside you that in any direction the routine street sights faded from continual notice—the freezing temperatures glowing on the digital bank clocks, the sleeping bags of homeless heating themselves over the sidewalk grating, the parking tickets fluttering against iced windshields.

In the toasty still life of the uncrowded coffee shop the windows offered an overcast street view of the afternoon's lull in the few hours before rush hour picked up at the onset of polar darkness.

"Their vote-out was nothing more than public humiliation masked as a legal proceeding," you said, regaining your forceful courtroom demeanor, "but excommunications aren't legal matters. Does my employer find out? Does my license face review by the state bar? Is there a fine? Outside church, what else changes? I'm still working, still earning a salary, still making plans. Only difference is my Sundays are freed up."

"So are you done with church?"

"Didn't they decide that for me?"

"Weren't they clear that this isn't a shunning? They told us you're still welcome."

"They announced everything to the whole congregation and had the nerve to consider the matter as privately handled? Now I'll always be known by them in their words as 'the fornicator.' How's that not a shunning?"

Your shoulders sunk, and your eyes shifted to the cold buildings outside, and for the first time I could unselfconsciously gaze at you. Then I watched you recede with each word like heavy steps walking away.

"They also had the nerve to tell me I should be there to watch my own excommunication because, as they put it, it would be good for me to see the consequences of my sins."

There is nothing more contrasting than time alone and time together. Even in the closed-eyed silence of either, one is so much colder. The questions I had for you risked refusal, so I let the blanketing of silence warm us.

"Did you know anything?" you asked.

"I didn't know how they did their business, much less when it comes to discipline."

"I mean about me and Tara."

"I should've known," I answered too quickly. "I knew you guys were spending time together because Tara never spends nights at our place anymore. I guess I maintained a necessary denial up until the meetings."

"They held more than one?"

"The second was me being questioned by one of the pastors in his office."

"I'm sorry, but what the hell did they want?"

"To know more about me as it related to whether there was a history between us. They knew I came from their alcohol-treatment program, and I let them know you referred me."

"In the church meeting, how did they break the news to everybody? Did they say how they knew about Tara?"

"An elderly lady asked, and all they said was that it was discovered."

"*Discovered*? They just go with whatever they suspect. Enough people there probably saw me out and about with Tara enough times to ask. I wasn't planning on hiding anything. Pastor Kraikmeyer held meetings with me and would report everything at the elders' weekly board meeting. I was less bothered the more serious they were because how many trials or grand-jury hearings have I been a part of where the cases at hand risk real prison consequences? Whatever happens, don't ever let a pastor intimidate you."

"Does Tara know about any of this?"

"Would it surprise you to know that between Tara and me she's the one most hurt by all this? She doesn't understand the reasoning behind why the church is treating me in a 'hostile way.' She worries she's cost me."

Again, silence. I gazed out the window at a city bus plowing through curbsides of slushed ice to sidestep Tara vividly coming to mind, sitting with you on the edge of a bed while you talked her through her frustration. I've seen her cry after performance appraisals with our boss. When they first hired me they'd call Tara and me in together to save the time it took to hammer the both of us over a whole list of late arrivals, dress-code violations, customer dissatisfactions, and any missed deadlines. Our recent appraisals occurred separately, and at least for me incurred less criticism. Tara might return to her desk in tears before composing herself enough to ask me for help. She takes facing consequences harder than I do, mostly, I imagine, because when her Adderall-hurried mind is slowed during moments of heavy reality and forced introspection, or from a weekend hangover, she for once catches a passing glimpse of the raw wreckage of a mostly ignored, pill-and-booze blurred reality.

"Tom, I'm sorry. I didn't expect it to come to this."

"No, I'm the one who owes you an apology. This is my mess. I didn't mean for you to have to see it."

"I don't think any less of you."

"Everyone else does."

"I don't."

I wanted to ask you for drinks at the adjacent sports bar, but you had to excuse yourself for work.

Thank you for the long hug.

And when can I see you again?

And it's been too long already.

And when will we talk again?

Resigning back to my desk for the workday's last few hours, Tara marched over.

"Where were you?"

"Discussing, uh, a case."

"With Edith?"

"No."

"Well, ten minutes ago she came looking for you. She wants to see us. I told her you were coming back from a late lunch."

My instincts shifted from explaining away lost time with you to scrutinizing my desk the way I knew Edith did when finding its occupant absent. I was glad for the invoice printouts neatly spanning my desk. Edith's overwhelming eye for detail left plenty of red-penned edits on every printout for me to look over and find positive effort with, and thus less likely to catch the glossy copies of *Vogue* beneath all the paperwork. And beneath my desk was a single pair of spare shoes—black ballerina flats, as opposed to the stable of snow boots, open toes, ankle-strapped heels, and beach sandals beneath Tara's desk.

"Another appraisal?" I asked.

"I don't know. If she wants us in her office it can't be good."

"Let's get it over with."

You've heard of Edith, our difficult boss? Her decades anchored in government auditing earned her a workplace respect that is a point of such forceful intimidation that during her impatient moments we lose sight of what she really looks like—hair cut short, rounded reading glasses, oversized dresses. We joke about how her closet full of bulky dresses must smother anyone wandering in, not unlike our experience in her office.

Which is why Tara and I entered together.

Edith ordered her door shut and kept us standing.

"Have I discussed the Phoenix audit with you?"

"Not lately," Tara said.

"How experienced are you with the Phoenix contract?" Edith eyed me. Part of her intimidation came from already knowing the answers to her own questions.

"I've . . . well, we've represented the contract in the weekly conference calls and issued all the technical directives dating back to last summer."

"Both of you have? Well, good. I don't have anyone else to go, and that leaves me defaulting to you two."

Edith wanted us in Phoenix for the contract-mandated annual audit and inspection of hardware facilities.

"Sit down. Tara, do you have a date tonight?"

"Um, no-o?"

"Not with that top you're wearing?"

Tara brought her hand to her neckline, checking its plunge.

"I must say, your outfits have been pushing the limits of what's appropriate for this office, as has been brought to your attention before."

"Yes ma'am," Tara said.

I was glad for leaving on my coat.

"Nicole, this goes for you too. I'm not sending you to Phoenix for a tan. When I tell you to dress professionally that means modestly. Closed-toed shoes, longer skirts, collars. Tara, what does that mean to *not* wear?"

"Sandals, crop tops, beach shorts."

So there you have it. I'm going back to Arizona in a few weeks. But to go with Tara, the bright promise of sunshine falters like any bit of living warmth weathering the cold. In the early-evening darkness after work I found a seat at a bar and drew upon the hours since marching into your office. By listening, I deferred to however critically you viewed the church's handling of your matters with Tara. I deferred to her wanting me to take charge of renting the car in Phoenix by not bothering to yet tell her that my license is suspended. She asked me first thing after we left Edith's office, and since I already knew the Phoenix area and since Edith was easier on me and trusted my lead, it was only fair in Tara's mind that I drive her around. I deferred again when she wanted to hold audit planning at the nearest happy hour when I asked her if the two of us could stay late to discuss. I deferred despite my aversion to drinking as a response to ending up traveling with Tara, the girl with the guy who, by whatever privation, I ended up without. Waiting for her in the bar was more deference. But I couldn't let myself fairly despise Tara because no matter how much more responsible I was when it came to work or otherwise keeping it together I was the one you had to pick up off the floor—signing me out of jail, sending me to alcohol treatment, and defending me in court. And I'm the one without an active driver's license to put to use behind the wheel in case this trip becomes me picking Tara off the floor.

$\sim$

After a few Sundays of maintaining my church attendance my shaky start with the pastor appeared behind us. Similarly, no one remembered you, or to put it kinder, I hadn't heard your name since my sit-down with Pastor Kraikmeyer, whom I only see in passing.

After last Sunday's service, when shaking the hand of a different pastor, the head pastor who usually preached, final tensions unwound as to what of me registered any suspicion to you. He didn't recognize me nor my name.

"We're glad to have you, Nicole. How do you find yourself fitting in?"

"Slowly but surely I'm working my way in."

"We encourage joining one of our weekly Bible studies or volunteer ministries. The children's Sunday school is always in need of more teachers and caregivers. Whether you intend to or not every member is better for getting childcare trained, even if you can't help right away."

I gladly agreed to stay another hour for the training, refreshed by how sincerely he wanted help.

Childcare training consisted of filling out paperwork alongside four other volunteers, which wasn't the idle formality I was expecting. Not when one of my signatures consented to a criminal background check or when the following questions forced an admission of last summer's arrest.

Have you ever been convicted in any court of a felony, or any other crime, for which the judge could have imprisoned you for more than one year, even if you received a shorter sentence including probation? If YES, please detail circumstances:

Pled guilty to DUI, I wrote, unsure whether the dropped charges technically risked a longer sentence if the judge rejected the deal. I had to be honest since I couldn't be sure who among their pastors might recognize my name from their alcohol-treatment program.

Are you an unlawful user of, or addicted to, marijuana or any depressant, stimulant, narcotic, or any other controlled substance?

I reread this question, making sure alcohol wasn't included before checking *NO.*

Have You in the last three years deliberately used the internet to view pornography?

From what I recall there's church-sponsored rehabilitation for this too, self-admitting, and overseen by their pastor of family counseling, who called me later in the week to set up a time in his office when we could review my application. He agreed to Friday at three o'clock, a downhill hour when I could duck out during the rest of the office's scramble for excuses to jumpstart the weekend early. The walk from downtown into Capitol Hill was bitterly cold. Icy winds sailed through the bare trees and cleared Chinatown's block of usual sidewalk musicians. At the street crossing where your office building angled into view further down the block I peeked from the hood of my coat to wonder what might be if I turned up the sidewalk and convinced you to a round of drinks. The winds froze away any color of hope, so I walked on, my hair blowing until pulling my hood back over. And reaching the church, the modesty of my coat was one less uncertainty when walking the glass hallway of pastors' offices, along which I kept my head down. The receptionist waved me back. Her disarming smile was a reproach to my mostly blank demeanor of keeping my eyes on the carpet. She wasn't the one walking into more questions or tired of testing the empty air with more unsure conversation once the door closed.

If you've worried any more about dragging me into any of this, remember that I'm plenty to blame, too, which is why, unlike during my reluctant time with Pastor Kraikmeyer, I didn't hold back. I told him about last summer's messy arrest, preceded since college by alcohol abuse, which I assured was definitely worth addressing during their resulting alcohol-treatment program granted by the judge as part of dropping the more severe charges.

"Sounds like you picked a very effective lawyer," he said without realizing the irony.

"Yes, and he's referred a number of other clients to your program."

"I'm glad we were able to help you, Nicole. Have you kept away from alcohol since completing our program?"

"Mostly. More importantly I've wised up to how senseless drunkenness is. Too many times I've regretted something I've said or lost the next day to a hangover. It's not a habit worth keeping."

I didn't sound like how you might know me, but I did truly mean what I told him. There was nothing good to show for the nights I'd centered around drinking.

"It will be a daily battle for some time, Nicole. But it sounds like you've begun finding freedom by realizing your sins. And how would you say you are now, spiritually?"

Spiritually? I'm never ready to articulate a passable account for my own spiritual state, no matter how many Sundays I was asked by fellow churchgoers offering this as their Christian greeting.

"I go to church regularly. I'm constantly praying. I take time to read the Bible. All of which are ongoing improvements."

"What else? Anything you're having difficulty improving?"

"My mom died a year ago, and coping with it became this big confrontation as to what really becomes of us after death. I'm not sure the Scriptures can always be so reassuring when it comes to the impossible questions."

"And did you repent?"

"For what?"

"Did you repent for doubting?"

"Isn't doubt an uninvited thing?"

"Well," he hesitated, "as opposed to actively looking to unsettle your belief?"

"I'm surprised if doubt needs repentance; doubt is always unsolicited on my part."

"You have a point, and overall I think you've come a long way since last summer. So much so, I'd like to have you join our Sunday school volunteer team. I'll have your name scheduled on the rotation of volunteers."

I thanked him and was glad I'd questioned doubt as anything that included our culpability in initiating doubt because I never go looking to disbelieve—rather, it's disbelief that finds me and leaves me to silence its crisis and find my footing once again.

Doubt's eventuality as a choice is a choice inasmuch as they say love is a choice, yes, if the choice is to whom you live out your love. But where our affections drift and shift like smoke, isn't that decided at an inaccessible depth of soul? I might ask why, why,

why you (?) and never receive an answer. I can also distract myself to a point, but all that does is deepen the ups and downs when love's loss relentlessly strikes.

I caught sight of you on a street corner a few icy mornings ago, from behind, and stopping to watch you walk away, my innermost self surfaced to depart in your footsteps down whichever street you disappeared and revisit our reality where we were together in Las Vegas, where I might again wake beside you. I'm only awake this early every morning to responsibly earn my keep, but how I long for that fast-burning reality of us, that irresponsibility of you and me happy together.

Again I helped Tara. I put together the presentation Edith wanted us to deliver in her office by the end of the week to convince her of our audit plan, but come Friday Edith rescheduled for first thing Monday morning, which meant combining the hectic Monday commute with an additional rush from work to the airport during the hours before our flight. If Edith's reason for delaying us until we lifted off was to force a better-dressed Tara off to the airport in presentable attire when the contractors met us in Phoenix, it worked. Tara was in the office before frosty daybreak, rehearsing our presentation, faithfully close to the lines I'd emailed her, wearing a dress of knee-length hem and elbow-length sleeve.

When ready, Edith called us into her office, and while I connected the laptop to the projector, she ordered Tara on a coffee run. Tara returned as we began: "The information-technology contract is our busiest contract—"

"False," Edith said. "IT is our busiest contract in terms of logistical contracts. Overall the engineering-design contract is busier in terms of dollar expenditures, which leads me to the question— what do you mean by 'our busiest contract?'"

"The IT contract has the most invoices," I answered.

"Right, meaning it'll have the most invoices to audit?"

"Correct."

"And," Tara said, "as part of their phase-in period for winning the contract we'll be recommending updates to their tech manuals and product inventory."

"Thanks, Tara, so can you explain why we're auditing a contract that's just started?"

Tara looked my way.

"Because Phoenix re-won the contract. Our audit will cover invoices dating back to their previous contract as part of closing out that previous contract."

"Good, Nicole. What did you study in college?"

"Political science, and I also earned a paralegal certificate."

"You wanted to be a lawyer?"

"At the time."

"Do you feel like your work here makes use of your college education?"

"Only in a vague sense do we rely on our academic backgrounds for operating in the business reality of contracts and budgets."

"We? Tara, what about making use of your college education?"

With Edith's eyes dropped to her notes again, Tara checked me with a glance. "Not really."

"Not really?"

After silence from Tara I answered by listing off the classes required by my political-science degree to demonstrate how indirectly my core curricula related to what she hired me for: "Industrial Organization, Macroeconomic Policy, Labor Economics, Wage Theory . . ."

Turns out the safer answer was simply "Yes," as an expected lead-in to elaborate on how college helps better understand the contracts we manage. Edith lectured as much before leaving us for another meeting. Her frustration spilled into her parting point: "The contractors you'll be working with will insist on paying for lunches and dinners. Letting them pay is taking an illegal gift and will turn up as an ethical violation when the legal department interviews you for contract review. And you can't let them chaperone you to concerts and sporting events."

However upset Tara was to come into work early, I was every bit as angry afterward, if not more, as we wheeled our luggage from the building and found our way out of the cold and onto the metro platform.

"What the hell?" I vented. "Edith can't just let us go to the airport without making sure we feel like shit?"

"You should know by now—nothing's ever easy with Edith. Besides, she ate it up when you listed all those classes."

"Screw her."

"Just enjoy it. We're free."

Still, her bitter points soured the satisfying ease it took us to metro to the airport, pass through security, and board the flight.

Our first flight was to a colder Minnesota. On liftoff my window seat looked north over the frozen Potomac. Views of the White House and National Mall quickly ensued until lifting into the shallow layer of clouds that held the afternoon skies in gray hostage. The vast cloud cover billowed west and after an hour parted over the waters of one of the Great Lakes. While Tara napped in the aisle seat, I compared the maps in the back of the airline magazine to the overhead views from my window seat, over what I guessed were Lakes Erie and Huron. The next lake I was certain was Michigan. Over Wisconsin the dull snow cover was interrupted only by the leafless brown ridges of forest between the farmlands. Descending into Minnesota the snowed grounds of the forests whitened through the bare trees along the Mississippi.

I awoke Tara on landing. "Minneapolis is my favorite airport for walking around. All the terminals are connected by a perimeter of walkways."

"It's not LAX," she whispered.

"LAX is always under construction."

"But at least you're in L.A."

As Tara lead the way to our Phoenix gate, I trailed behind to appreciate the airport's northern theming of Minnesota gift shops, tavern brews on tap from across the Great Lakes, and the low-ceilinged row of gates boarding propjets to Fargo and Bemidji. Further along the larger terminal's ramped carpet, the Phoenix gate was instantly noticeable by the relaxed passengers lined up for boarding. The sight of girls our age in black leggings and baggy gym tops hanging from one shoulder prompted us to remove our coats.

Forget Minnesota and the rest of our wintered-under nation; cheating the freezing temperatures by flying into Phoenix was an awakening as intense as the unfiltered sun welcoming us over the Rockies. On our final descent Tara leaned over to join in the view out my window of the sun's spectacular reflection flashing as a single wave across Phoenix's many backyard pools. My goodness did I miss the desert sun coloring anew the adobe pinks, rust reds, and fairway greens. It was like our eyes worked again. Yellows and oranges and harbor blues flowered brightly in the crushed margaritas gleaming along the bar tops of the airport restaurants.

The need for a ride evaporated once the contractors, two older men named Ron and Gary, spotted us holding our coats with crossed arms and decided to indulge themselves in handling our luggage and driving us around.

They drove us to Tempe. In the delay of rush-hour traffic we thawed under the sun falling across the urban valley and over desert mountains. In the back seat Tara and I rolled down the windows. We unpinned our hair and let the heated breeze flow deep to our roots. So warm was the sun on my bare arms that in the rearview mirror I could see my summer self smiling. I needed a redder stroke of lipstick, but the brighter look was pretty much there, starting with the tinted lenses of my sunglasses reflecting the passing palm trees.

In their front seats Ron and Gary were also smiling. Between the lines of their questions they wanted to know our ages: "Is this your first job out of college?"

And: "How long have you worked as contract auditors?"

And whether we would let them show us around: "Is this your first time to Arizona?"

Tara: "Yes!"

Me: "I graduated college down in Tucson."

"Would you want to meet up for happy hour at the hotel bar after you settle into your rooms?"

"Yes!" Tara enthused.

Suddenly it felt like an obligation to spend the evening as their well-treated client. I didn't even want to drink. What I wanted, when we checked into our ninth-floor room at the Embassy Suites, was to fully dress the sunnier part. Tara would drink with winning approval for the both of us, but I would look my best, too. We tossed our coats and scarves across our queen-sized beds and opened our suitcases to lighter clothing. Tara had me fasten the top button on the back of her yellow sundress, and I went with a silver skirt and sleeveless violet blouse.

"You wouldn't happen to have red lipstick I can borrow?"

Burrowing into her leather makeup kit she found both the shade I was hoping for and a joint, which she held up.

"Tara? You took that on the flight?"

"Not in my carry-on."

"You should know better."

"But you'll smoke cigarettes?"

"Yes, because cigarettes aren't grossly illegal."

"Haven't you heard? Pot's grossly *legal* here."

"I think you mean Colorado."

I was reminded of Dustin smoking out our high-rise suite in Vegas. If anything the long-awaited life back west was best summoned by smoke and lipstick. We compromised on smoking cigarettes instead, blowing the smoke into the bathroom's exhaust fan and flicking the butts into the toilet. We gave ourselves a last look over before heading downstairs. All nine stories of the flowering, inward-facing atrium of balconies matched most anything midrange along the Strip. A narrow canal numbered with koi fish meandered the length of the lobby. Drinks were served along the canal to a host of tables where the contractors waited. Bearded Gary was bald, and Ron's hair was fully gray. Both were overweight. Finishing a round they lit up on sight of our dressed-up selves.

Tara luxuriated in running up their tab with more chardonnays on the way, billed to their corporate account. It wasn't worth cautioning her with Edith's warning. Not with Tara catering to Ron and Gary's attention all evening, nodding along to their high praise of Phoenix's Mexican dining scene, before agreeing to dinner at a cantina down the road. I was glad Tara was the one taking

To Tom

up the task of cheerfully relating to them until she assented us to Ron's offer for line dancing at a western bar near the Arizona State University campus.

"How late are we going to be out tonight?" I asked Tara at the bathroom mirror.

"It's only nine."

But with the East Coast clock in my head clanging midnight, I wanted to be done for the night like Gary, who left after dinner. In Gary's absence Ron spilled his problems on us when we took a seat with him at a cowboy bar. I had no guess as to whether his wife's sudden relocation to Texas to take care of her ailing mother might be cover for estranging him. Nor did I have a response to his son dropping out of college without explanation. To avoid another round I went outside for a smoke beneath the stringed lights of the open patio. Tallying my drinks at four I tried dismissing the count as deserved relaxation for returning to Arizona, but I was too tired and worried about tomorrow. In the graveled distance across the grounds of a decommissioned train depot glimmered the condo towers and parking garages along Mill Avenue, Tempe's primary bar corridor. I was familiar enough with the campus surroundings to find our hotel on foot from Mill, but I couldn't leave Tara. Not even with her leaving me as the only one caring about tomorrow's work in lieu of the partying she was bent on having. I watched the lightning galvanize the big skies storming over the mountains, too distant for thunder or rain. After my mom died I wondered whether Arizona would become less of the home I'd left, and so far, on both of my recent returns since her Tucson burial, the only comforting sights were in the skies. The sun and lightning, best appreciated in stillness. Everything else moved along.

Back inside the bar the lights were lowered, and Tara and Ron blended into the dance floor. I took my seat at the bar and waited, watching tiny bubbles surface in a beer sent my way by a stranger, though at some point Tara was spooked and suddenly wanted to leave.

"He wanted to show me his place," she told me in the cab.

"Now?"

"He wanted me to see his pool and rifle cabinets."

At the sound of our early alarm Tara remained motionless in her bed. My patience with her lack of help and keeping me out late turned to frustration. In my head I blamed her for needing more sleep, for having to watch over the work, and, after a shower, for having to rustle her from the dead planet of her hangover. How late would we be if I ended up waiting however long for her to wake? Better off sharing a room, we kept silent distance from each other's waking routine. While Tara showered, I did my makeup and hair before she did the same while I booted up the laptop and reviewed our presentation.

"Tara, how ready are you to present?"

"I'll have you look me over."

"I mean, how well rehearsed are you?"

"I'm not ready, Nicole, I'm sorry."

Looking up to see how she'd at least cooperated with my suggestion to wear the black-and-gray business dress to appear as formally East Coast as possible, my frustration waned to the reassurance I took in making sure she was out of bed.

"Can you click through the slides while I give the presentation? Each time I say 'next?'"

An hour later Gary picked us up from the lobby and drove us to their commercial complex in Mesa. The ride there, with the sun glaring off the windshield, the windows rolled down, and radio newsbreaks announcing paradise temperatures, recalled my Tucson commutes of alike winter mildness during the dead of the nation's frozen months.

Their factory facility amounted to three buildings consisting of a customer call center, the hardware-assembly floor, and a distribution warehouse flanked by container trucks backed into loading zones.

As soon as Tara saw Ron in the assembly plant she covered her mouth and nose before muttering about the industrial fumes worsening her hangover. Ron handed us face masks before touring us through a series of automation labs and onto the assembly floor trafficked by forklifts moving pallets stacked high with boxed orders. At each stop Ron introduced us to his laborers as "the Washington DC clients we make equipment for." I should've been the one most impressed—it's welcoming to see a heavy-booted, dirtied-jeaned, hard-hatted workforce on their feet, manning machinery. Instead they were the ones impressed. In our smoothed black pencil skirts and matching blazers and all the way from Washington, to them we meant bold business for the instant I saw myself mirrored in their collective gaze as a flash of relevance. This was *making it*, this was *arriving*.

Their admiration held until the workers slowly returned to their stations once Gary started us down a long hallway to the call center's conference room where factory management was seated. Edith was waiting on conference call. She had everyone introduce themselves before ending with us. "Nicole, Tara, you ready?"

Our presentation explained that before starting orders under the newly awarded contract the past year of orders under the expiring contract required auditing, "which is why Tara and I are here. Next slide."

"How many invoices were filed last year?" Edith cut in over the speaker.

"Nearly nine hundred," I answered.

"And what percentage will our audit strategy cover?"

"A minimum of twenty-five percent, so we'll be looking at over two hundred."

"Are the invoices ready now?"

"They're being printed as we speak," Gary answered.

After the presentation the invoices arrived in two boxes, and the conference room cleared out, leaving Tara and me at the big cocobolo table.

Edith stayed on speaker: "Tara, why didn't I hear from you during the presentation?"

Tara had no answer. Nor could she answer how many invoices were filed last year or what percent required audit.

"Besides not knowing the contract, did you at least pay Nicole the courtesy of listening to her present for the both of you?"

"Um, I clicked the slides for her."

"Do you know how to audit the invoices?"

Silently, so Edith wouldn't know, I pointed Tara to the laptop screen and had her read aloud the slide explaining the matching of purchase orders to deliveries.

"The technical direction letter initiating a purchase under the contract is verified against—"

"Work through lunch if you have to."

Tara spent a few moments calming down after Edith hung up. Once she touched up her makeup, I guided her through how to meticulously match the dollar amounts from the technical direction letters to the corresponding unit orders shipped, which required matching to the weight signed for on the delivery receipts. From Tara's compliance emerged her quiet concentration and trust in my help; her mind, like a toddler's finally sitting still, steadying to the tedious paperwork. I'd rarely seen this tranquil Tara before, so quickly I knew her to race to the next distraction that she gave endless, caffeinated narration to, whether at work googling blouses or soliciting drinks at the bar.

"What do we do when the dollar figures don't match the orders?"

"We notate the order number on our discrepancy spreadsheet and save the purchase letter and its receipts."

With interruptions only for coffee refills, we worked until Ron returned at two, asking us to clear out the conference room for the scheduled factory meeting.

Once back at the hotel I called the shower, to which Tara suddenly needed a shower, too, thinking nothing of the morning showers we'd already taken and realizing nothing of the excuse I was making for disappearing to our hotel room, supposing instead we'd ready ourselves for another late night. So long for our peaceable hours together, I looked out the window in knowing resignation, watching the weather in the skies thickening to threats of storm. So I gave Tara the shower first while I kicked off my heels, fell into bed, and took a nap.

The nap aired out my mind. Two hours was the right amount of rest needed to face another late night. I wasn't looking forward to drinking, though a sangria did sound like the perfect complement to wherever the evening's mild air would take us. I'd let myself drink for two hours—the operative currency of time in Arizona.

I redressed before going down to the lobby and taking a seat with Tara and Ron who'd been drinking for the time it took Dustin to drive up from Tucson during my nap. Dustin was waiting in the lobby when I appeared downstairs, oblivious to Tara and Ron having anything to do with me until I waved him over to their table. Our round of introductions came with a new round of drinks. Ron, drinking straight whiskey, wanted to return to last night's cowboy bar.

"We should go get pizza or tacos out on Mill Avenue first," I said, with the aim of later ditching Ron at the bars. It's so difficult to get time with anybody. After a quick dinner Dustin listened to Ron's stories of working stadium concessions "back when I was your age" at the old Cotton Bowl, seeing in person the seventies-era Dallas Cowboys championship teams. They talked as we walked, a unity that went well with drifting on to the next bar of our crawl along Mill Ave. We settled into a tequila bar because two of Dustin's former roommates were there.

"These will be the drunkest guys you'll ever see," he promised as our IDs were checked at the door. When Ron was asked for his ID he lifted his hat to show the grayness of his hair to the bouncer who laughed and waved us in.

"They drink until they can't keep their eyes open," Dustin warned.

Seeing his pair of friends, along with several others, hunched over their sprawl of emptied glasses as we added ourselves to their table, I had a sudden aversion to the dull scent of beer thick in the air. Running around and drinking all night was how I'd always kept up with everybody, and suddenly I wanted out.

I gladly deferred my shot of rum to Tara. She swallowed it down in one motion before cramming a seat for herself between Ron and Dustin. In the dimly lit bar the strongest light shone from the neon signs of Phoenix's sports logos—Suns basketball, Diamondbacks baseball, Cardinals football.

"So, you're a Denver Broncos fan now?" Tara called out Dustin's orange shirt.

"No, Cowboys all the way."

"So, but, tonight, yeah?"

Tara deserved public-intoxication citations, along with Dustin's friend who ordered the table a round of Irish Car Bombs.

"Okay, and with those I'm going to bring your bill," the waitress said.

"So let's pretend I was your girlfriend," Tara offered Dustin, "we'd live in a Washington row house with a Broncos flag on our mailbox."

"No, a Cowboys flag," Ron shouted.

"Anywhere but DC," Dustin said.

"And we'd share a bed, a big bed—who keeps calling you?" Tara turned her attention to Dustin's buddy's phone.

Dustin leaned over to tell us that his buddy's girlfriend was calling around to find out where they were. "He ditches her to go out and get super drunk several times a week."

"And we'd be home together every night," Tara shouted to Dustin over the dance music, "in a house so big we'd be like children on a playground."

For as hesitant as the process has been, I'm glad, God willing, to be gradually giving up drinking. Alcohol turns me into a place where nobody's home. I pushed away my Irish Car Bomb and glanced toward the doorway, counting the reasons to leave. For one, I was at the point of not caring if Dustin was left with the burden of dragging Tara back to our hotel. And why was Ron, at his age, insistent on tagging along? Picturing myself in his shoes, out drinking at double my age, soured my willingness to further crawl the night's college bars. Plus, it was already late enough for the bars to lower their lights to the dance music and start charging cover.

That was when the very upset girlfriend of Dustin's buddy's charged past the line at the door and found our table by recognizing Dustin, who did what he could to calm her down and deny having seen her boyfriend, who by chance happened to have stepped out the back door to piss on the side of the building. Ron butted in on the racket, inviting her to dance. She ignored Ron, or more likely hadn't heard his pushy offer over the thudding music. How is it that nightclubs are the place to socialize when others can barely be heard or seen in the packed darkness? Numbed by my surroundings, I left with a severe sick-and-tiredness of all the clubs where I'd wasted late nights. Walking the desert air, the calmness down Mill Avenue to our hotel summoned memories of previous visits. The independent bookstore owned by a retired history professor and occupied round the clock by his elderly gray cat. The streetlamp under which a boyfriend once bought me a rose from a corner vendor. The gravel lot where Dustin once had his car towed and I had to drive up from Tucson to sort it out. Mill Ave was here in pieces, as an empty stage of storefronts, lots, and lampposts, but absent of the life that once remembered, stung with loss. No cats or flowers or boyfriends or stepping back into those years to escape these. No more Arizona, almost.

At 2AM Dustin called needing cash for the taxi idling outside the hotel. He also needed help shouldering a wasted Tara to our room. Propping Tara onto a luggage cart, she gestured warning of imminent vomiting as we wheeled her through the lobby and into the elevator. In our bathroom I removed Tara's overcoat and held back her hair as she convulsed over the toilet. After resting her into bed and tucking in beside her, I was upset until falling back asleep. My anger persisted at the sound of the early alarm; I remained angry with Tara for lacking the wherewithal for work, which left me facing the rest of the audit on my own. I was angry witnessing the nothingness alcohol has to show for all its consumption because I, too, have nothing good to show for all my drunken weekends. I've said so much I wish I could take back. I've wasted money. I want nothing to do with drinking. Nothing anymore, not a drop, which I've promised in counselling, but for once, for the first time since my first sip, the prospect of giving up alcohol didn't come across as a standard to live up to but instead as wise freedom from the profane drunk I'd been. I could smell the alcohol from Tara and Dustin as I readied myself for work.

Should I have awoken Tara for work? Still drunk, she was unresponsive. Hopefully Edith wouldn't call. I didn't know what to say if she asked for Tara. When Gary picked me up beneath the hotel veranda I told him Tara was sick.

Settling into the same windowless conference room from yesterday, I wanted to get the audit over with, but without any help, even from Tara, I was looking at a full day of tracing dollar amounts to the unit weights summated on varying documents. A number of the delivery receipts were foreign, and the brief detour of picturing their destinations were squashed as instantly as they occurred in mind because their numbers were too often hand scribbled and harder to read. The hands on the wall-mounted clock knew to slow when they couldn't be ignored. Checking the clock was like getting stuck behind a driver who doesn't care if you're in a hurry.

Tara's absence persisted as disappointment made all the worse by having to finish her half of the audit. Who knew how she felt when confronted with her own irresponsibility, for instance if Edith found out, but it's striking how easily all of us can distract ourselves from answering to the cold constants of responsibility and loneliness. When all along I can't forget you; I can't forget that it's Tara who has you to run to. The clock remains mystically still until Edith's call breaks the spell. I told her the audit would be finished sometime in the afternoon.

"Can I speak to Tara?"

"She's sick. She couldn't work today."

"I'll call her myself."

Edith's call motivated me through another stack of papers. Dustin texted: *Tara woke up to take a call. She's upset.*

See if she wants lunch? I answered.

Tara was worth a listen if Edith fired her over the phone. But evidently Tara wasn't quite fired—*I'm so sorry*, she texted. Edith's call could be counted on to frighten Tara into helping compile the audit report tomorrow. Ignoring Tara's calls I finished the last of the audit around three before packing up the paperwork and heading back to the hotel. In our room Dustin was leaning back by the window in the office chair, dividing his bored attention between the TV and an open textbook on his lap.

"Did Edith call?" I asked Tara.

"Yes."

"Well? You said you were sick, I hope, because that's what I told her when she called me and expected the both of us to be there working the audit."

"I'm so sorry." Tara felt guilty enough to ask if Dustin and I might want to get dinner while she stayed back to start the report.

"Okay, but do you have a cigarette?" I downplayed how appealing her offer sounded as I untied my hair. As Dustin looked up restaurant options I kicked off my heels in the bathroom before changing into a sundress as soft and weightless as the desert air. Without Tara (or Ron) to babysit, it was just Dustin and me, like kids again, on our bikes with pocket money Mom had spared us for ice cream trucks. Or, in our older case now, we bought smoothies. To finally exhale back in Arizona, I wish I'd never left. There was nothing so comfortable or freeing as wearing a sundress in the dead of winter. Like Santana I'd gone East for a promising next step only to find its crowds and frozen proving grounds nothing more than tiresome competitions.

Our departure back to Washington was delayed a day due to snowstorms closing airport destinations all along the East Coast. With another refreshing day in Arizona, Tara rode along with Dustin and me down to Tucson so I could visit Mom's grave once again. Tara observed Tucson in sobered silence, first on showing her the University of Arizona campus where Dustin and I finished undergrad, before standing afar when I, by and by, kneeled at Mom's grave.

Tara wasn't fired. On our return to the office Edith read over our audit report, offering no reaction as we stood at her desk, which is the best outcome of Edith scrutinizing anyone's work but nonetheless intimidating to wait through. At last Edith dismissed us. Through the morning Tara gazed out the windows, where newer layers of weekend snows whitened the graying mounds of slush plowed against the curbs. Windblown snowflakes swirled from the tops of buildings. Was Tara exhaling the worries of the bullet she'd dodged? After driving the audit home it's easy to believe I kept her head above water, and I can't tell if she sees it the same way. I can't help but wonder what she tells you about work. When I'm not upset with Tara I don't know what to think of her, and who knows what she thinks of me? Better to get along without knowing, which must be true between many others I tread the daily waters with, like Edith. At this point, how impossible it is to know another soul.

I wasn't sure whether the pastor's questions would ever leave their eye, but eventually they moved on from noticing me. It's like they weren't sure how to address whether I had anything to do with you. Since then going to church has gradually calmed into the lone certainty of my Washington routine. Or rather, church carves a dependable refuge within my weeks of not knowing what's next. It's refreshing to hear preached from Psalms God's willingness to hear our frustrations. There's an immersive comfort in adapting the evangelical view from the vantage point of their vocabulary. Their use of the word *encourage*, for example, carries a spiritual depth when spoken between members of the congregation. To encourage prayer, study of the scriptures, and a life of holiness is for one believer to uplift another, which in turn motivates prayer and Bible reading into the determined habits of a long-sought place of order for my often-worried mind.

Along with avoiding alcohol, it's a relief to more seriously practice the faith. My conflict with alcohol, as you're well aware, deescalates when I can walk into church fresh off a sober week. I felt exactly this unburdening on the Sunday after the Phoenix trip with Tara, realizing freedom from the guilt of entering the sanctuary after a typical week of boozing. It's *encouraging* enough to sit through the recent sermon urging us to understand the senselessness of drunkenness. A sober mind is vital to our sanctification, he preached. *Sanctification: the spirit lead strengthening of our faith through walking in likeness to Christ's example.* Justification, on the other hand, is the immediate moment of conversion, which I'm sure you can more exactly define, but the point is how these terms

To Tom

mean so much more when internalized for personal commitment. Please don't think I'm giving you a lesson or trying to point where you might be off track; rather it's me beating myself up because it's clear how few of us care to follow through with sanctification because theoretically it never ends. Last Sunday's sermon on the subject avoided the obviousness of just how much day-to-day distraction encumbers the traction of sanctification. The sense of life as short can be countered by considering anyone's experience of so much change, so much back and forth. One day I'm drunk, and now I'm professing sanctification. *Professing*: as in how few professing believers follow through . . . and isn't that the point?

Volunteering for the children's ministry every few Sundays has so far assigned me watch over the two-year-olds. More experienced volunteers warn of how tiring it is to wrangle a classroom of nearly thirty terrible-twos, but I find them an easier bunch than their reputation deserves. Unlike with infants, who can't articulate why they're crying, a two-year-old can point to what's wrong, like a missing "blankie" or just "Mommy." Most who are crying for their parents can be calmed by being held. There's one little girl, always in a frilly ice-blue dress, who cries for us to hold her the whole time. When I put Ainsley down to answer other little demands, such as toddlers fighting over a toy fire truck, she cries until I hold her again. I sit with Ainsley on the floor and calm her by pointing her attention to the other toddlers climbing kitchen sets or barricading themselves into playhouses. Soon enough another little girl will join Ainsley on my lap with a book. Two years must be the age when stories become irresistibly fascinating; the pair on my lap soften to perfectly attentive silence as I read picture books of mostly Bible stories like Daniel in the Lion's Den and Jonah in the Whale. They fall asleep in my lap. Already I can see in their angelic faces the prettiness of their always tall and slim mothers. The best moment of childcare is seeing their faces light up at the return of their parents. They sprint toward their mommies or daddies calling from the doorway. Of the church families I've come to know, I met most of the parents through childcare, mostly in the moments of making sure their child's shoes, diaper bags, or blankies are handed back. In fact, if you're willing to hear more, it's worth mentioning how easy it is to meet others while watching over the toddlers. Others, as in that potential, interested someone. Everyone wants to know if I'm seeing anybody. At church they have to know *who*.

Because Paul and I are the only caregivers who Ainsley allows to hold her, we've formed a natural togetherness in passing her back and forth. Ainsley would fall asleep to the deep voice of Paul's storybook reading. Whenever Paul makes a point to converse with me during childcare, it's his diesel-deep voice that echoes his most pronounced quality.

"So, you changing a lot of diapers today?" he jokes.

"Nah, the pair of newlyweds are gladly handling all the dirty diapers."

"I guess they want the practice?" Paul said. "If I really wanted to avoid diapers I'd schedule myself to teach the three- or four-year-olds."

"The thing with the threes is once they start talking they never stop. In the middle of long expositions their friends will toddle over to corner you with more newsbreaks from their little worlds."

"Do they cry instead?"

"Babies cry until about two, then they start sounding out words. By three they string together phrases. Like frat guys, I guess. Whatever they want they let you know right away."

"Hold me," Ainsley said at my ankles, opening her arms upward. I picked her up to look out the fourth-floor window facing in the direction of East Capitol Street's back approach to the Capitol Building. I'd pointed out the shapes of the familiar buildings poking over the rooftop altitude of Capitol Hill's snow-topped row houses, trying to get her to sound out the shallow "triangle" of the Supreme Court's roof, the "stick" of the Washington Monument, and the "dome" of the Capitol, but Ainsley kept her fist jammed in her mouth.

"With the two-year-olds," I said to Paul, "their primary sophistication is in processing stories. When reading aloud they'll crowd around you like a bonfire and follow a fairly advanced narrative."

To Tom

"How much of their excitement for story time is nature verses nurture? When they see you sitting down with a book do they rush over because reading is a condition of closeness with their parents?"

"I think stories are inherent from the day we start learning language."

Paul's enthused goodbye, before I parted into the wintry afternoon, lingered as warmly in mind as the excitement of the toddlers reuniting at the nursery doors with their parents. Knowing I share the same age as several of the younger moms offers no further similarities. Single, ever diverging, floating; missing out, I worry. Church seizes on many chances to parallel parenthood with the relationship of God overseeing his followers, but lacking the role for myself, my answers to how to fill the coming years passes more and more unsustainably. And when you come to mind, I don't know when I'll find someone.

There's another reason why children are on my mind. Santana is suddenly in the process of regaining custody of her two-year-old, Bianca. Before returning from Las Vegas, she called me earlier in the week to ask whether I might have room for her to move in. I told her "sure" paying more heed to Bianca than Tara, who remains gone as long as she's sharing your bed. If you noticed my missed call, my impulse was to instead have you tell Tara to let Santana live in Tara's room, where she maintains no presence despite her parents continuing to pay her rent. It's an arrangement Tara keeps intact to avoid the obvious prodding of where (and who) she's really living (with).

Meanwhile, Santana's story for why she was suddenly returning with Bianca wasn't clear, both over the phone and as she retold me on our metro ride from the airport.

"I'll have to fly back to Nevada in another month to formalize custody of Bianca through the family courts."

"Hi baby Bianca," I answered her big eyes, in astute study of mine, before asking Santana why Martez's family was handing back custody.

"They don't need her anymore. I haven't seen Bianca since we took her through the Bellagio. You remember the argument I was having when you and Tom ran out of the suite? I was arguing with Martez's mom. She was there to take Bianca."

"They don't *need* Bianca anymore?"

"Because Martez is pleading guilty for the lesser sentence. He's expecting three years behind bars like it's a good thing!"

"I still don't understand what his legal issues have to do with Bianca's custody, but I guess Tom's advising Martez to take three years given the severity of risking drug-trafficking charges to a jury's discretion?"

"Given the *initial* drug charges," Santana qualified. "Three years is playing right into the prosecution's game of overcharging to force an admission to lesser bullshit. The only connection Martez had to actual drug distribution is operating a nightclub where trafficking allegedly occurred. Martez wasn't even there when ninety percent of it went down. But because he happens to run the club he's charged the same as the dealers."

"Tom won't let Martez agree to an unfair deal."

"Who's to say the judge will find Martez guilty?"

"But if the judge does agree to their guilty plea . . ." I cut myself off as we stood for the metro slowed to our stop, realizing the stubborn denial of her wishful thinking.

Time with Paul was as innocent as walking from the school bus with your sixth-grade crush. He wanted to get to know me, he said on our recent walk from church, before asking for my take-aways from the sermon. I was compelled with Paul beside me and for our small, meaningless talk that upheld our shared presence down this street I'd walked so many times alone.

"May I take you to dinner this week?" he asked.

"Sure," I agreed, no sooner sensing the weight of his plans for a more official relationship: *Well, we met in childcare*, I pictured Paul speaking for us after a few dates, answering to the sudden attention surrounding his proud exhibiting of me, *Nicole*, his new girlfriend.

I blamed your excommunication for my suspicions of why I felt under the watch of the church, and my moments with Paul gave stifling reason: Any time a girl, me, associated with a boy, you or Paul, the audience demands a full explanation.

My first clue was one of the pastors' wives, Mrs. Kraikmeyer, who asked me in the hallway if I "liked" Paul.

"Why him?" I deflected despite knowing how Paul and I were simmering for all to see.

"Well, is it true? If you two make plans for dinner, you're welcome at our place."

Mrs. Kraikmeyer was an older woman in the big-dress style of Edith, cradling her purse to her chest, and I wanted to ask her what else the *audience* wanted to know, but my expression, failing to mirror her happy interest, cut her questions short. I don't know what answers she deserved, and what is it with everyone's innate attention to everyone else's romance or potential thereof? Why are relationships everybody's addictive fixation, especially for those who've already found someone?

Over Mrs. Kraikmeyer's shoulder I caught sight of Paul down the hall, and knowing he expected to walk me home again, I signaled him outside to the icy steps where we wouldn't be easily overheard. Feeling watched constitutes its own presence, more felt than Paul's as we started on the sidewalks back. Again, Paul asked me about the sermon, and again I didn't remember well enough to indulge his delving into the key takeaways because the sad uncertainties of work and you, along with Santana and her baby, occupied my thoughts. This happens when I have too much on mind: me drifting into the disengagement of gazing nowhere, of hearing only the winds gusting through the bare branches, of suddenly having nothing to say. The Sunday-afternoon stillness of frozen streets and empty parks reinforced my sudden detachment, the weariness of nothing left to do or see.

When we reached sight of my place, Santana was vaping on the front steps with her bundled toddler. She spoke in Spanish to Bianca's admiring first sights of snow—*nieve*—before turning her attention to Paul.

I introduced Santana as "my roommate," and as for Paul, Santana so plainly sized him up as my find from church that I didn't bother qualifying him as anything more than "Paul."

"So, Wednesday night?" Paul turned to confirm our dinner plans before wishing farewell.

"So, Wednesday night, oooh?" Santana echoed once Paul was far enough down the sidewalk. "I've been rooting for you to meet someone tall, dark, and handsome!"

Santana wanted to know more, like how far along we were when it came to "seeing each other." Were we "dating?" Were we "girlfriend/boyfriend?"

"You find work?" I changed the subject.

As the three of us, Bianca included, stepped inside Santana restated her plans: She was going to waitress the evenings around my daytime schedule in order to divide our downtime caring for Bianca—her with Bianca in the mornings, me in the evenings.

"And if Tara returns, guess who's stuck with the blowback of agreeing to this living arrangement?"

"I should've planned this with you sooner, but it's all happening so quickly," Santana pleaded.

I reminded myself of how much I wanted to help her during our time undergoing treatment together, but the unburdening I meant for her was instead taking root toward housing her toddler too, whose unsettled custody left doubt as to where Bianca legally belonged, the reality of which quickened when I recognized one of Bianca's books among Santana's belongings—*Oh, Cuan Lejos Llegaras! (Oh, the Places You'll Go!)*

If Santana was going to leave me caring for Bianca while she waitressed in the evenings, didn't I have leverage for further explanation? So when she brought up Paul later that evening, I raised the stakes: "Tell me why, again, Martez's family is suddenly ceding Bianca's custody?"

"They don't want Bianca because I'm no longer a threat to sue for child support. I can't sue Martez for child support if he's going to prison because there's no income to sue him for. Before his arrest he promised he'd sign over joint custody. He saw how upset I was with his family taking full custody and even wanted me to move in with him in order to raise Bianca together. I'm hoping his legal issues blow over so we can get back to our original plan."

"But if you're getting full custody, why stay in Washington with Martez behind bars?"

"Having Bianca with me gives me visitation rights to Martez."

"Prison visitations are how you'll wait out the three or four years until Martez finishes his sentence? Returning to Vegas until Martez is out isn't a bad idea. I can't house you in Tara's room forever, but if returning to work the casinos pays well enough I'll go with you and find paralegal work somewhere. We could split the costs and live together."

"Vegas is dead for me. My mom died there. My dad's a lost soul, and I can't support his indigence if I go back. Much less be near Martez's family, without custody of Bianca."

"Or we could look for work in Phoenix?"

"Thanks, but I'm here until things work out with Martez."

I certainly wasn't telling Santana to settle on waitressing away evenings of slots and poker tables forever. If anything I was recognizing that in Vegas her good looks would earn premium dollars. Even now, only hours off her flight, her prettiness flashed from her casual appearance of a young, jetlagged mom—her jeans baggier, her tied-back hair growing out of its bronze highlights, and the arches of her eyebrows flaring from behind the black rims of her reading glasses.

I hadn't understood why, when her mom had suddenly died, Santana didn't put her Washington life on hold to will Bianca under her proper care. But I guess she'd already lost custody by then. And anyhow, that was all before I met her. Before I could speak my regards.

I'm not sure how to take being the subject of Paul's careful plan if his intentions with me fall suspiciously under watch of his pastors. If that's the case I'm surprised nobody has discouraged him away from me given their insights into my recent events with alcohol and you. Nevertheless, when can it just be the two of us? Paul and me? Does church have to play overseer? Are they expecting to know everything between Paul and me, just like they were asking me about you?

That was my greater concern, if you can believe it, as I wondered ahead to dinner with Paul, and not Santana and Bianca settling into Tara's vacant room.

"I'm frustrated about other stuff," I promised her, when, as we shared a vape on the doorsteps, Santana cautioned how upset with her I might be. "We're both under a lot of pressure lately, and it's getting to us."

"Thank you," she said and nodded in relief that I wasn't confirming how increasingly frantic her decisions were becoming. "Who knows what will happen next?"

So what's next? I wanted to find out from Paul as soon as we were seated in whichever restaurant he wanted to keep a surprise until Wednesday night. He did let me find out we were dining downtown because when he insisted on picking me up. I told him if reservations were downtown I'd be working late that night anyway so why not meet me outside the Metro Center stop and walk from there. I brought my makeup to work, logged eleven hours, and spent another half hour dressing up my hair and makeup in the bathroom once the cubicles cleared, save for Edith, typing away in the only lighted office. Before stepping outside to meet Paul down the block I ate an untoasted bagel to damper my appetite.

A surprising sense of redemption rushed over me when I saw Paul's tall stature outlined in the fog venting from the sidewalk gratings. These sidewalks I'd hastened along in nightly darkness were rescued from their crowded anonymity with Paul striding beside me. We could walk into any of the passing cafés and hotel bars under mutual confidence. For the first time I didn't need you warming to mind whenever I peered into the glow of street-side restaurants and spotted couples at their tables alleviating between them the loneliness often following me home.

Paul chose an Italian restaurant, which I took as a good sign because every couple eventually has their Italian restaurant. The windows looking out into the cold were curtained, and the inside lighting was dim. *Intimate* lighting, as they call it, for once fitting the word to my liking.

The waiter brought bread, olive oil, and menus.

Paul asked how my day went. We took turns answering. He said he kept his coat on at his desk and sipped hot coffee all day because his building lost central heating.

"Wouldn't your boss let you work from home?"

"It's winter, you just get used to always being cold."

He said DC winters didn't have the bite of the Minnesota winters of his boyhood. "Besides," he added, "I prefer freezing over melting in the humidity of July."

We carried the same back and forth you and I once had over whether DC is a winter or summer city.

"I get it," I said, "if you're raised in the Northeast or the Great Lakes states then maybe Washington feels like a swamp, but it's only a swamp for a few weeks in July. Otherwise you're bundled in hoodies and coats until baseball season."

"That's the point: the swamp. Isn't Arizona only a dry heat?"

"When it's a hundred and five degrees it doesn't matter what kind of heat it is. The desert sun sits on top of you."

I should've just agreed because Paul appeared confused, or didn't believe me, and after our orders were placed the conversation sobered to the business of us, as in his *plan* (or whoever's).

"If all goes well, I mean, if you're up for it, what d'you think about dinner at the Kraikmeyer's in a week or two?"

"What's the occasion?"

"Well, have you met Pastor Kraikmeyer?"

"Yes, and his wife too."

"They just want to get to know us as a couple."

"She was asking me nosy questions about us the other day."

"It's a thing they do as one of the church's pastoring families where him and his wife host a couple for dinner."

"It sounds like they already want to know too much."

"Pastor Kraikmeyer has been a blessing since my college days. He mentored me through picking a major and finishing it. After college he encouraged me to aim for a job in Washington so I could continue membership at District Baptist. The Kraikmeyers have always wanted to help me."

Help? No matter how well their wishes were, Paul couldn't perceive their help for what it was: an obligation to live up to the strict, dare I say, invasive terms of their help. Their expectations were too much, and Paul didn't know any better because, to hear him wait on their plan for us, church obligated full disclosure and deference to the pastors when it came to too many deciding matters. What to study in school, what job to take, where to live, and with whom—was it all a regular course of church membership to solicit the pastor's advice? As for Paul and I dating, I'll fail the strict conditions and stages of dating that we're together expected to be chaperoned through. How can Paul and I ever really know each other if we're responsible for how our relationship is lived out in the critical minds of others?

"Can we at least spend more time getting to better know each other first?"

"I guess." Paul collected himself.

His options, which I watched him think through, were to turn down the Kraikmeyer's invite, promising them a later week, or, over the course of our arrived pasta entrees, to work on me with that carefulness of his. He must've felt caught between me and them, but as an emerging couple we were already under pressure and both differently disappointed. Outside the winds were picking up. Stray snowflakes blew from the tops of buildings. Washington is a winter city.

"Let's let it warm up before we do dinner with the Kraikmeyers," I offered, an evening that by then I hoped to divert to attending a Nationals baseball game together.

"All right," Paul said with a shrug, his eyes on his dish.

"We could have a barbeque with them when it's nice enough outside."

When our check arrived Paul asked how I was getting home.

"The metro."

"Right to your address," he said, neglecting any insistence on driving me back, a lack of decency suddenly reflecting how contended he felt by me. Why can't I be somebody agreeable and careful like Paul and not overthink his intentions? Instead, something mean in me that was never mean enough to get what I wanted (like Tara always did) but mean enough to still bruise Paul's thoughtfulness, stranded me on a cold repeating of my walk home after your excommunication with the same snows unthawed along the lonely sidewalks. All my hype for Paul was for replacing you, for drowning out with him what calls me to you, a hope, like his for me, too high for him to live up to.

The rest of the workweek's coming load of audits demanded enough concentration to crowd Paul out of mind, as well as Santana and you too. Yours is an absence felt always, never waning like the rest, which begs introspection on how few occasions you and I have spent any amount of meaningful time together. Did it take only half a dozen times together to now have you waiting in mind for the rest of the competing static in my head to die down? Was our time together only our few appointments meeting over my DUI case, the trips to Blacksburg and Las Vegas, and the time I walked into your office? About once a month is sadly all I've had with you? It's a thought whose running letdown doesn't lightly fade when withdrawing to the numbers at my desk. It's a sadness like the cold morning outside that once escaped keeps you trapped inside. Nothing is more impersonal than sifting through fields of data that have nothing to do with me, save for getting paid, while all the while you and Tara, Bianca, Santana, Dustin, and my mom have become what's left of me, the unrest of others coming and going.

But the world of numbers at least constitutes predictable footing. I focused for a few hours, free of other pressing thoughts, until I heard Tara take a call.

"Hey, babe, feeling any better?" Tara said to you from the other side of our shared cubicle. "Okay, just stay in bed today . . . there are extra blankets in the second drawer."

Closing my eyes, we're warm beside each other, beneath all those blankets. Let's call in sick to the rest of the world.

To have you on mind is to sentimentalize how inexhaustible the well is; why stray when so many others are comparatively drained? Yet how many more real occasions will we have together? Time spent that even in its receding memory burns white. Perhaps five more times, if I have to push for it. Or never? And yet when I close my eyes to rest next to you it all seems an endless rush.

I opened my eyes, interrupted; Edith was calling me to her office. In Edith's office, under the dry breath of the overhead vent, she asked me to shut the door and take a seat.

"How would you recapitulate your on-site visit to Phoenix?" Edith asked without lifting her eyes from the warp speed of her typing.

"I believe we were effective."

"We? I believe *we*, as in you and me, can admit who carried that audit. As the year moves along I'll have more on-site visits than auditors qualified to handle them. I think you're ready for more. I saw a headline on Lake Michigan getting so frozen over that its entire surface can nearly be walked across. Which is reason enough for me to book you to Chicago next week, before it warms up in another few months."

"Next week?"

"Like I said, Nicole, don't thank me yet." Edith nodded. "You're prompt, always available, and ready for more. You've earned more work." She looked up from her keyboard to enjoy my surprise. In the corner the plastic leaves of decorative shrubbery rustled in the central heat.

As intimidating and difficult as Edith could be, it was a small victory to know she saw the better of me over Tara. Comparing my work reputation to Tara's was a win, but sitting back at my desk and overhearing her still on the phone with you, who was really getting what they wanted? For the first time I really wondered what Edith's life was like outside of work, because goodness, what if work is what we resort to excelling at because nothing else in life is going according to what we're truly living for? Chicago in February? I'd quit my job for you, but how can I openly admit as much?

When Paul finally called to follow up with me I was already off to Chicago.

"I know I'm partial to my home state, but you should pay a visit to Minnesota sometime."

"Yeah, well, Chicago called me here. Besides, if it matters, I flew through Minnesota not too long ago."

To Tom

"What'd you think?"

"One of the better airports for walking around."

"When you land back in Washington may I give you a lift from the airport?"

Paul wanted to "talk," he said, which I took as him asking me to let him make up for how our date had ended. But when I landed, the four nights in Chicago felt intended for me to hopefully come around to the idea of going to the Kraikmeyers.

"I'm not going to the Kraikmeyers next week," I told him on the ride from the airport.

"They just want to get to know us."

"Paul, I'm not going." I drew my line before blurring it a bit. "Not yet anyway."

Silent for the rest of our ride over the frozen Potomac and into the Capitol Hill neighborhood, we barely exchanged goodbyes when I stepped from his vehicle.

Burning orange above the street was Tara's bedroom window. If she was back and mad about Santana taking up residence, Paul had left me upset enough to face her head-on, but on huffing my way inside, my expected evening of anger was softened inside the doorway by Bianca's wide eyes. Before I could kick off my snow-caked boots, I kneeled to welcome her little footsteps rushing my way.

"Nee-coe!" Bianca pushed her way through the unbuttoned front of my coat and let me lift her.

"Look at the cupcake I have wrapped in my coat!"

Bianca giggled, warm in my grasp.

~

Come Monday my deskwork of more auditing provided no escape from a weekend of legal concerns over my new "roommates." From beside an unsuspecting Tara, I excused myself from my desk to call your office, but your secretary said you were in court all week. Texts and emails to you went frustratingly unanswered. Then again, if Tara living with you warranted her finding out the advice I needed from you, her reaction to discovering that Santana had stolen occupancy of her bedroom wasn't worth the risk.

Forgetting how much I (and Tara by extension) are in violation of our lease's strict forbiddance against outside parties taking up residence, am I risking eviction? Obviously yes, but am I exposed to any further legal risks with Bianca, only two, living with me several time zones apart from her lawful guardians until Santana can settle her custody?

On Friday morning's metro commute, my legal worries hit me hard enough to relive my dad appearing alongside me in court, with you as my lawyer again, unless, if I can ever get through to your office, you can assure me that I have nothing to worry about. Then Paul came to mind, but thinking about him offered as little headway as wondering why nobody on platform after crowded platform bothered indulging in the morning cigarette I also needed. With each underground stop so drab, leaky ceilinged, and dimly lit, what disinvited the masses from going ahead and lighting up?

Bianca has warmed up to me very quickly. Now that she's used to me holding her and fascinating her with cookie dough and candles and my earrings and bracelets, she celebrates my arrivals home from work by climbing onto my lap with a book and sitting as contently as little Ainsley, her warmth a lively weight in my arms as I read to her. It's dark by the time I'm home from work, and I usually get an hour or two with Bianca before Santana, on nights not working, announces that it's time for a bath—*te lavo*, or bed—*acostarse*.

It's also a comfort to arrive home to an apartment kept more actively tidied than by Tara or myself. Santana's deep cleaning of the coat closet unearthed the many abandonments of previous renters. "Basura." She piled their leavings at the back door for me to greenlight their disposal. After rescuing a teddy bear, Bianca gladly helped me fill a trash bag with crumpled lampshades, musty sofa cushions, running shoes missing laces, and carry-on luggage with zippers too rusted to open.

Santana soon found waitressing work across the river in Arlington, filling the evenings around my daytime work. Having gone through her first week, she waited until Sunday morning to ask me to watch Bianca while she waitressed one of those brunches serving bottomless mimosas.

"I can't skip church today," I told her. "I'm teaching Sunday school for the first time."

The same pastor who'd interviewed me for childcare duty had approached me with a lesson binder the Sunday before and asked about "moving up to serving in the bigger kids' class," ages five to nine, recommending me for the same reasons Edith praised me: promptness and availability.

"What if we check Bianca into Sunday school together? Maybe you can take her home once you're finished teaching?"

"I wish you'd given me a heads-up because it's too late to find a babysitter."

We walked Bianca to church, holding her hand at either side as she picked over icy patches of sidewalk. She was in a playful mood, meowing and barking along the way, and excited to climb the front steps herself, though still grasping our hands. Inside, Santana's familiarity with the building brought back memories of meeting her in the basement for alcohol treatment. At the childcare check-in desk, I hung back while Santana signed Bianca into the two-year-old class until Bianca cried "mama" in protest to us leaving her. I introduced Bianca to Ainsely, happy to see me again, which occupied Bianca's attention from Santana and me going our separate ways—Santana to Arlington and me upstairs with the lesson planner in hand.

While the rest of the teachers prepared for Sunday school by setting up chairs and tending the check-in desk I was left alone to rehearse this week's story of David and Bathsheba, whose raw themes of murder and adultery sent me reflecting on what age I'd come to know the Old Testament's more severe stories. It wasn't like recalling from college exactly when you'd taken this or that Spanish or math class. This was a matter of always knowing; as far back as I can recall Mom took Dustin and me to church. It's safe to say I learned of killing because of Cain and Abel (last week's lesson), of infidelity because of David and Bathsheba.

As have the children, I noticed, once eventually settled into their seats.

From your Sundays attending, you'll remember after the morning service's welcoming hymns the children are dismissed from their parents' laps, and the boys and girls are lined up separately to simplify the headcounts in the hallway. One of the pastor's little girls helped me count attendance; Emily and I verified thirty-seven girls and thirty-one boys according to the roster printed from the nursery's check-in desk. Emily's younger sister, Charlotte, newly graduated into the older kids' class and scared of heights, didn't want to climb so many steps, so I stayed with the girls, marching her hand in hand up the staircase spiraling four floors up, above the toddler's nurseries to the higher views of the Capitol Dome and Congressional buildings. Taking their seat in the large classroom the girls were noticeably all in dresses, with sisters often matching in color and the littler ones swinging their legs in chairs too high for their feet to reach the ground. The boys wore polo shirts and required constant silencing from their excitement among friends.

Having previously cared for the two-year-olds, and now coming home to Bianca every evening, I instantly noticed the developmental progress between the toddlers and these five-to-nine-year-olds. They were more aware of each other, fostering their little friendships by sitting in groups of three and four with those they knew from playdates and birthday parties.

They were highly aware of their age, informing me (and reminding each other) with the same earnestness in which their dads might announce their profession on introducing themselves.

Once eventually settled into their seats I started by asking if anyone could raise their hand and answer who King David was.

Nearly every child raised their hand.

"Can anyone answer what this week's story of David and Bathsheba is about?"

Calling on the proudly raised hand of one of the pastor's little girls, she cleared the air: "Betrayal, murder, adultery!"

Even remembering I'd also learned these stories under those harsher Old Testament terms, I still underestimated the children;

her answer fazed only me. The story was therefore free to be taught as is, in its harshest wording, which might be the point of how the wording of the Bible came together. Since scripture presents sin in its most destructive terms, when sin is learned as a child directly from the Bible, its strongly negative terms like *murder* and *adultery* take impressionable hold as enormously irresponsible wrongdoings.

I also underestimated the detail to which they knew the story. They knew, when asked for raised hands, how David loitered home from war to his rooftop. How in his idleness the sight of Bathsheba bathing corrupted David's judgment. The children pretty much told the story as mediated through my questions. How David plotted to have Bathsheba's husband, Uriah, killed ("murdered") in battle as cover up for his unlawful pregnancy ("adultery") with Bathsheba. How upset God was to send his prophet Nathan to tell David a parable of a man rich with livestock stealing the lamb of a poor fellow to serve his guests as dinner. And how David, in his affair with Bathsheba, was in fact the heartless rich man, and as consequence God would bring violent unrest among the children of his household.

The children knew the Bible well enough to teach each other, as they did, the dozen of them allotted to my drama class, when came their turn to reenact the story. I sent them rummaging in the supply closet for costumes and toy weapons before assigning dialogue. When the time came their lines took a back seat to prolonging the combat scenes of both Uriah's staged death and all of David's children battling at the end. The few early-arriving parents looked on as even the little girl sitting on a platter in a lamb costume joined in with a plastic sword.

After the main service finished and the children were all picked up by their parents, us teachers were cleaning the classroom when Sharon thanked me. I admitted that in my difficulty of planning a story heavy on adult themes I'd left out too much.

"I noticed. It's all sin," she said.

It's a story they've heard read from illustrated Bibles by their moms or from the scriptures their dads covered at the dinner table.

Still, it was strange to hear of David's adultery with Bathsheba his wrongdoing termed as *sin* as Biblically defined and understood by even the five-year-olds, when day-to-day I'm so distanced from ever considering the word *sin* in mind or conversation.

Sharon's bigger problem was that by skimming over several scenes the lesson and resulting reenactment didn't eat up enough class time to occupy the children until the parents arrived.

"That's why we kept the kids singing hymns," she said, wanting me to be sure of the inconvenience I'd caused, "and had to resort to Christmas carols."

My bigger frustration turned out to be running into Paul at the nursery's check-in desk when I went to pick up Bianca. He figured I was there to see him. He hoped I could make time for lunch, "to talk about some things."

"Not today." I told him the honest truth. "I'm watching my roommate's child. In fact, I'm here to pick her up."

Paul's silence sought further explanation. It was fair to wonder why I was watching "Bianca," as I asked for her.

I couldn't decide if Paul remembered Santana on my front steps a few Sundays ago like I suddenly needed him to, because Bianca was clearly not my child, as he naturally considered, not with her romantically darker features and night-black hair and eyes contrasted by her caramel complexion.

"Let's talk later," I told Paul.

"Sure thing."

Once Paul handed Bianca over I hurried from the church to avoid further explanation. Later in the workweek I texted Paul to set up a time to meet, ready for what would turn into too many questions. "Yes, well, do you remember my roommate, Santana?" I wanted to explain. "Bianca is her child." When Paul wouldn't respond to my second and third texts, I stepped outside for a smoke break. He was leaving me in the cold, of course. It took no imagination to realize that Paul seeing me with Bianca was enough; she was his needed out from us having to work out. *I'm not going to fight it*, I told myself, lighting a second smoke. At some point Paul might break the news to me in more apologetic words, in the slower setting of a coffee shop, but what I didn't expect when I showed up the following Sunday for more Sunday school teaching was for the pastor of childcare to summon me to his office.

I should've remained standing when Pastor Kraikmeyer pointed to the chair across his desk, as before, when interviewing for childcare weeks ago.

"Nicole, since our first meeting how have you liked serving our children's ministry?"

"It's going well. The children are great."

"Well, I thank you for volunteering, but what I want to get to is whether you know Bianca." He looked down, searching through a printout of last week's attendance. "Bianca Solorio? Who was checked into our childcare program last Sunday?"

Wishing it was Santana here to explain, I answered, "Yes. Bianca's mother was with me at check-in."

"Why was Bianca checked in under your name?" Would he really have noticed without *someone* prompting him to check?

"Because I was the one picking her up afterward. Her mom was working the morning in Arlington."

"Are you her babysitter?"

"I end up watching Bianca a lot because her mom is temporarily living with me."

"And her mom is Bianca's guardian?"

"I figure so." I shrugged. "But I'd rather clear it up with her before guessing." What if he somehow pieces together that Santana had only months ago also underwent his rehab program?

"You don't know?"

"I don't want to speak for her. I can tell you that I know Bianca is with her mom right now, back at my place."

"Well, I don't want to overwhelm you, but because we're a licensed childcare provider, we're required to look into questions of guardianship or neglect, which I know sounds severe, but a few of our volunteers did their part to have me ask you."

"Thank you," I dismissed myself. I fled down to the basement where hopefully the bathrooms were empty without the busy foot traffic to risk overhearing me sob out my anger. I kept my head down, hair falling over my face.

Stepping my way back under the insufficient hallway lighting of the basement recalled the beginning days of Santana and I in rehab—a time of meeting you too. I was at a loss with Paul, though for speculative reasons that nonetheless made sense: he no longer found me worth the constant explanation he was under obligation to give his mentors when accounting for me, so, to end everything, and without regrets, he only had to raise a few questions about the little girl I was witnessed with. Having me explain Bianca was enough to end everything while alleviating any explanation on his part. Or any concern as for how I was let off because wouldn't the church step in and take over?

Forget Paul; I'm at a loss with everything else. Why do you have to matter so painfully? Especially when it comes to the months you've taken up with Tara, who I've kept in the dark on how privately I've raged. I cried because what would competing with Tara or propositioning you accomplish? Humiliation, along with reliving the loss that in my mom's death renewed all my unanswered prayers for relief in her absence.

Mourning the loss of my mom became a sort of comforter secondary to alcohol, both of whom I'd regularly met with, like a series of interviews from which the job was eventually given to alcohol. Today's tears masked faint bathroom odors of bleached tiles and the paint whitening the overhead pipes. I cried my makeup away; its reapplication delayed me from children's church where up four floors of stairs I kept my head down.

I took a distracted seat on the little girls' side of the classroom and let my attention buoy in and out of the rough waters of the story. Lot's wife was turning into a pillar of salt.

One of the little girls raised her hand. "What's the wife's name?"

"The story doesn't name her," Sharon answered.

Sharon's lesson ended with Lot escaping the destroyed cities of the plains, the details of which I meant to better keep track of because, of the half-dozen smaller classes that Sunday school was broken into after the opening story, I was assigned the story-review class.

Fortunately, after seating my kids around the table, the eight girls and two boys already knew the story, more so than taught by Sharon, who left out all sorts of difficult details anyway: *It's all sin.* The children knew how Abraham was visited by the Lord along-side two angels, and after dinner, after foretelling the coming pregnancy of his wife, Sarah, they stood overlooking the plains, contemplating the destruction of Sodom and Gomorrah in the distance, and when the two angels departed, Abraham turned to the Lord and counted down how many righteous men it would take in either city for God to spare them from destruction. The children said God destroyed both cities the next day, allowing Lot to escape but turning his wife into the pillar of salt that Sharon ended her story with as warning to obey the Lord in all things.

They were proud to show off how well they'd learned the Bible stories they'd been taught by their parents, adding to each other's retelling around the table, eager to please me as they would their parents. The beaming trust of these children assuaged how intim-idating the same bond was to maintain between fellow adults, whether it was in working for Edith or Tara angry or the pastors of the last hour, some of whom were parents to these children, who until Sunday school was dismissed and parents waited for pickup, I stood as queen over their soft presence. Or, as one of the little girls invited herself onto my lap, was I their throne?

"Can I see your hair?" She undid my bun with an innocent fascination evoking Bianca, letting my freed hair flow between the fingers of her grazing hand. The classroom door opened, and in came another little girl, crying.

Sharon stood over her in the doorway, asking on the girl's behalf if I could exchange an upset Charlotte for two of my boy students she needed to play the Lord's angels during the story reenactment. Charlotte sheltered onto the lap of her older sister as two more friends peacefully gathered near, calming her with such heartbreaking sweetness. My little hairdresser was now down at the helm of my dress, working to untie the ankle straps of my slingbacks. She placed my shoe on the table, and two other little girls rose from their seats to find the fashion brand.

"Lucky," they checked aloud.

"My mommy has Jimmy Shoe shoes," compared another.

"Jimmy Choo, sweetie?"

"Jimmy Choo choos," the pair chanted, until the rest joined in. Louder they *choo-chooed*, jumping from their seats to link hand in hand and skip together to the beat of their chant. Asking the girls to please quiet down, they in exchange circled closer. Two smaller ones pawed at my dress as chants dissolved. A dimple-cheeked girl held up a red scrunchie, asking me to remake her ponytail, and the rest followed suit, requesting their hair redone. Their gentle appreciation swelled over me as each waited their turn.

"You all look so wonderful in your pretty dresses."

At this they beamed with ever more the thrill I was surprisingly gaining from their closer admiration of my pearl-stud earrings, which I let them touch, and my trimmed eyebrows, which a kindergartner reached up to trace with her finger.

"Like elf princesses." I assured them of how pretty they could look forward to growing when in a few more years they'd pierce their ears and try perfumes and makeup.

When the time came for classes to gather back for the closing story reenactment, my assigned girls didn't leave my side. They piled into my lap or surrounding chairs, clutching my dress and sleeves, beaming obliviously to the skit unfolding at the podium. Even as young as five it's profoundly uplifting to hear that you're pretty. I can barely remember myself at their age, with Dustin a toddler beside me, but whenever I've since taken compliment of my looks it's an unexpected exhilaration above any encouragement I could've hoped for.

It was a good send-off from such sweet angels; to see both loved sides, their affection I'd prompted, and to relive their younger selves again—a send-off because with the pastors keen on Bianca's custody I couldn't see how I'd be allowed in the Sunday school anymore. The letdown rushed over me as soon as I left their radiance. It was almost worth having Paul beside me if people like Mrs. Kraikmeyer were going to keep noticing me anyway, particularly in this moment of aloneness outside the church again.

Who knows how it came to this? But forget Paul, I started home, the icy sidewalks biting cold through my slingbacks. At my back the Capitol Dome remained visible through the bare trees along East Capitol Street.

Turning up the front steps I'd taken contrast of the dome's unchanging existence—how comparatively I exist merely as reaction to whatever subjects itself rigidly around me, how hopeless I am to force anything on my behalf. It's a disappointment I could easily enough dismiss back home thanks to the company of Santana and Bianca. But through the front door the racket from inside was more violent and the mess more reckless than Bianca was capable.

"Whose shit is this?" Tara's angry voice shook from down the hall.

From the floorboards of the hallway I began picking up Bianca's rag dolls, the diapers to stuff back in their packing, the plastic matting Santana and I changed her on, and her outfits all trailing into the bedroom doorway.

"Tara, let me explain." I should've known there'd be no calming Tara. She was horrified.

"This is *my* room!" She hurled more of Bianca's outfits at me when I rushed in. "Who's living here?"

"Tara, no!" I gathered what more I could of Bianca's clothes from her grasp.

"You know I live here!"

"I'll fix your room back to how it was!"

"That, and kick out whoever's sleeping here! It only takes one call to the landlord to evict you, and this," she held up one of Bianca's baby bottles to the window that I hadn't noticed was open. She held it there long enough to make her point before tossing it out. Reaching for another bottle on the nightstand as the first shattered on the sidewalk, I hurried to stop her.

"Tara, please!" But Tara flung back another bottle, the blunt force of which struck the side of my face. I fell as I reached her, grabbing her blouse as though in a panic of drowning, bringing her down with me. The strike hastened from me a separate awareness beyond itself, taking lightheaded escape through deep breaths of exhaled fear, from which I felt the cold universe brewing wherever in the room I drifted out of body. There was the silence of outer space and the strength draining from my arms as I held Tara's wrists at bay. Then there was only Tara's unnerving screams as her energy escaped in long exhaled cries until her arms finally went limp against my grasp, and she rolled off me. Our entangled collapse made for a tight fit on the narrow-carpeted space between the bed and wall. We settled shoulder to shoulder, face-up, slowly regaining ourselves. Tara diminished to a rhythm of bitter sobs while I took detached solace in the constellation of plastic glow-in-the-dark stars Santana had plastered across the ceiling for Bianca to practice counting. *Uno, Dos, Tres*, I exhaled. My gaze angled through the bare branches of the open window and found nothing in a sky of the same lasting blankness that I saw whenever daring to look up from the well of myself. A well from where I've shouted; would it have cost you anything to peer down and extend a hand?

Silence as aftermath, rather than hollow answer, closed over Tara as she wiped her tears. I thought of maybe a drink, but on the nightstand where I'd snuck many an evening's last pour of vodka or whiskey, instead gathered more of Bianca's baby bottles. So I watched the silence of the window's lace curtains yielding gentle in the cold and felt the insistent pulsing of the soft bruising spanning the ridge of my cheekbone.

"I am so, so sorry." Tara's tears picked up again. "Please, if you can please forgive me, Nicole. I wasn't throwing the bottle at you. How can I get so angry with you when you've been so nice to me? And always so helpful at work? I'm so sorry. You don't deserve this. It's not you I'm angry with."

I should've known it was you she was falling apart over.

"Please forgive me, Nicole."

So how could you, whatever it is you did?

I could've guessed, probably the obvious, before Tara finished pleading her apologies at an outdoor volume that paid no carefulness to me lying beside her. Through the open window exchanged the winter cold for her regrets.

Worrying we'd be heard more than we already were, I found her hand with mine, calming her in my grasp, as though holding Bianca when she needed quieting.

"Tara, it'll be all right."

"I'm so sorry."

"I forgive you."

I've looked up from this well of myself for how long now—with how many more years of shouting unheard? But holding Tara's hand was like having someone else with me at rock bottom. Together we could look up and share in the emptiness of no answers from the many faces coming and going, peering down on us, promising escape but after a time recruiting us to answer to them. Looking up at Edith, our dads, our pastors, and vodka, I cannot shoulder their demands, not to mention what to do about housing Santana and Bianca? It's the reality of work, church, and roommates. And the disappointing reality of where our irresponsibility leads. To court, to rehab, to excommunication. Adulthood is the costly upping of responsibility until a breaking point is risked. Until it's no longer worth shouting about, though let me shout anyway. Let me shout for you, for anybody who might hear.

But not now. Not with police-cruiser lights suddenly flashing through the open window, alternating in red and blue orbits across the starry expanse of ceiling. How long since our racket had ended? Half an hour?

"Somebody called the cops." Tara leapt up.

"Tara, stay down," I whispered. "If they knock, they won't have anything to report if we don't answer. They'll leave."

The encroaching cold chilled the damp skin contact of my blouse that under the trauma of fighting Tara I'd hotly perspired through. I pulled Tara back down beside me and yanked the disheveled comforter from the bed to shield us from sight. We huddled, waiting, listening to the outside, until over our breaths the slam of a car door shook us.

"Stay down. We can't let them see my face."

"Oh my gosh, you won't press charges?"

"Of course not." I pulled the covers over us. "But because we're roommates they can arrest us for domestic violence, which is more severe than simple assault charges."

"I'm so sorry."

"Hush."

The knocking on the door finally did the job of silencing Tara. Through several series of knocks we waited out the long, unanswered intervals. My only sense beyond listening was that of my vision adjusting beneath the blanketed dimness to see the grinning Disney princesses patterned across Bianca's comforter. At last a lengthier silence, broken by the startle of a car door opening. I exhaled when it slammed shut. Ice slushed beneath tires. The ceiling was blank again when we sat up.

"Can you go with me to work tomorrow?" Tara asked, looking my face over.

"Together?"

"So I can do your makeup and cover the bruising?"

"I'll just say I walked into a door." I touched my cheek.

She returned a smile, and her shoulders eased as she took fresh stock of her room. The baby bottles, bedtime readers, and pasted-to-the-ceiling plastic stars glowing in winter's early darkness. Outside hummed the nearest streetlight. The cold air stiffened with the imminence of another snowfall.

"A baby girl?" Tara judged from the princess-themed bedding.

"Bianca."

I told her everything I've told you. How Santana needed a room after returning from Vegas with Bianca. Tara listened with a resigned patience I'd never experienced from her, offering contrite attention rather than reacting with obvious questions or again with tears over what had so upset her. Should I ask? For her sake I wasn't sure. Or is it for your sake I should avoid asking? To start asking questions contrasts my rush from having to give one explanation to the next, from defaulting to explanation wherever the day goes, at church and home, before the coming workweek of more explanation. Before the cops were back for more explanation? We traded concerned glances at the sound of the downstairs

To Tom   147

door again. It opened to Santana's steps, followed by the little pat-
ter of Bianca's.

"Santana, up here. I'm with a friend."

Santana slowed her approach in the hallway and flipped on the
lights. Bianca darted from behind Santana's knees.

"Nee-coe!" She rushed onto my lap where I shared the carpet
next to Tara.

"Bianca, baby, this is my friend." I gestured to Tara who eyed
Bianca with equal fascination. "Can you say, 'Hi, Tara?'"

I introduced Tara to Santana as "my roommate," whose room
this was. Noting the mess of the bed and hallway, Santana asked
Tara if she was moving back in.

"Yes." Tara relocked gaze with Bianca. "But how long do you
and Bianca need a place to stay?"

Maybe it was Bianca warming my lap or Santana closing the
bedroom window, but the hopes I suddenly had in Tara for offering was as warm as when I'd helped her on the Phoenix audit.

Tara moving back in, along with the church questioning Bianca's custody, would buy the leverage it took to hopefully convince
Santana to reconsider returning West. You should've seen Tara
extending her arms and Bianca carefully moving over to her
lap, effectively overlapping their short histories in the bedroom
belonging in different ways to each other.

Later that evening, when the time came to sort out sleeping
arrangements, I defaulted to Bianca's eager insistence that I spend
the night in "her room." Tara took my bedroom while I fell asleep
early in a nest of bedding on the carpet beside Tara's actual bed
that Bianca innocently believes is hers, only to awake in the most
nameless of wee hours. In the basin of my sleeplessness gathered
the deep night, first reaching its enduring cold, then, as from distant shores, came the calm tides of Santana and Bianca breathing
in their sleep. Sleeplessness is as much a gathering of worry; gone
is the moat of daytime busyness keeping at bearable distance the
loopback of reliving police lights on our ceiling or of Tara's violent
anger or having to explain Bianca again. Church has backfired. It
isn't the promised refreshment, not as it proves itself an unsettling

atmosphere of not living down Paul anytime soon or of getting cornered for more answers pertaining to Bianca or you.

I must've fallen asleep because it was Tara's voice pulling me into the unwanted morning dark. Beneath her whispering she patted my shoulder until I turned from my side. Before registering her words the sharper sound of my alarm pulsed from down the hallway.

"How do you silence your alarm?"

"Unplug it." I sat up.

"It's time to get ready for work anyway."

With bleary compliance I let Tara seat me beneath our bathroom lights to do my makeup. Examining the bruising on my face, she started with an oily foundation, packing it thickest at the darker center and covering the outer yellowing with a small, dense brush. In the mirror I watched her apply a layer of setting powder to match the surrounding skin before finishing with a concealer that shined in the mirror's border of bright bulbs. Tara started her makeup once I took over for my eyebrows and lashes. Finishing with lip gloss and ready to dress and head out the door, I looked much more awake than I was. Gaining the day's first wakeful footing required a smoke until I could settle in with a hot coffee at my desk. I vaped outside in the gray daybreak of our icy walk down East Capitol to the underground metro stop.

With work persisting as my only certainty these days, it's entrapping to find life yielding only at your desk, standing steady under Edith's rigid office rule. Maybe that's how Edith rose to intimidating prominence—she'd sunk all of herself into a career once the hope for family life dimmed and disappointed her strict terms? No one knows anything of Edith's private life, whether she's married or has older children or what they might be up to; or what she drinks, with who, or where. Edith is such a forceful workplace personality that in answering to her she becomes our working life. But I wonder if this is common to having a demanding boss, and more reluctantly, if my best option is a similar career-engrossed path if the ever-pictured future of having my own family recedes.

The difficulty of picturing Edith's personal life so readily supposes a lack of one that after coffee and a few hours at my desk, how surprised was I to see Edith at my cubicle? Did she notice the swelling on my face?

"Can you check on Tara? She's crying in the bathroom."

"Yes." I turned to her desk to check her absence.

"What do you think is upsetting her?"

"A boy," mind you.

"Can you talk her out of it?"

"I'll take her for a walk." I pulled on my coat and gloves before grabbing Tara's scarf and coat draped over the back of her chair.

In the bathroom I heard her restrained sobs. The stalls were empty, save for the last where Tara sat slouched on the tiled floor, tempering her tears into fists of toilet paper.

"I'm so sorry, Nicole."

"I forgive you. Starting yesterday."

Tara motioned me to join her in the stall, tucked away from sight like we were behind the bed again.

"I want to talk, but not in here." I offered her coat.

"What about work?" Tara stood.

"Edith understands if we need time."

"Did she notice your face?"

"She only noticed that you weren't at your desk."

On any warmer day we would've walked the few blocks to the wider clearing of the National Mall. The grand museums, war memorials, and great Capitol Dome always lifted my mind from the office and gave a passing sense of belonging to DC's importance. Now the Mall was divinely white in the swirling morning snowfall, and in the wind we couldn't hear each other over the arctic gusts tunneling between the buildings. Our walk to the corner coffee shop was snowy enough. Above us the rise of buildings gradually vanished into the whitening density of snowfall. Across the street from the Dunkin Donuts where we took a window seat, only a darker church steeple remained visible and appeared freely floating above the ghosted outline of its stone tower. Tara checked her makeup in the reflection of the graying window.

"I don't want to touch up my makeup if I'm just going to cry again."

"We don't have to talk about what happened." I'd rather let silence fall between us like the snow because I already knew the bad news.

"Tom and I," she sighed, "had a falling out."

I sighed, too, knowing it's your fault; I sensed the guilt causing her meltdown fully shifting to you.

Tara detailed my general suspicions: you set your sights on another girl, and Tara fought against being replaced. The details jumped around like unconnected dots between which the blank spaces could be filled with my assumptions.

"Do you think Tom had wanted out for a while?"

"We were living together for months. What kind of asshole treats relationships like a contract you break when you want out?"

Tara looked away, searching for words that worked.

"Tom's a bastard," she said, "and I hate that this is all a lot of work down the drain."

"Not getting what you worked for is hard to cope with," I said, unconvincingly. The disappointing truth is us both wanting you. She'd taken you much further, in relative part because I'd gotten nowhere. Tara has no clue I've wanted you all the same, and if it's allowed us to sit peaceably in the cleared air of having taken her punches, I'm thankful she doesn't know.

"I guess I'm paying for allowing myself to need him so much."

"Needing each other is part of getting close to someone."

"He didn't need me if he left. What do you think?"

"It wasn't meant to be," was all I could come up with.

"He let me get attached to him while he waited for the next girl. While I stupidly let myself believe we'd work out."

"Can I ask . . . how far did you hope to go with him?"

Tara raised her eyes to mine, interrupted from her protracted gaze within. Could she know I was asking for my sake?

"I don't know. The joke's on me for wanting anything."

"I'm sorry."

"For what?" Tara dug through her purse.

"Wanting Tom isn't a joke."

"Of all days to forget my Xanax. Let's get a drink."

"Tara, I mean it. I'm sorry. You gave yourself to somebody, and it didn't work out. Someone else is the riskiest thing to lose yourself to, but it's nothing to be ashamed of. I want the same thing you had for a time. Having someone I can safely lose myself to. Did you take piano lessons as a kid?"

Tara wasn't listening as I digressed.

"I remember tirelessly practicing during the week leading up to every recital. I'd get so lost in concentration that my entire self became the sonata I was playing. I wouldn't realize how sublime of an escape it was until I stepped away. Time had gone by without any notice. How much time has to go by before I find someone? Meanwhile I'm left to go on believing that in finally finding him I'll have that same sublime world to safely lose myself to. And together we're protected from what worries us alone, like growing old and having kids."

"That's scary," Tara whispered.

"Losing . . ." I stopped short of saying your name before recovering . . ."being alone?"

"And time. How it just passes on by."

I knew what Tara meant in wake of losing you.

"When what you work for goes to waste—"

"What about you?" Tara asked.

"I need to talk to Santana tonight."

"About Bianca?"

"Yeah."

When what you've worked for goes to waste, I wanted to finish, the underlying time lost might be the costlier loss. Walking Tara back to work, for a few steps I let my stride linger behind to sneak a glance in the direction of your office building.

The next cold morning I followed the determination of my glance down the snowy street to find you smoking on the sidewalk. I wanted to see you, to really look you a long goodbye, to burn you into final sight before we recede from each other for good. At some honest point the excuses to go finding you are dead on arrival, but I'll admit to forcing our eye contact by walking right up after noticing you from across the street.

"Nicole?" You hesitated.

I waited until you asked, "How are you?"

"Hopefully better than I look." I hadn't meant any reference to my facial bruising, the sudden self-consciousness of which I tried to deflect. "Hopefully better than I look freezing out here on the sidewalk." But it was too late.

"What happened?"

Figure it out on your own, I wanted to say.

"Guess."

"Boxing?"

"Yes, you missed Sunday's title fight."

"I'm sorry?"

"My opponent threw everything she had. She was quite motivated."

You looked away to ponder, exhaling smoke before returning your attention to me.

"Someone really assaulted you?" Nothing gets past that protracted, cross-examiner's glare of yours.

"Tara. It was more of an accident." My watering eyes hastened the moment I'd meant for you to figure it all out.

"I'm sorry."

"For what?"

"For missing the title fight. I don't know. If there's anything I can do . . ."

"There is." I would've appreciated a hug, but catching you off guard was more useful. "Can you make a call for me? As a lawyer?"

"Depends; who am I calling?"

But once in your office you refused.

"I'm not calling Santana about my client's case. If her and Martez were married then we could maintain confidentiality. Doesn't he keep her updated?"

"Yes, but Santana's unrealistic. She thinks it's worth sticking around Washington and fostering hope for Martez to get cleared."

"If she won't heed him, then I don't know what to tell her. In another month he's is scheduled to plead guilty."

"Which will result in jail time?"

"A reduced sentence, yes."

"You can't tell Santana that?"

"Why does she need to hear it from me?"

"Because one of the pastors was questioning Bianca's custody, which I don't think Santana fully has. Which is where I was hoping you could talk to her, from a standpoint of offering her legal advice, maybe on behalf of Martez?"

"Why's the church questioning Bianca's custody?"

"We checked Bianca into childcare while Santana ran off to work and I taught Sunday School."

"I don't know what I'd tell her, but my advice to all of you is to quit going to church."

"I can't talk any sense into Santana when it comes to Martez facing jail. The more we're realistic with her the more I'm hoping she'll consider what's best for her."

"Like what?"

"Santana and Bianca have been crashing at my place, and now that Tara's moved back in who knows how long I can keep them? Santana might as well move west with me."

"You're moving?"

"I need a blank slate. I'm done with Washington."

Thank you for checking up on me later in the week. Your call was a sweet gesture and made for a softer evening. *I don't know,* I brooded after our call, *who knows when I'll ever find someone?* Until then I'm tiresomely sized up as unmarried. As you pointed out, among evangelical culture, to be married or unmarried is treated as defining status, as a core identity. Single, I had to hear it termed, to again remember your words, when Sunday I ignored your advice and was back in church, ready to deflect questions about Bianca. But no one followed up on the previous week's questions of proper legal custody. Though, as fallout, I was replaced from my scheduled teaching duty, leaving me to attend the sermon.

In his sermon the preacher called on the single men to open their eyes to marriage, to see in God's plan for our life that marriage is a vital part. I don't disagree that marriage is change for the better, but in unmooring from Paul I wonder how elusive subsequent attractions might stubbornly be for me when greeting the eligible men in the sanctuary or in spotting them handsomely dressed in the pews. In my silent nights no bolder dream of any man watches over me. Why this wasteland of disengagement, where mutual attraction is maddeningly beyond my will?

The preacher closed his sermon praying for those who were single and desiring marriage. Remembering in the pews your pessimism over what a fixation marriage is for evangelicals and how whether you're married or not is how you're known, I worry that continuing Sunday attendance will only amount to a sinking awareness of what I'm without—my own growing family. Singleness: nothing to show. Alone is the more accurate status as time goes on.

So I meant to answer for Bianca's custody not only for the sake of closing the matter between us but also as a last act before leaving their church for good. But nobody asked.

Only Bianca asks where her mom is, as she does most any night when Santana is out waitressing the evening shifts.

"Tomorrow," I assured her near bedtime. "Mommy will be with us when we wake in the morning. Which must seem like years to a little cupcake."

With two hands she took the bottle I'd returned from the kitchen and stood next to me. Offering her a seat in my lap she refused so as not to interrupt her view through the glass back door of the alley. I assumed her adorably serious fascination was held by all the snow which shone with celestial whiteness under the motion-triggered floodlights. I couldn't tell what triggered the floodlights until turning off the lamp and kneeling beside Bianca to catch the startling green eyes peering over the back steps.

"Can you say *kitty cat*?" I whispered.

"*Gato.*"

I carried Bianca over to the door for a closer look.

"Tail." I pointed. "See the bushy tail?"

The cat's ghost-green eyes fixed their intensity on Bianca. Overwhelmed, Bianca slid from my arms to the floor, pressed both little hands to the cold glass, and cooed.

To Bianca

SURELY YOU'LL KNOW MORE OF HOW YOU CAME TO LIVE IN Arizona by the time you might read this. For how long you'll stay, who knows, but as I intend, you'll leave Washington as soon as your mom is ready. I plan to move with the two of you there, following the sun to where I'm from and taking it as a sign to start over alongside you, where in Arizona I hope you live your childhood as contently as the evenings we spend reading through picture books before bedtime.

Earlier this evening you fell asleep on my lap as we read through your illustrated farm-animal book. I could tell you were ready to drift off when you rested your head in the nook of my shoulder and gave up naming aloud more animals as I pointed to them—"*pollo*"—and responded with their English names.

"Yes, pollo *and* chicken."

It must make for a long day to face two names for everything, along with all the rest that comes with being traded off between your mom and me, given how soundly you sleep in my arms. I carried you upstairs, passing by Tara's room where your crib sits empty, and nestled you for the night between two pillows positioned in parallel to prevent you from rolling off my bed while I returned downstairs to writing my thoughts for you.

When wondering where to start, there's so much beyond your understanding and best not to share until well into your adolescence. Even then, how much of your early years will your mom rather keep undisclosed? Especially if the three of us can get moved back west before you can attain clear memory of these months you've spent in limbo, either without your mom or now crashing undercover with me.

Tara arrived home, as she often does after your bedtime, stomping the snow from her boots and asking if you were put down, before marching upstairs in prolonged, tired strides. You'll only hear from me about Tara, my roommate and coworker of the past few years, who your mom has only known since moving in.

Tara wasn't upstairs more than a few minutes before I smelled the earthy musk of the joint she'd lit.

"Tara, the baby!" I said through her open doorway.

"I know," she relented. She hadn't even waited to change from her business attire.

"You promised no more smoking inside."

"Nicole, she's asleep."

"Could you at least open your window?"

"It's freezing."

"Or close your door?" Which I did for her, softly so you didn't wake.

Smell, I've heard, is the most memory-inducing sense, so rushing again to your adolescence, if some strange waft ever strokes a distant familiarity you can thank Tara, who by then will still be smoking and maybe selling. My memory returns me to the high school football game where I first caught its fumes rising from beneath the bleachers. Marijuana is one example of what I'm getting at when wondering about what age it's appropriate for you to learn what I can account for.

Where do I begin? You're two years old. You were born Bianca Evangeline Solorio in Las Vegas, Nevada, to Santana Solorio. Your mother was twenty-three. After your birth she returned to cocktail waitressing the casino floor of the Bellagio until moving to Washington, DC, once your father's side of the family gained full custody of you over a year ago. The two of you live with me in Washington. The Capitol Dome is visible through our street's birdless overhang of trees skeletonized by winter. Winter is nature's ghost town. Its streets are policed by deathly cold nights. When your mom waitresses the late shifts, I put you to bed with two pairs of socks on your feet. Tonight I fit Arizona socks on top. The sun silhouettes a cactus stitched at your ankle. My desert girl.

Tara isn't very mindful of the responsibility a baby accrues me in patrolling what goes on in our apartment. Like a few evenings ago when she pouted off my interruption of her smoking upstairs. Or when I remind her to keep the volume down when she comes home late. Tonight, though, she left her boots in the foyer and stepped silently upstairs, which made hearing her surprise on flicking on her bedroom light all the sharper.

"Nicole, get up here!"

Your friend Squibbles, as his collar read, was lounging atop Tara's bed as fluffy as one of her pillows, licking his paws in happy obliviousness.

"First a baby, now a cat?"

"I didn't realize he was wandering the house." I lifted Squibbles from the bed. "Another reason to shut your door."

"Since when do we have a cat?" she asked over Squibbles's baritone groans.

Do you remember Squibbles? It's easier to appease him, of course—just set him on the couch to finish licking his paws, but in Tara's defense the living circumstances of our apartment change faster than she should have to put up with. Your crib still sits beside her bed. Tara's easy on you as a sort of apology to me, but a cat she'll hold over my head.

My point in telling you all this is to say that having to repeatedly explain yourself is as miserable as winter and sorely unnecessary. All of your adult life you'll be sized up for competition and subjection, Tara being only a minor offender compared to my more ambitious coworkers pining for whether I'm seeking other jobs or higher-profile projects they're in the running for. Or my scrutinizing relatives who at every chance wanted my reasoning for going the paralegal route rather than to law school. Or it's church folk asking too much as prelude to begin mentoring me in ways that by the time they're asking whether I've dated my own defense attorney or where your mom is I want to run. And answering is giving too much of yourself away, or worse, letting yourself be stolen. I'm convinced that part of growing into responsible adulthood is refusing explanation to those whose questionings will tire you out.

So I braced for a fight when Tara came down to pour a nightcap. Passing by she eyed Squibbles on the armrest of the couch, flexing his paws on the upholstery.

"Whose cat is it?" she asked from the kitchen.

"One of our neighbors."

"Then why isn't it there?"

"I'm not sure which house he belongs to."

"Doesn't the collar say anything?"

"Only Squibbles."

If pouring herself a drink was an obedient substitute for not smoking, she then entitled herself to asserting her own house rule.

"Can we not keep cats in the house?"

I reached to pet Squibbles's head.

"Can we wait until it warms up?"

But Squibbles bit me as I answered Tara before hiding beneath the coffee table.

"Can you keep it out of my bedroom and let me finish the last of your vodka?"

"Sure."

"Good. I already emptied it."

It's exactly this sort of back-and-forth tension that wears me out and risks bringing about the worst in me as though I'm again fighting to *retain* myself (the opposite of explaining myself away). Yet let me warn you, the more I resort to this retaining of myself the more it fosters a pessimism that I worry hardens me from caring about those who are good and right to care for.

I think of my younger years spent seeking to love and be loved, and God willing, you too will seek the same wherever you're led. But at this point, who do I have left to love? My mom has passed away. My dad and brother live in other states. I have them as incompletely as any coworker or roommate. Who else, I worried, until I had you at every waking and crying moment to fearfully and wonderfully care for? Please know the marvelous gift you are to me.

It's my bedtime now, and I'll go upstairs and fall asleep beside you. Tonight I layered you in two outfits and put you to bed face up inside a fleece hoodie that I zipped to your chin. You don't come close to filling my hoodie; it fits you more as a sleeping bag, the empty sleeves limp alongside you. I pull the comforter over us like a cozy tent. More than any gift, you're a giving of myself to you. With you there is no retaining myself.

You're happiest to rule the apartment and task your mom and me as your maidservants. You hand us bottles to fill and picture books to read. You point to the couch for a search of its cushions for your pacifier and to the kitchen cabinets to rummage the pots and pans beneath the counters, pleased as anything to sit on your diapered rump and bang away. You're accustomed to having your tiny voice and the shining expectations in your dark eyes answered and can appear, likely even to Squibbles, more excitable pet than baby girl.

When you and the cat first spotted each other through the frosted borders of our glass back door the world around you stilled with innocent wonder.

"Tail. See the bushy tail? See the kitty ears?" I had pointed over your shoulder, but you were fixed eye to eye with the cat. Was this one of your cuddly bears morphed to feral life? It had to be—the jumpy tail, sharp eyes and ears, and smoky colored plush of fur—all too much for your dear fascination. And to the cat's green eyes what exactly are you? Your diaper, when it's all your trouncing around the apartment in, always reminds me of a rabbit's cotton tail.

It's all such a joy to see the world through your delighted eyes. Even in the dark, when the alley's motion-triggered floodlight timed out and there wasn't much more to see than the cat's green eyes, the splendor was unlost. You didn't quite hear me announce your bedtime, and when I picked you up you fussed up the stairs and into bed. The cat protested, too, its meows carried inside, so why not go with the simple consensus and let the cat in? Might it be disoriented in the snow so deep it leapt its way through to the nearest lighted back door? Or was the owner gone for a thaw in Florida? Downstairs the cat's white paws were rasping against the

To Bianca   161

glass. Bringing him inside and checking the collar, only the name "Squibbles" was inscribed. No phone number or address. Squibbles, a hefty cat, weighed not much less than you. I carried him to our warmer bedroom and placed him atop the bed so you could again see him while I made him a bed of stuffing a towel into a shoebox. But Squibbles wouldn't have it; he'd already curled himself to sleep, and neither were you interested in seeing him leave sight of the bed. So Squibbles stayed at your feet with me beside you for the night.

Resting my arm securely over you, I felt your joy as your eyes beamed wet with dim hallway lighting that outlined the tilt of his ears and the soft rise and fall of his side. And I felt your peace as you drifted to sleep.

What else? Your birthday is May the eleventh. You're closer to turning three, so really, two and a half. When you're a little older, and winter comes not so cold in the Southwest, you'll whole-heartedly endorse this extra half year. From the children I teach in Sunday school, reaching their half birthday is a detail of utmost identity. They hop from their chairs as they correct me— five *and a half*! A brother and sister even exacted six and *three quarters*, a good way to begin learning fractions.

When they ask my age I count until running out of fingers. Then they talk me through "eleven, twelve, thirteen," until by twenty I insist not knowing how to count any higher. When I ask your age you react with two raised fingers. It's clearer than answering with a pacifier, or, as known from your mom, a *chupete*. You say "dos" when your mom asks "*años?*" You overlap vocabulary between the languages, handing me your bottle and asking for "juicy *biberon*." You overlap within words, too, asking for your *coh-binkie*. Your mom figured it out first: You wanted us to find your security blanket; by day your *cobija*, by night with me your *blankie*. Your mom also explained *gatojo*. It's your tripping of *gato* over *ojo* when Squibbles overwhelms you with his green peepers.

On the basis of those eyes and the touchable appeal of his winter-thick fur, Squibbles quickly learns that if he sits at the back door you will most vocally advocate for his entry.

"He's not a toy," I warn before unlocking the door. Once inside, Squibbles leads you on a merry chase. Ambling after him, often top heavy with your *coh-binkie* and *biberon* in either hand, you run from room to kitchen and all corners between. When he's had enough scampering he jumps to a surface beyond your reach and relaxes, letting down his wild nature from the anxiousness of time outdoors. Squibbles is your first encounter with anyone who refuses your little demands, and that he knowingly overhangs his tail just out of your reach is more than your short fuse can handle. After a shared cooling period Squibbles will let me bring you near him once I've coaxed him with pets on the head and scratches beneath his chin.

Then I lift you slowly near Squibbles, shifting your weight to one arm and guiding your hand over his fur with my other. It's a balancing act, not only for my arms but for lulling your excitement from an outburst that will send Squibbles dashing again. Or scratching. Like the night you first fell asleep to Squibbles at your feet, I can closely feel the glowing warmth of your excitement. It's a joy to see through your eyes the world rebirthed in a halo of innocence, a world I no longer saw for myself or without you.

You didn't sleep well last night, crying several times. It could be that you're getting sick or were cold. Polar winds pounded our windows, and the best I could do was hold you closer. Or you might be missing your mom while she waitresses another late shift. I think about her too, before falling back asleep. As with adults, sleepless nights must expose babies to the worst of worry, when daytime's fortitude of busyness is dissolved. Fortunately, it was Sunday; we slept until your mom was also awake. I warned her that she might be in for a morning of fussing, but you instead dispelled last night's unrest by waking in such a sweet mood of eye rubbing and baby yawning that part of me didn't want to leave because where else can innocence like yours find safe home? For us grown-ups, probably not even where adult holiness is preached. I took the morning to attend church, rushing off like someone who didn't want to be fired from a job for further lateness.

What stayed with me from this week's service was the harshness of its prayer of confession. It was delivered by one of the younger pastors with such savoring graveness you would've thought he was proud to surprise us with just how much of our day-to-day living is in need of relentless confessing.

For "our tiredness," confessed the young pastor from the pulpit, "we lift up an opportunity we took to wrongly prefer sleep more than you, God." For "our hunger," he similarly confessed our preference for food. He confessed our time exercising or shopping for clothes or planning what to wear as worshipping our appearance. I wanted to defend myself right there in the pew; there's never a moment to admire my outfit when rushing off to work.

He confessed our disappointments with spouses and children, "our failing to appreciate them as gifts from you, God." But then he confessed the daily idols we make of family and the caring of them through work and education, both of which also might be "hidden idols of our hearts."

It's introspectively exhausting to account for all our possible wrongs. Head bowed, I peeked down the airless rows to find the pews in eyes-closed contriteness.

"And we confess to admiring the beauty of nature but failing to acknowledge you, God, as He who chiseled the mountains and sanded the beaches we enjoy without a thought to your creation."

Dismissing the fact of no mountains or beaches in easy proximity of DC, I wondered if in never going far enough to admit our wrongs, do we in trying to, in prodding around in the dark well of ourselves, risk internalizing as personal guilt the many blessings natural to daily living? So what if dinner was quite tasty? Or wearing this dress is rather uplifting? Or if with longing I remember those many majestic desert sunsets?

I wonder if all this relentless confessing conditions us to seek *permission* to enjoy anything at all. I ask because I've started noticing that the joys I see fellow Christians profess without reservation are joys perceived or misperceived as joys exclusive to only the Christian life.

Hear me out: The other night when Tara arrived home with a box of store-bought frosted cookies for the office breakroom the next day you didn't hesitate to ask for and happily scarf one down. But within my churchgoing habit of grim confession, even the commonest of cookie enjoyments risks suspicion as the makings of idolatry. Frosted cookies before God? However, the same box of cookies shared in the name of moral generosity serves as that permission needed to finally enjoy a cookie. And Tara, who's no churchgoer, was more than pleased to share one with you. What she wasn't soon happy about was returning from a brief moment upstairs to find, at my unsuspecting back, you taking a bite out of each cookie and placing it back in the box she'd left within your reach. ("So much for the break room.")

But to my point, the reformed Christian who relearns to enjoy said cookie within only the context of scriptural encouragement risks misperceiving any common enjoyment as enjoyment exclusive to Christians. I, of course, don't mean for cookies; I mean this for marriage and parenting, two church-officiated responsibilities where it's particularly noticeable that Christians are convinced of having better marriages or of being better parents for taking to heart scripture's intent for especially marriage. Whereas church bases its theological teachings for marriage's spousal roles on the Bible's analogy of church as Christ's bride and Christ as corresponding head of the church, I'm currently preferring the more direct parenting analogy of God as our Father as it's brought to life in caring for you.

In all the unseen ways I can watch over you, to then ponder God watching over us. In your mom and I not missing a moment of your life, consider God knowing every moment of ours. To think of my responsibility for you and God's surely greater responsibility over us. And as for my panicked rush to find you when some few nights ago you briefly disappeared from my sight, consider what it is for us to run from His. Our scriptural understanding of marriage or parenthood doesn't so much as determine how fulfilling each is for us but instead better provides us new considerations of God, say as Father, that we wouldn't sense without living out either responsibility.

To Bianca

I have stated what a precious joy you are, a delight, and I need not be Christian or first seek permission to find the joy I have in you. I'll go so far as to add that my joy in your joy and wonder and housebound adventuring is by analogy the same joy He has in ours. Take how your excitement in spotting Squibbles waiting outside our back door becomes my excitement too. Once inside Squibbles is content to let you amble after him from a safe distance while he conducts nightly patrol of the TV room and kitchen for new finds to sniff out and claim as his—whatever suitcase, boxes, and gym bags Squibbles finds new to the room, he takes luxuriant rest atop, and it's then he allows me to bring you closer for petting. You're getting better at containing your up-close excitement of taking in his animated eyes, swiveling ears, twitching tail, and comfy purring. Think of your kitty happiness as mine for yours, as God's for ours.

The dirty laundry pile in the upstairs hallway is Squibbles's napping spot. (I learned from one of my mom's cats that laundry can wait, or else risk their claws—"They relish the salty smell," she vouched.) So one evening last week when Squibbles socked me away from washing his bed of gym sweats, I returned downstairs to find you rummaging through the foyer closet where Squibbles's earlier patrols had led you.

Take your delight in digging up the years-stored Christmas tree and how proudly you held up like a trophy one of the shiny bauble ornaments while the unboxed rest rolled green and red across the floor. You know exactly what Christmas is, and asking for it—"Navidah"—why not? With laundry delayed for another night and with the ornaments, frilly garlands, and a tangled nest of lights all scattered from the closet, why not clean up by decorating for Navidad?

I hadn't put up a tree in over two years, not since the Christmas before my mom passed, which, come to think of it, was your first Christmas. The tree, along with much of the kitchenware, was left by the pair of girls who'd lived here before, and it looked about that long since its last raising. Mounting the tree in the TV room, its boughs filling the back window, we were hanging ornaments when Tara came home. The sight of you wholly immersed in stringing the lights in tippy-toed satisfaction atop a chair you'd pushed over served as explanation: I'm just as happily spending another evening in your baby world.

"Will there be spiked eggnog too?" Tara asked.

"No, but I salvaged your cookies. I cut 'em in two and saved the unbitten halves in a bowl."

"I'll keep that in mind next time I get the munchies. In the meantime, zinfandel."

Tara went upstairs with a bottle, and after settling herself into wine world, after the tree was finished decorating and the TV room darkened, arrived back down and took a seat beside us on the couch where I'd gathered you on my lap to behold the synchronized twinkling of tree lights. The sight stilled you, a respiring warmth in my arms, the evening softened.

I was you held and beheld too, somewhere under the same overtaking quietude, regarded in my arms as when I've gotten out from under the city lights to witness the panoramic multitudes of stars over West Virginia or from the air, when landing for a layover and catching breathless sight of Chicago's skyline shimmering at dusk.

You soon fell asleep in peace. Tara and I conversed in whispers until eventually I carried you upstairs to bed for another night wrapped in my hoodie. Ending the long day with a shower, or so I'd planned, I found my hoodie, bed, and bedroom empty on return.

"Tara," I called downstairs, the glow of the Christmas tree reddening the hardwood steps, "is Bianca with you?"

"Keep the cat off the laundry," came her dampened reply from behind her bedroom door.

"Then remember to turn off the tree!"

To my relief you were downstairs at admiring distance from the illuminated tree. To the sight of you, rosy in the glow and hunkered in worshipful silence alongside the equally fascinated cat, I exhaled in similar tranquility so as not to break the timelessness of your wonder.

A sight for my wonder too.

And surely a sight for God's wonder, my own thoughts on God occurred as I labored my divided attention through the following morning's sermon. Our joy in others certainly informs us on God's joy in us. But this is a sincerity lost on too many believers who indebt their joy to the shame of their once reveled self-destruction. My time of immoderate drinking comes to mind, but confessing can't be at a cost of foregoing the redemption and, dare say, the Godliness of finding joy in others.

To an uncertain but hopeful degree I've always wondered what being a mother must be like. Uncertain, I say, because having a baby of my own seemed impossible to fully imagine without one in my arms, and hopeful, I say, inasmuch as ever knowing just how helplessly in charge of an even more helpless life remained from sight. To think at any length on motherhood yielded the overshadowing preoccupation of finding the future man I wanted to build a family with, and in that sense, especially given the dead end of recent prospecting, having a baby was a nonstarter to think about until I started arriving home to you every night.

If I'm honest there wasn't much proactive parenting on my part tonight. No reading you picture books or checking whether you needed a bath or taming an encounter between you and Squibbles. Tonight I changed into my pajamas early and sat you in my lap to relax in the Christmas tree's offseason glow. Squibbles has taken to the tree like anything else he discovers, first giving thorough study with his whiskery nose before trying his paws at climbing atop the ornament-laden boughs. Bells jingled, and a few bauble ornaments fell in his piney ascent until his top-heaviness tumbled the whole tree over. You giggled before just as happily making a game of fishing out the ornaments that'd rolled beneath the couch and TV stand for me to rehang once I propped the tree back up.

With Squibbles darting upstairs you turned your attention to me, scrambling back on the couch and standing on my lap as I retook my seat. As though to paint my face you traced your fingertips over the arches of my eyebrows, across the bridge of my nose, and on my glossed lips. You ran your fingers through my hair with an adorable concentration free of testing how close you can get as when you do the same to Squibbles's gray fur. You view Tara with similarly cautioned distance. She'll arrive home for the evening and join us on the other end of the couch with a bowl of ice cream or a glass of red wine. From my lap, you put as much attention into her as she does flipping through waves of channels.

Since moving back in Tara and I are slowly renewing our history of watching trashy reality shows together, mostly high-heeled drama excessing in public fits and drinking by naturally beautiful women, dressed to shine and shouting highly regrettable vulgarities. After settling on the Bravo channel, Tara peered over and noticed your bold study of her looking every bit the reality queen. She was dressed in a formal evening gown, her overbleached hair tightened back in a ponytail, stray wisps fastened by bobby pins matching her bright-red gown and lipstick.

"So, does Santana have any change of plans?" Tara asked.

"Still waiting to see what happens to Martez."

As necessary as it is to ask about the future of your *father*, she's in denial that your dad's plea deal will include prison time, and I don't want to tell her how waiting around and hoping otherwise, and hoping they can live together again and raise you, is a lost cause for now. The sooner she moves on the better.

With or without you I wanted a way back West, and pressing her again for what was next sunk my thoughts into my own worries, such as breaking the lease and walking out on a dependable job. It goes to show just how little my DC life keeps my head above water. I don't know how else to reflect on my continuing time in Washington without sinking into regret, the mire of which likes to return my mind where I last left off, thinking about Tom.

You were still eyeing Tara when, during a commercial break, she gestured you to leave my lap and cross to her side of the couch. For her latest trip to the salon, where post-Tom she's spending more time, she had her hair straightened so that when she fans it out for your fascinated fingers it divides like a veil. She also had her hair recolored. What I would give to have Tara's lovely blonde hair, descending as though from the clouds as similarly from her empty

To Bianca

head. To compare, if my hair fits into the blonde spectrum as wheat, parched and wilting, Tara's hair is a whole shiny, golden field.

And what I would also give to have the beautiful night sky of your mother's raven hair, dark and sleek; hair promised you as yours grows. Right now you're in the loveable toddler pigtails phase, but don't let that delay you from looking forward to blossoming into your mother's striking features. I can already see her mystery in you, as well as the bright eye you're eagerly developing for all matters of fashion.

Tara's face is to you a finished painting, and out of unfamiliarity and artistic appreciation, you withhold reaching for her brighter lips, powdered cheeks, and mascara-caked lashes.

"Has Bianca ever had her nails painted?"

"Never," I answered, realizing I was more and more speaking as your mother. "It's hard to get her little hands free when she's sucking her thumb or jamming a hand in her mouth."

"What about her toenails?" Tara pulled off one of your socks.

"Toes might work."

"I'm going to be the first to ever paint your nails," Tara happily told you. You realized what was going on when Tara presented from her purse a bottle of the same red polish she was wearing. When I pulled you back in my lap you kicked and fussed in excited protest, but I was only positioning your feet over the side of my lap for Tara to wipe off your toes for painting.

"Let me hold your feetsies." I grasped one of your ankles.

As stilled as you ever were by Squibbles in the window or beneath the glow of the Christmas tree, you settled into my lap, and your gleaming eyes followed each trip Tara's red-tipped brush took from polish bottle to toe and back. I guess this was us nurturing your little girlhood; from now on your feet will still at the scent of nail polish, long after you're too big for holding.

When Tara finished you continued gazing over your red toes until, exhausted by your own amazement, you started drifting off in my lap. Before you were fully asleep I made the mistake of trying to put your socks back on your feet, but this alerted you to defend your toes by crying.

"She's worried socks will wipe the polish away," Tara realized. "Okay, okay. No socks for cupcake!"

You clutched hold of my thumb to assure that I'd keep my hand from your socks while you fell back asleep.

Tara killed the overhead lights, and beneath the glow of the TV (and adjacent Christmas tree) we leaned back with glasses of wine and whispered. By her second glass our back and forth was mostly Tara venting about Tom, her ex. Her reasons for loathing him mounted more freely the longer we stared at the glowing screen's celebrated gluttony of public insobriety, indulgent fashions, catfights, and infidelity, the quasi reality of which fused my letdown of longing for Tom into pleasantly weary imaginings of us hand in hand, running through the show's same drunken garden parties, summer pool sides, and bars faster than the chorus of arguing can unfold behind us, all as Tara kept whispering next to me in the dark.

Tara isn't anywhere near coming to terms with Tom tossing her aside, and she wouldn't almost nightly descend with wine into confessing to me her depths of abandonment had she any clue I'd similarly wanted Tom. My chances with him ended with a whimper as opposed to the bang Tara reels from, so I'd taken my distance without a word. You see, I couldn't close in on Tom as impulsively as Tara had because he was my defense attorney. I hired him after my DUI arrest last summer, which is how your mom and I met, during our night awaiting release from a shared cellblock. (In mentioning this, I realize at some point I owe you the whole backstory.)

But staying on Tara, I couldn't, and can't even now, seem to uproot my own private emotional stake from still wanting Tom no matter how agonizingly clear Tara conveyed his uncaringness.

"I gave him so much," is her refrain once the wine sets in.

If anything, listening to her confirmed the bulk of my meticulously built logic where almost like church I visited when needing particular convincing of how I wasn't missing anything: Patience—there are other, better Toms out there; Nothing with him could last anyway, and the earlier I knew this the less heartache; The difference between having a man and not having a man is what we make of it. Or all in our heads. Or not worth defining.

I didn't even have to run into Tom to test my logic. It collapses inside me whenever I walk by his building on K Street. Part of actively upholding this logic became bypassing his office building by taking a different sidewalk path from the metro exit to my office, because raising my eyes to his eighth-floor office window is like confronting a wall that no resolve of patience and hope can overcome. A wall that I was painfully on the other side of, and to hear Tara and to have her beside me, all I could do was hold you closer because my willingness to go against all good sense and scale over to Tom surged back. Give him whatever it takes. Even wisdom must admit to patience killing passion.

"They should only use girls' names for hurricanes," Tara's third glass of wine regretted, "because Tom and I were sailing smooth until hurricane whatever the hell was her name showed up."

My glass of wine regrets too. I wonder, in watching trashy reality shows with Tara, whether I should've thrown the same drunken tantrum the pretty cast members do over all the same losers they've slept with. But seeing tables flipped and wine glasses hurled against walls, not even another glass or bottle of my own can bring me to imagining my anger as violently acting itself out. Besides, as another point of my logic held, when you can't stand someone, it's a great advantage to not let them know. Tara doesn't know.

If Tara had asked me a few nights later, I'm glad to tell you that by then we're closer to an answer on leaving for Arizona.

While your mom watches you during the day, she'll take you to visit your father in prison or make calls to Tom, his lawyer, trying to gauge a way forward that includes your father. In the evenings, when she has a night off from waitressing, we'll talk after you're put to bed. Earlier this week she wanted to know the details of my push to get us to Arizona. How were we getting back? Driving, flying? *So what gives?* I asked, because I knew my weeks of campaigning hadn't persuaded her.

"Martez is working on scheduling a hearing to plead guilty."

"Tom cut him a deal?"

"And I'd like to wait until his sentencing before moving because it's the last time I'll see him for a few years. Tom's trying to convince Martez to plead down to lesser prison time rather than risk worse at trial."

Let me take you back to when I said you were born in Las Vegas to Santana Solorio. Your father is Martez, age thirty-seven, a second-generation Colombian-American whose parents immigrated to California in the seventies.

"What's Martez agreeing to plead guilty to?"

"Oh, stupid stuff. Drug trafficking. Allowing the sale and use of cocaine and ecstasy at his nightclub."

By the time your future parents met in Las Vegas, your dad was part owner of a nightclub at the Bellagio. Their first encounter was a job interview. Your dad hired her to dazzle in a red dress and VIP host the tables reserved for bottle service. And so, you were born a few years later.

"Do you think Martez knew about the dealing?"

"Not enough to go to jail. He's maybe guilty of keeping friendly terms with dealers who took advantage of his club to sell until the place got raided, but he's always been friends with dealers. Once enough of them were arrested the investigators turned them into witnesses against Martez so the police could revel in taking down a so-called drug club."

In case you're wondering again, your mom and I's first encounter was sharing a night in the district jail. I was arrested for trying to drunkenly escape a tow lot by plowing my car through the front gates. On that same July night your mom was waitressing at your father's club when agents stormed in and booked her as part of a roundup of bouncers and servers so they could shut down the place.

"How much time is Martez agreeing to?"

"Three years."

Jail is where I also met Tom.

It was Tom, a regionally known defense attorney, who your dad arranged to retrieve your mom when she'd called your father

To Bianca   173

for help the next morning. We'd shared the long, uncertain night conversing on the common ground of both our own mothers' recent passing, and come morning, and badly needing a lawyer of my own, we had Tom tell the guards he was there for both of us. I hired him to better courtroom results than your dad's getting.

So, where were you in all this? You hadn't yet left Las Vegas. Your father's side of the family, namely his mom and sister, hijacked custody of you, insisting on raising you in Vegas so that when your mom followed your dad to Washington they kept you there, not believing her a dependable mom by the added evidence of her leaving with your dad for Washington.

When I found out after meeting your mom that she had a child she, at some point, made the defense that their insistence on raising you was to eventually gain the legal custody needed to prevent her from filing child support against your dad, whose ventures in Las Vegas, Los Angeles, and Washington made for a sizeable portion to claim.

"Santana, we both need new lives. I've been done with Washington for as long as you have, and I'll quit my job when you get back if you'll move with me to Arizona like we've talked about. Let's go to Phoenix and find work and an apartment and just live our lives raising Bianca."

"Okay," your mom whispered.

"We'll make a road trip out of it."

When I'm most put off by your mom clinging to your now incapable father, such as when our conversation ended, I hope you're never angry toward her. So why bother telling you this if it's too early for you to remember? Because no truthful account of your earliest upbringing can be given without revealing the irresponsibility of us adults—Tom, Tara, your father, myself. You'll have your youthful irresponsibility, too, your remissible teenage rebellion of getting wasted and trying marijuana and skipping class that I pray isn't preceded by our example of adult irresponsibility. *Do not remember the rebellious ways of my youth,* so say the Psalms, *but remember me according to your lovingkindness, Lord.*

Please understand that adulthood isn't one day lightly woken to; adulthood is more often what's gradually stumbled into with disappointment and regret and loneliness. So when it came to growing up we kept drinking too much—Tara, myself, and your mom—and we fell in love with dead ends because nobody wants to understand that disappointment and regret and loneliness are hardly shameful marks of personal failure but rather naturally occurring inevitabilities, similar, I'll risk saying, to the inevitability of aging, but rejected all the same because, of course, none of it is proud living.

It's why I believe the pastor's common inclination to teach on either sinking feeling as discontent between God and the believer's incorrect reaction, as though any disappointment is by default disappointment with God and requires confessing. Your life will have inevitable points of loss, and may you pray, pray, pray when high tides of disappointment swell over you. But never beset yourself with worrying how God might answer you any less. As a parent lovingly watches their children so the Lord watches over those who look to him, so say the Psalms, for God remembers we are dust.

What really peaks the regret and loneliness of my lowest moments is when I dwell on my age, the point at which both regret and loneliness converge most painfully, which leads me to explain how I've come to view my unrest as a brooding over time itself: I'm twenty-six and graduated college four years ago, when I was twenty-two and positively expecting marriage and children to transpire as easily as finding my first real job. It's as easy to regret those past four years as it is to look with the same amount of years ahead, to when I'm thirty, and worried all the worse what a waste of time it will be if I'm still aimlessly alone.

Let me preach more abstractly: Might it be that youth disguises aimlessness as adventure, so that in my past times of unrest, of subsisting on minimum wage between semesters, the days passed more purposefully than these earned years of higher-salary work and achieving the successful Washington life? Like a bucket to be filled, time once passed according to the youthful distractions

To Bianca   175

and interests abundantly filling it. Now, as an adult, time passes according to its unconcerned self, the days passing differently, one burdening the next as something to be filled for the sake of being filled.

The problem of time is having to wait, because that's what the passing days too often come across as—a blind wait. Yes, and like most any girl I want a spouse and children, but it's not entirely because I'm a girl, as a pastor might remind me. Unrest is something deeper, yet is it solved, I dare ask, by the same methods as youthful distraction? If instead of getting drunk and setting my mind after Tom, I anchor my future with a spouse and children for the sake of unquestionably occupying myself like everybody else, comfortably filling time, then what keeps marriage and kids from counting as another, albeit mature, form of distraction? If productively working and even caring for you is distraction, then what's the vital difference? It's a difference of responsible and irresponsible distraction, where responsibility is to live uprightly, irresponsibility is to destruct, and distraction is what keeps us from giving full attention to time. To having to wait. To remembering we are dust.

Pardon me for digressing, and for ever suggesting whether you're merely my latest and greatest distraction, but when it comes to you, I've given much thought to how you've bettered me in the mere months I've cared for you. You're a wonderful, beautiful, blessed distraction from what I was becoming.

At first I kept your mom's word of returning west to myself. I worried that if in mentioning and openly planning anything, the promising fate of our move together would be undermined. The closest indication I've since made of Arizona is to read you your illustrated Sonoran Desert book each evening, pointing to and letting you name the cactus, coyotes, jackrabbits, snakes, pepper plants, and red mountains as I let my mind linger in expectation of going west.

It meant formally making plans to leave Washington, partly by readying for the questions demanding explanation at the news of our move. I began with Tara, but as it turned out, she wasn't much better at understanding the implications of us leaving than you, a toddler, getting the news spoon fed to you each evening. On the first night, after putting you to bed with a promise that was more a goodnight on your mom's behalf, I went back downstairs to start on Tara.

She offered me a seat beside her on the couch to share in more or less the same evening she's carried out since Tom dumped her: a glass of wine, pajamas, and a few hours of booze-fueled reality TV.

"So, I'm planning to move in a month or two," I said during the commercial break.

"Where?"

"Back to Arizona."

She didn't respond; the show came back on, and she waited until the next commercial break.

"You're leaving me?" Tara sounded surprisingly hurt, which begged more explanation.

"I'm only in the planning stages, but yes. After four years in Washington it's time."

When the episode ended I was ready for a backlash about ending my portion of the lease or quitting my job, but she was more upset with the car alarm pulsing down the alley.

The next night I told her that I planned to keep lodging you and your mom until we left.

"Washington isn't working out for her either?"

"No." I should've left her at no. "She wants to stay until her boyfriend's hearing."

"The baby daddy?"

"Yes. And now that he's going to prison Santana's plans for all of them to live together are over."

"What are they always running away from?"

That was Tara for you, or the red wine, piercing to the emotional marrow without ever closing in on the practical ones.

The car alarm sounded through the alley again.

"Is the cat outside?" Tara asked. "Maybe the cat's triggering the alarm?"

To Bianca

"Squibbles?"

He answered for himself, marching into the room on hearing his name and happily jumping between us on the couch.

"Maybe it's the clumps of snow falling from the trees?"

"Did you hear it go off last night? I was so pissed I couldn't fall back asleep."

Tara was better rested at work the next day, finishing her coffee before starting in on my plans for Arizona.

"What are you going to do for a job?" We were at our desks, and I hoped coworkers weren't listening. I avoided answering with any substance, because questions seemed her way of telling me that shepherding you and your mom to Arizona was a bad idea.

I could defend the confident amount of savings I'd fostered going back to my first paychecks here as a contract auditor three years ago—there was certainly enough to secure us a lease while your mom and I sought work in Phoenix. Rather than answering Tara, I excused myself to the restroom to hide in the farthest stall where Tara weeks ago cried when alcohol and pills weren't within easy reach. I huddled in the stall with my breathing and worry, bracing for tears. What if we run out of money? I wonder if all parents go through moments of wanting to apologize for the world their children are born into. What if this Phoenix life I'm striving to set up doesn't do you or your mom any better? Either way there'll come a day when your mom and I are powerless to keep you from not always getting what you worked for or the uncertainty and disappointment inherent in growing up, and the weary competition, not for the foods or fields of old but for the luxuries that allow us to look down on those without. Tara had Tom, and if she ever knew I wanted him, too, she would win everything. Theirs is the world I'm sadly apologizing for.

When the tears didn't come I left the building for a walk around the unthawed block. Gusts of bitter cold swept through the long hallways of downtown buildings, at the open end and above which grimaced the wind's damp source of dismal cloud cover. I can tell you that the Arizona I'm hoping for is a parting of those long winter clouds, along with so much more.

In a literal sense I'm not asking too much. Many restful evenings can be made of sipping Sangria to long, similarly colored punch sunsets over desert fairways in breezy Phoenix, its pavement warm enough by March for bare feet, which as I describe it, sounds like the escapist surroundings that emotionally snowbound Tara is lately attempting to piece together with zinfandel and reality shows.

But in practical terms I worry that I'm asking for too much. I'm hoping for a new job to support us, a job that likely won't pay as much or carry the salaried certainty I have here in Washington. I'm hoping for the well-being of a new home centered around you and her, with my brother, Dustin, crashing when needed.

A new life is a lot to ask for, especially on a day confronted by the chores of ties to unbind. The lease, the keeping your mom convinced, and at some point my resignation letter due to Edith, who to list as a professional reference is like asking for a life raft away from her safe ship. I wanted to give up walking and huddle in the sidewalk wind, like in the stall, but this was no place to cry. How air can harden, as opposed to soften, say at dusk in Florida. What makes air *hard*? The cold. The bullying morning rush hour of jackets, scarves, and mittens before ultimately seeping through your bundled layers. This was air at its arctic hardest—a tough morning.

Tara didn't ask or nag any further when I settled back at my desk. Later in the evening, when she dressed into her pajamas for another night of TV, I kept you and Squibbles in my room, leery of what questions or scenes wine would bring about downstairs. When you fell asleep Squibbles curled beside you in my bed for the night. It was then I heard Tara downstairs, yelling.

"Tara, please," I hissed from the top of the stairs. "I just put the baby down."

"The damn car alarm is going off again!"

I stepped downstairs to hear. "Yeah, so? It spazzes out every night."

"Help me do something about it."

"Tara, you're drunk."

Half the reason she'd turned her attention to me was because her latest bottle of wine was empty.

"Talk to me until the alarm dies down." Grasping my wrist she drew me beside her on the couch. "Are you really leaving?"

"Yes."

"And quitting your job?"

"Not quite in that order."

"How are you going to get there?"

"We're taking Santana's car." It was better to get this out of the way now than tomorrow at work.

"What about the lease?"

"I'll be turning in my thirty-day notice."

"What about the car alarm?"

"What about it?" I could smell the wine on her breath as she leaned her drunk head on my shoulder and hear the alarm again down the street.

At her desk the next morning Tara slumped beneath the towering stack of itemized charges that overnight had doubled in height. Three-hundred-pages thick, I guessed, unmotivated and sulking because if I went ahead and started our shared work while she kept her head on her desk I was only setting her up to notice my eventual absence. I'm tired of the unspoken jockeying between us, the ruling tension of which was at the moment relieved by her expressionless sleep.

When Edith called us into her office regarding the expected paperwork audit, Tara didn't rouse from her desk.

"Nicole," she welcomed when I appeared in her doorway. "How's Tara?"

"At her desk."

"Still hungover? I caught her breath in the elevator this morning."

A bleary-eyed Tara stepped from behind me.

"When can the two of you have the paperwork I left on your desk turned into an audit report?" Edith asked.

"Can we get something back to you in a few weeks?"

"Will you still be here in a few weeks?" Tara asked.

Edith eyed me so intensely I wanted to hide.

"Anything I need to know, Nicole?"

"Yes," I said, since Tara blew my cover.

"You're leaving?" Edith for once looked fazed.

"I'm resigning before the end of the month to look for paralegal work in Phoenix."

"You're quitting before you've found another job? This isn't like you, Nicole."

My empty response was to nod.

Back at our desks, Tara shot first, firing off anger not surfaced since her outburst over Tom dumping her. She fussed up a storm blaming last night's disruptive car alarm rather than her obvious hangover for why she was so "out of it."

"You couldn't wake me up when Edith called for us?"

"You couldn't keep quiet about my plans to leave?"

"Well, you *are* leaving."

"That's not your bridge to burn." I handed her a cigarette to signal her outside. But outside she said nothing, save for asking for another smoke.

I considered the usual course of reaction, which called for apologetic recognition of her dismay before easing into an understanding tone, but the smoldering anger in her eyes meant there'd be violent hell to pay when she returned from her own faraway depths. I'd seen this inward act before, the rumbling before her temper erupted. But what had me more on edge was Edith bewildered by my decision to leave.

Edith's surprise sent me back into a spiral of bitter doubt. Again, I didn't opt for the usual course of reaction; rather than again walking myself through the logic of my plans and the well-rehearsed case for spurring a move west, I lit another cigarette and smoldered alongside Tara, numb to the chilly breeze and pissed as hell that quitting work and moving and looking for a new job couldn't for once be taken casually, especially when as soon as I left I'd be out of the minds of those who wanted to know.

Through the afternoon we stewed at our desk, saying nothing over the tower of reports that loomed between us. Attacking the reports with both duty and defeat, I was suddenly unbothered by how costly the risk was in quitting this job. Nevertheless, we made for good little workers, summoning just enough composure to numb our contention and sustain productivity until it was time to go.

Ever since Tara moved back in after splitting from Tom, she insisted on commuting together. We sat next to each other on the metro if rush hour didn't force us to remain standing. Crowded around us were faces submerged in their phones, absently reflecting the same day's muffled drudgery. A few men always ventured glances our way (girls!), but even during our most disagreeable days, there was steady comfort on our island of mutually knowing each other among waves of passing strangers.

Commuting home was also when my mind shifted to another comfort—the warm, smiling expectation of you.

"What?"

"Nothing."

Tara and I were safely talking again.

"You're smiling about something."

You're the happily secret life I get to live. It's because of you I can smile after a frustrating day that more or less justifies rallying with Tara around a bottle of wine and trash TV. But when I see how happy you are to see me arrive home, skipping to me in open-armed thrill, all the competition with which we strive for identity through work and boyfriends melts into an afterthought of snoozed alarms that I can for once take casually.

You have a softening influence on Tara too. From the other side of the couch she'll look away from the TV to gently smile at our nightly reading, and with you on my lap, sounding out the pictures of our books, Tara will take up petting Squibbles's gray fur and scratching beneath his chin.

Putting you to sleep entitled Tara to a stronger pour, and once I was back downstairs Squibbles moved onto my lap.

Remember I warned of the unpredictable hell to pay? It began with her determination to drink to the point of painful confessions and tears.

"Join me."

"I'm here."

"I mean drink with me," her second, larger glass said.

Her third glass was more demanding. "Look at the snow falling. They'll cancel work tomorrow. No reason to stay sober."

By her third glass I uncorked a red blend.

"I wanted to marry Tom."

So did I.

"I don't blame you. Tom was . . . he stood out." I couldn't tell if she was listening. She leaned her head back, her gaze lost to the ceiling.

"Tom wouldn't discuss a future beyond just living together. I wanted something with potential."

"Marriage and kids and all that?" I hoped Tara didn't catch my surprise as I lowered the lights and sat back down.

"He never brought up marriage, so I did. I opened us a bottle one night, and after a few glasses I asked if he ever looked forward to marriage. He didn't have a response. I wonder if that's when he decided to find someone else."

"I'm sorry."

"I've been trying guess what he thinks about why we fell apart. Do you think men ever worry that marriage leads us to a life of childcare and housework? I get how much effort Bianca takes and what it takes to be a mommy, but I think men are scared to literally ask us about it because motherhood is our thing, right? It's supposed to be a given, right?"

"So you're asking whether men are hesitant about asking women about their role as a wife? Because they don't want to be accused of not understanding in the first place?"

"Right, but it's more like men might think being a mommy is tedious and might be scared they're really asking us to do all that cleaning and cooking and staying put."

"Do you think Tom thought that?"

"I don't know. I'm probably just overthinking it."

"Well, I'd like to be a mommy someday. A baby would for me hold more meaning than my job, which is also tedious and probably more frustrating. I guess the tradeoff of becoming a mom at the expense of our job is naturally worth it presuming that motherhood is preceded by a loving husband."

"Tom didn't love me." Tara teared up. "And I'm not even sure if he or other guys understand that loving us is how to convince us that we're okay with their plans."

"I'm sorry." I looked her way.

"Did you like Tom?" she asked after a few sobs.

"Tara, I wasn't allowed to. I was his forbidden client. He asked me to alcohol rehab, not dinner."

Tara gave this a little laugh before her tears swelled over and she closed her eyes. Once she was asleep I didn't leave the couch either, drifting off to the glow of the TV and the snowfall.

Tara heard it first; her rustling nudged me awake.

"Nicole, help."

"What time is it?"

"Put on your coat and boots." Tara flicked on the light. "I'm dealing with this once and for all."

The maddening car alarm and fury in her voice cleared into my shallow alertness. Tara stormed out the back and into the snowy alley, leaving the door open, which I arose to shut against the night's icy gusts. Catching sight of her down the alley and realizing where she was headed I took her original orders to don my boots and jacket. Ahead I could see Tara's boots were untied and wobbling at her ankles. Her crossed arms held shut her unzipped coat when I caught up to her several row houses down, standing at the back gates, the pulsing headlights of a ringing SUV piercing between the fence boards.

"I wonder if anyone else got woke up?" She scanned the alley for lighted windows, her breath fuming in the cold.

"Someone will see us."

"Here, help me over."

"Tara."

"Help me, and I'll share whatever I'm smoking tomorrow."

"What about when I'm tested?"

"You're quitting."

"My next job?"

"Just hold the trash bin steady."

She grabbed a branch overhanging from inside the back lot and in one acrobatic motion hoisted her thin frame high enough to plant a knee atop the trash bin. Before the lid fully caved she balanced herself over the gate like she was climbing onto a stage. This stage, then, that she lowered herself down to using the gate's cross boards for footing, was where the SUV blared. Snow swirled like confetti from an overhead darkness broken only by the blinding high beams pulsing to the alarm's primal beat.

"C'mon," she said unlatching the gate.

How Tara next rushed into furious action was characteristic of her temper. She scoured the lot with a determination that outpaced my racing mind, the throbbing reality of the car alarm, and the madly barking dogs several lots over. The dense snowfall slowed in relative suspension above us.

The snow accumulation was deep enough to crunch underfoot; Tara's hurried tracks paused beside a grill, and from an adjacent stack of icy cinder blocks she lifted one. Too bulky for stable maneuvering, she corralled the block and took several slick steps toward the blaring SUV before thrusting the cinder block against the driver's-side glass. The glass cracked without giving. Maintaining her grip, Tara took a batter's stance to rock the block back before ramming it clear through the window. At this frenzied point I noticed this was an older SUV, because after Tara pulled the door's pin lock, she opened the door to reach behind the steering wheel and yank on the manual pull knob for the headlights, which already flashing, now remained constant.

I suddenly noticed the cold wind cutting into my hood.

"We're done, let's go!" Tara darted from the back lot.

Out in the alley I closed the gate behind us, before retracing our tracks that were already filling with snow. Trailing our sprint was the bark of dogs and several windows that had flickered on over the alley. I glanced at our dark window, worrying someone had seen us, though the only definite witness was Squibbles, watching from the back doorstep, his large, nocturnal eyes not the least bit concerned.

To Bianca

"What kind of person leaves their dogs outside in a snowstorm?" was all Tara had to say as she held open the back door for Squibbles and me, locking it behind us.

It wasn't until the car alarm timed off, when I was back upstairs getting into bed with you, that I realized Tara meant to drain the battery and leave no juice for the alley's nightly interruption.

It was still dark out when my radio alarm activated to scratchy announcements of school closings and city-wide telework for federal employees. I sat up at our window; the snow had stopped, and looking down the ghostly predawn of the snowed alley, the headlights were considerably dimmer. I rolled over and curled back to sleep next to you.

In the weeks leading up to our move to Arizona, I took over making sure to spend time telling you our upcoming move while your mom took several steps to pave the way for taking you west. First, she quit her job. Then she flew off to Las Vegas for a week to work through Martez's family defaulting legal custody of you back to herself. My preparing your toddler expectations wasn't unlike when I talked you through the upcoming turning points of your daily routine, alerting you of approaching dinners, baths, and bedtimes helped to smooth over the speed bumps of your gently paced routine.

I also talked you awake most mornings while your mom slept off her late shift downstairs and Tara took longer than I did readying herself for work. I'd wait to leave for work with Tara by whispering good morning until you yawned and rubbed your eyes.

One morning this week I laid in bed later than usual, laboring my thoughts over ending my portion of the lease between bouts of snoozing the alarm. If your father's hearing was only a few weeks away and we were planning on starting our drive to Arizona right after, I was still on the hook for nearly another month of rent due to the requirement of a forty-five-day notice to end tenancy.

I snoozed the alarm against the mounting weight of overarching realities: the forty- and fifty-hour workweek, student loans, filing taxes, figuring out medical insurance, reactivating my license at the DMV, friends growing up and losing touch, parents aging and dying. The matters of adulthood are confounding and anticlimactic. The only responsible reaction seems blind busyness, all for the sake of forgetting this very busyness and what in darkest thought lurks behind. Yes, in the great history of things behind us are the times of famine, plagues, barbarian invasions, and dying in childbirth, but when your parent dies and your days cycle in loveless routine, there deepens an impression that all the worst of history isn't so far from us, lurking near enough to fire a few warning shots our way.

But in waking next to you, and through the demanding hours between putting you to bed, I notice the vision you're giving to my blindness, a direction to my hurry, a loving center to my routine. You fill an emptiness I've carried for too long.

By now you've heard the idiom *better to give than receive*? In terms of caring for you I'm starting to wonder if the benefit of this dynamic goes just as much to me, the lover, if not more than you, the loved.

Consider the surgeon satisfied by the benefit their surgeries provide their patients. It's the patient who regains sight or walks again, yet who's the enabler of their healing? Yet the surgeon isn't obligated to delve any deeper into the lives of their patients the way I'm immersed in the entirety of yours, nor wonder how their patients ultimately turned out. What I'm trying to tell you is that even with us moving together, eventually I'll have to face longer-term questions of how long I can realistically remain a part of your life, because I'll miss you. I'll miss our evenings of singing along to the TV and fixing up your hair and sitting you on my lap with a book.

Consider God who comes to mind when I need to step away from reality overwhelming me: would He, by "father" God analogy, ever similarly go through seasons of missing us? Or rather, would God be capable of missing anybody, or allow Himself to, and in what scenario would this play out? I don't know if I'm even asking the right question, but I like asking because it envisions Him as caring for me in the knowing way I care for you and tames the stony sense of God as unattainable standard.

To Bianca

Psalms says that God knows us more than we know ourselves. The verse is an affection for us that, without the advantage of reflecting on the oversight I have into your life, I had always passed off as comfy saying. It should result as my devotion to you that I can account for your small years in ways you cannot understand.

Your dad's drug charges haven't cleared; he will plead guilty in a few weeks, maybe prompting your mom to move with me.

Until then, restful Saturdays like today are harder to come by than the weekly reprieve from busyness that Saturdays are meant for. When I rolled out of bed to brew coffee, I didn't bother checking whether Tara arrived home late last night, nor did I know her whereabouts until she texted me to join her for brunch in Arlington, no doubt with her clubbing buddies, punctuating her invite with a cocktail emoji. I responded with a selfie of you and me snuggled on the couch, just the two of us, until we heard Squibbles meowing on the back steps.

Letting Squibbles inside, he whisked past my ankles and huddled into the shape of a bread loaf atop the vantage point of the armrest. Since that night Tara tossed a cinder block through the SUV window, I now glance down the alley whenever opening our back door. The car alarm hasn't sounded since—Tara's covert mission accomplished, or as she saw it, peacekeeping. The assured silence was that of the neighborhood sleeping off the overcast morning. Balmy temperatures reached above freezing, hastening the drip-drip of snowmelt in the gutters.

By the time we got around to flipping on the TV, the children's-programming block that your mom has you watch was ending. Surfing other channels for what followed indicated a sea of early-afternoon college basketball tipoffs, so I took another cue from your mom and bundled you up for the park. You know Lincoln Park well, pointing ahead as its familiar clearing veered into view with still another residential block of ice-slushed sidewalk left to push your stroller through. Before I could unbuckle you at the gate of the jungle-gym enclosure you twisted from your stroller and scampered for the other toddlers gathered on the mulch footing of playground.

To my amusement you were greeted as a regular. Little voices welcomingly mispronounced your name, before one of the moms gave the definitive "Bianca."

"*Donde es mama*?" She gently asked you.

It's when you pointed her attention my way that I was caught off guard by the stinging recognition of her as one of the moms I'd worked alongside in the nursery at the church. An attractive woman in her late thirties in faded jeans and a bright-orange ski jacket.

"Nicole?" She remembered my name.

I wanted to duck behind your stroller.

"We haven't seen you in a while," she said on behalf of the church.

I could only guess how much my caretaking of you has spread around from the pastors who'd weeks ago questioned me about your custody. As she looked to you with revived curiosity I could tell she was piecing together whatever she'd heard. How the little girl whose guardianship the pastors had questioned me over was in fact you, at the moment hand in hand with her toddler daughter. Together the two of you were treading muddy circles in the playground's thawing puddles.

"We miss you working in the nursery. Will we hopefully see you volunteering again?"

"Not this Sunday."

"Have you spoken with the pastors?"

"Bianca's mom lives with me, if they want to know."

"Mama." You overheard us.

"Yes, Mama's home." To avoid further questions, I retreated beneath a tree to make a few calls to anchor the arrangements of our road trip. "Destination Arizona," as billed to my brother Dustin on inviting him to fly out to DC in a few weeks to join us on our cross-country drive. I also called Brad, a former colleague, to ask for the "big favor" of crashing in the extra bedroom at his house in Phoenix until your mom and I found an apartment. Both were willing but wanted a few days before confirming.

Before long you were crying. Your merry chase of the bigger kids led through the slick footing of a puddle, and there you sat, crying with your muddy hands extended, needing to be wiped and warmed. I held back at your stroller to fish a cloth from your diaper bag. Like a pit-stop crew I cleaned you up and sent you racing again, but after another half hour you were once again crying, tired and due for a nap and a bath.

Tara was hogging the shower when we returned. When she finally emerged from the fogged bathroom with a towel wrapped around her hair it was your turn.

"Santana's taking off from Vegas. She'll be here at the end of the day." I announced your mom's text message.

"Wake me up. I want to go with you guys to the airport," Tara said, surprising me. "Until then I'm taking a nap." As did the rest of us after your bath.

You and Tara fell soundest asleep, each in your own bed, while Squibbles drowsed downstairs. Only later, as the afternoon darkened into evening, did the sadness sink in that with your mom returning with full custody of you, these might be the last hours of the passing months that I can throw myself into caring for you. Yes, this whole winter I'd known our exclusiveness would sooner enough end, and for responsible reasons I'd helped to set in motion, but now the reality of the space growing between us to make room for your mom's full responsibility hastened sharply as though aware of the winter by feeling locked out in the snow and already no longer keeping warm beside you. I'm scared of missing you, Bianca. The latest reality of which occurring via another text update: *Boarding last leg to DC, landing in 3 hours.* I've been scared as evidenced by throwing myself into plotting a new life together out West.

When it was time to go to the airport all I could do was throw myself into the excited anticipation shared among the bustle of us getting ready. Even Tara, helping me to her mascara and giving final critique of our makeup, could appreciate the adventure made of picking up your mom.

Tara drove the refreezing streets, crossing to Reagan National Airport over the dark Potomac, which was too crowded with floating ice to neatly reflect the spacing of electric lanterns burning along the neighboring bridges.

Once parked I left your stroller behind to instead carry you on my hip, and from the parking garages the three of us took the glass-paneled walkway bridging the main terminal over the taxi-congested arrivals. We waited at the ground-level baggage claim near the base of escalators carrying passengers from Chicago, Minneapolis, and Denver as announced by the intercom numbering their baggage carousel.

"Santana!" I waved at the packed escalators. It was only when your mom returned a wave that you recognized her, gripping tightly around my torso and nuzzling your tears into my neck.

"Bianca, baby, come to Mama."

All of us calmed you down as she took hold of you. Between our mix of Spanish and English greetings and retrieving from the carousel her bags the commotion of our little parade made for an international incident leaving the airport.

Your mom and I rode in the back on the other side of your car seat; she held your hand and hummed you a reassuring tune while with your other hand you grasped my thumb.

"DC hasn't changed in the week you've been gone," Tara joked on regaining a glimpse of the cold city over the bridge.

"I never felt like I really lived here." Your mom said what I was also coming to understand about Washington—that we were never truly inside the city but rather always viewing its marbled world through a window, just like now. Like lights through this starless tunnel of wherever our Washington years were passing us through stood its floodlit monuments and domes above the dark river.

But for a much as Washington felt closed to us, we were all very much on the inside of the world revolving around you, narrating to your mom the details emerging from our time in her week away.

"Bianca still won't let us take down the Christmas tree. She cried when we tried."

"And where's the man of the house?" your mom greeted the cat.

"Skibbles!" you answered.

Dropping from your mom's arms you proudly led her over to Squibbles resting on the armrest and showed off how I showed you to pet him, starting with his head before gently moving over his smoky-gray coat. Squibbles yawned with indifference, briefly opening his sleep-heavy eyes.

When it was soon your bedtime your mom followed along on our nightly ritual of changing you into pajamas, tying your wild hair back, and standing you on a stool to brush your teeth over my bathroom sink. Your mom had "her way" of brushing your teeth, she contended. Handing over your toothbrush like a symbolic passing of the parenting torch disrupted my instincts to not give you up the rest of the night. I flicked on the night-light for when your mom would turn out the lights and put you to bed beside her before I returned downstairs to the couch, whispering along to the Spanish lullabies I could hear her singing to you.

Remember my mention of the space that would have to grow between us starting the day when your mom finally regained full custody of you? Tonight recalled the hot August days marking each first day of my grade-school years when waiting with my backpack at the bus stop the moms of new kindergartners were in tears as they sent their little ones off for their first-ever day of school. Wouldn't their child be back home in the afternoon, every afternoon, and dependent on their parents for how many more years? I was dismissive at the time, but those moms sympathetically came to mind as you rightfully slept beside your mom while I lay awake on the couch with Squibbles warm at my ankles. Yes, the day had to come; Santana is your mom, and you're hers to raise, but please know how immediately I came to miss the evenings when you were all mine, when nothing stood between us. Nothing except the little lullabies I found myself humming to Squibbles in the dark.

⁓

Your mom and I had a lot to plan for during the two weeks leading up to us moving West. There were any hectic number of details to work out when deciding whether to rent a small moving truck or drive your dad's SUV, which in turn dictated how much of our belongings could be packed, and I just assumed I'd be paying for fuel and hotels. Instead of worrying I found myself surprisingly upset. My anger went deeper than my frustration with your mom's sudden unwillingness to consider life beyond your dad's hearing scheduled for next week.

"Not to sound unsympathetic," I lectured, "but you've had months to plan for life without Martez, for Bianca's sake."

For the first few mornings following each previous evening's broken tries to talk through our plans, I awoke on the couch surprisingly upset. It's wrong to dwell in anger, but in my case anger has less to do with your mom and more often serves as an outlet for an inner restlessness that when stakes aren't as high surfaces as an anxious questioning of why I live where I do. Why Washington, I've been asking since my mom's death.

"But what if the judge only gives him probation?" Santana argued. "Then there won't really be any reason to leave. He can live here with us."

"What am I supposed to do when my job ends in two weeks? My lease ends too because we agreed to move away."

"I guess I didn't realize how *decided* everything was."

"What I don't think you realize is that Martez is *agreeing* to prison. What do you think the odds are that the judge will remove prison time from a pretrial agreement? Judges usually want to impose *stricter* sentences."

In my less-stormy moments I'd confronted myself as to whether my helping hand with you and your mom had given way to demands for her to follow my plans, but you know what? I've decided to leave with or without her. Dustin will fly out, and we'll rent a moving van and drive it to Arizona. Much of my anger is a despairing over leaving you and going it alone. If somehow I get used to the idea of letting you go it's already taken longer than the unrestful nights I've spent mentally letting go of my job. This process of letting go lingers as an ongoing forgiving of myself over essentially tossing away the personal meaning I'd worked for in amassing overtime hours and publishing audit reports, that once sworn off, was merely distraction taken for responsibility and compiled like data for the sake of having something, anything to hold onto.

Should we sadly part ways, I can't imagine ever truly letting go of you; I love you and will miss you. For as much as I've latched my sentiments to not only you but Tom, too, in a different way and against my aching interest, I can reluctantly relate to your mom similarly holding onto your dad.

Your mom spends nearly every morning of her first week visiting your dad at the penitentiary near the Baltimore Airport. Once Tara and I leave for work and the morning's interstate congestion dies down she loads you into the car seat of his Porsche and drives the forty-five minutes into Maryland.

I hadn't realized the determined frequency of her visits until Saturday rolled around and I awoke on the couch to you fussing for me to free you from your playpen. In the direction of the sizzling from the adjacent kitchen I said, "Santana, I babyproofed the whole house. It's fine to let Bianca wander."

"Cupcake is really clingy this morning, and I'm keeping her out of the kitchen while I cook."

"I'll hold her on my lap." I picked you up. "We'll read one of her books." But your mom insisted on accustoming you to the playpen. To this refusal I stepped over the playpen's green mesh walls and joined you with a book. From the kitchen your mom surrendered an amused laugh while you scrambled onto my lap, kicking up loose cat fur across the playpen, which until this week was solely Squibbles's prime napping spot safe from your excited reach.

"Nicole, are you good to drive in the snow?" your mom asked. "I need your help visiting Martez."

"Not with my license having been reinstated only last week." An annoyed response that duplicated for the snow, too, recalling its predicted four-inch accumulation as I took notice of the whitened alley through the nearest window.

"His confinement allows for daily family visits."

"Would you rather me stay here and watch Bianca?"

"Since Martez and I aren't married I'm not allowed to visit as family without Bianca."

She planned on visiting for the allowed hour while the Porsche's seat warmers were supposed to enhance my waiting in the lot.

After breakfast we bundled up, and for the first time since the suspension on my license expired, I took the wheel driving us north. Toward Baltimore the snowfall thinned from a haze to a gray-skied clearing of office parks, chain hotels, and box stores.

At the Baltimore Airport exit your mom paused from applying her makeup to gesture directions from the off ramp to an access road that drew parallel to a lengthy stretch of tall, razor-wire fencing bordering a snowed field as the prison complex came into view. The front-gate security guard was thrilled to see your mom again, waving us through after she indulged him in a brief back and forth.

"All right, one hour," she promised as I parked.

To your fussy protest of the cold wind tunneling into the back seat as you were unbuckled, she said, "Cupcake, it'll be baking warm once we're inside!"

She walked you by hand, but less than halfway to the visitor's entrance you plopped onto the frozen pavement and refused to stand, kicking off one of your boots in a loud tantrum, your pigtails bobbing high on each side of your head. I watched as she carried you and your boot the rest of the way, wondering, as you cried over her shoulder, at what age do first memories begin taking shape? Turning three in another few months, and guessing how close you might be nearing your own first memories, your tantrum a protest at having the first memories of your dad via prison visitation. There were many happier moments worthy of surviving as your first memories—Squibbles ascending the Christmas tree, painting your nails with Tara, and our evenings reading before bed. How grateful I am to foster a world commensurate to how much we've adored you. And how surprised I was to see you soon walked out of the prison entrance, toddling hand in hand not with your mom but alongside the tall stature of a man in black slacks and tucked in a collar shirt . . . *Tom?*

To Bianca   195

From the driver seat I stepped out, puzzled, letting him speak first as you darted for me, wrapping your arms around my knees.

"Santana mentioned you'd be outside."

"I shouldn't be so surprised to see you here," I admitted.

"Bianca wouldn't calm down, so Santana asked if I could take her to her *tia*," he explained as I picked you up.

In the familiarity of my grasp you wound around to regard Tom with wide-eyed study that not only contrasted the aversive self-consciousness that overcame me when near Tom but likewise absorbed without interpretation the depth of consequence between him and me: Tom was once my lawyer, too, when, and for some months since, all the affection I profess for you had as silently as a sunflower faced him.

"How's it going in there?" I asked.

"Bianca isn't the only one having an emotionally difficult morning. Half the reason I was glad to bring her outside was to give Santana the letdown she needs with Martez."

No sooner did your mom's tears flood to mind, streaking dark with eyeliner down her cheeks, then was I taking grateful stock of wearing my new cuff boots, dressiest pair of dark jeans, and a light layer of blush in following your mom's lead this morning to not skip makeup after braiding your hair and mine while she went all out with the eyeliner, lip gloss, and glitter.

"She's really breaking down in there?"

"I've walked her through his plea deal how many times now, making sure she's aware that he's willingly agreeing to incarceration, and it's taking his assurance to undercut her denial. For months she's held out hope that the judge might treat his plea deal with more lenient terms, but when it comes to pleading drug felonies the judge won't budge."

"I'm sorry," I said. For Martez pleading to jail time or Tom empathizing with his client? For your mom hurting or you caught unaware in the middle?

"What do you say to an early lunch?"

"Of course." *Of course, of course, of course,* my heart beat.

"There's a diner back by the interstate."

"But doesn't Bianca need to stay with Santana?"

"Yeah, but I OKed it with the guards. They know me well enough from all my visits to my former clients."

At the diner our waitress greeted Tom by name before taking our orders for a round of coffee and a donut for you.

"Many former clients," Tom playfully whispered to you.

"Speaking of former clients," I teased.

"It's refreshing to finally run into one of my clients outside of court or prison."

"Thanks." I wanted to convey so much more to Tom, but there was no way to ease into the bottomless well of how overwhelmed I was to find him seated across from me, his very presence retaining its initial suddenness as though reborn each moment. Imagine gazing down a long road that outpaces your anticipation of each mile, from coast to coast; this is what it's like to see Tom again, my lifted spirits skipping to the raw possibilities between us, numerous as miles, narrowing toward the horizon and fading beyond, despite all my wishing otherwise. I was more aware of Tom than of you leaning against me in our booth as the waitress refilled our coffee. Calm and warm in my lap, you wiped your hands clean of the sticky donut glaze.

"Santana tells me you're moving back to Arizona."

"Did she say if she's going with me?"

"It's an option if Martez goes to prison."

"It's more than an option. It's a practical next step for life without him, but at some point I have to let go," I said, drawing you back onto my lap, a contrasting physical sentiment Tom thoughtfully observed.

"What about your plans?" Tom asked. "With or without Santana and Bianca?"

"I'll crash at a friend's place in Phoenix until I find work."

"Does District Baptist know?"

"Should they?"

"They'll start calling if you disappear."

"Then I'm probably due for a call," I said.

"Once in a while they email me well wishes."

TO BIANCA   197

"How do you answer?"

"I don't."

"Neither will I."

"Make it easy on yourself and tell them you found a new church in a new city. It'll save you the guilt I went through when they excommunicated me."

"You weren't excommunicated because you left town."

"You're right, and I should never've involved myself with Tara. Before you set foot in their sanctuary and witnessed me getting voted out I was in good standing and encouraged to date one of their members. When our relationship didn't work out I blamed the same pastors who later had me excommunicated."

"Why are you telling me this?"

"Because looking back now I would've never involved myself with Tara if I hadn't been so pissed off with how my honest attempt at a Baptist girl broke under the weight of so much intrusive help. They had to know everything, and it wore our relationship down. Do you know the difference between having responsibility versus having authority? For all the responsibility I see you taking for Bianca you ultimately lack Santana's authority as her mother."

"Yes?"

"When I was dating Sharon at church we took responsibility for each other while everyone else was content to swoop in and presume authority over our relationship. Too many pastors and busybodies expected us, in the name of helping, to answer for all that went right or wrong between us."

"Sharon?" *From children's church?* I wanted to ask without diverting his larger point.

"It's the same frustration I used to have with my clients," Tom continued. "Where I felt responsible and took the blame when they ended up getting more prison time than expected. But my clients are up against the judge's authority, not my responsibility. For every responsibility you have try to get corresponding authority. That's the point I want to make."

"Tom, I'm not sure that authority isn't too much to expect in most every instance or counters the risk of responsibility. Won't a pastor argue they're responsible to God for their members? And can't a judge similarly argue that even though they're the authority over a particular case they're still responsible to the justice system? The only authority I really have is over my own life. Whatever I take on as a responsibility beyond my personal authority is done at my own risk. In the case of helping Santana care for Bianca the reward has outweighed the risk of answering to the oddity of it."

"Rather than involving myself with Tara, sometimes I regret not convincing Sharon to ditch church with me and take up things under our own authority."

"She would've refused. I've worked with her in the children's Sunday school and can tell you she's completely beholden to church. I went through a similar experience with a guy there named Paul. He wanted some kind of institutional permission for the time we spent together. For as brief as we lasted we were already answering to the same questions you probably faced."

"I like your plan to cut ties and leave for good. It's what I mean by taking authority over your situation. I just wish I had someone worth disappearing with."

"Same here," I said, patting your belly and presuming you weren't going with me; *same here*, presuming Tom's obliviousness to my timely candidacy, seated so plainly across from him.

If this didn't close the book on my months of hope for Tom, your mom called, breaking my contemplative gaze, lost as though down a long road over Tom's shoulder.

"Where're you guys at?" She said, her teary frustration audible.

"We'll head back." I flagged down our waitress.

Your mom was in the front passenger seat when we parked beside the Porsche SUV. Through the tinted passenger window her shadowy outline appeared, head in hands, breathing warmth into them, but upon opening the door she was actually sobbing, her makeup smeared.

"When do we go?"

"I can drive us back as soon as I get Cupcake buckled in." I opened the back door to your car seat.

"I mean when are you leaving Washington?"

"Next weekend." I hesitated with your buckle. "When my brother lands I want to be packed and ready to go."

"All right." She lowered her face back into her hands.

All right, what? I wanted to ask without spooking into retreat the fragile need in her voice.

"I'll see you two Friday, at the courthouse?" Tom spoke from behind the wheel of his adjacent ride.

"Yes, with Bianca," I said, focusing on your mom rather than the elaborate goodbye wishes I usually staged for remembering Tom until our next encounter. You could say I'd taken authority to leave the diner, sending Tom out to heat the car while I'd awaited our check for the coffee and donuts because in your mom's voice I was confident of her sudden need for me. She needed me, not in the way we'd spent the morning facing the embodied disappointment of men, but side by side, moving on together. And at the moment Tom drove away, I needed her too, her occupying presence keeping at much needed bay my usual post-Tom letdowns.

On the drive back your mom detailed her morning behind bars. How your dad confronted her tired questions on the likelihood of probation instead of jail, asking her how many times Tom had walked her through the plea deal. To her answer of "all week" your dad wasn't so nice in reminding her of being made aware of the plea deal weeks before. And yes, no argument, she was probably in denial, she agreed, and late in facing life without him, but couldn't he let her hope for a miracle? No, not if your dad had to hear another word ignoring the three-year sentence he'd spent the months since August resigning himself to, already in the cell where he'd spend it. Three years with which your dad told her to make grateful use of her own freedom. Cornered into admitting her lack of thinking ahead, she mentioned my options for Arizona, a move your dad immediately supported, the new life she needed, he reiterated, until by the end of their visitation she well enough understood the move as a fresh restart that would probably bring change for the better. How we could even take the SUV.

In only a matter of days you would begin with us the move that would take you to Arizona.

"Let's have a drink tonight," she said.

"Tara keeps flavored vodkas in the freezer."

"I noticed."

The Friday of your father's sentencing was my last day of work, the sites of both just blocks from each other. Two Easter candy baskets awaited as goodbye gifts on my desk, which addressed how to occupy you for the two hours I had you with me in the office before we reunited with your mom at the district court-house. You were with me for the morning to free up your mom as she readied herself to see your dad for the last time in who knows how long. Your mom was a spasm of anxiety so I took you on my commute, your little hands clutching my windbreaker and your eyes widened at the concrete sights I wouldn't miss. The under-ground metro, the ascending Chinatown-station escalators, the busy sidewalks until in the office you let go for a run at the Easter baskets. Nobody expected any work from me on my last day, even if I wanted to, especially once they came by my desk for a goodbye and spotted you seated at the feet of Tara and me with both bas-kets overturned and chocolate on your face.

"We're babysitting her." Tara narrated the unexpected sight to the girls gathering around our desk. You basked in the oohing and aahing adoration, indulging even Edith by refusing to admit who could be eating all those chocolates, before she reminded every-body that it was a workday.

"I'll have her back to her mom later this morning."

"Promise me you'll be back to let the office host your last lunch today?"

"Yes, of course." Martez's sentencing was due to finish by noon.

If you were to notice shadowing my expression the intimida-tion of entering the courthouse for the first time since last sum-mer, some other time I can explain the personal low point of my own court appearances last summer, which, alongside my mom's passing, set my path in motion to interlace with yours.

Inside the entrance of the courthouse your chief concern was keeping grasp of the Easter basket you refused to hand over to the security guards until I assured you they'd return it after sending

TO BIANCA 201

it through their metal detector. The Easter basket's arching handle was too tall for you to hold without dragging the basket across the tile as your mom, waiting on other side of the detector, led you by the hand down the long hallway.

Reliving the full anxiety of pleading guilty last summer was unavoidable upon entering what turned out to be the same courtroom where I was sentenced, where your dad and Tom now stood before the same all-knowing judge, Sheila Parks, whom I didn't bother guessing whether she recognized me as I took a seat beside you after putting you on your mom's lap. As last summer's regrets flooded the courtroom, it likewise was by her hand that as your dad and Tom stood alongside the prosecutor, the heavy seas of her embodiment of those memories parted way for the sentencing hearing to begin. Despite the stakes your dad faced, the judge didn't conceal her apparent boredom with the mechanics of the hearing, a boredom I realized wasn't so evident when I was the defendant under her focus.

"How do you plead to the offense of maintaining public nuisance by presiding over property used for illegal distribution of controlled substances?"

"I plead guilty, Your Honor."

"Let it be noted that the defendant has entered a plea of guilty. What was the District expected to prove if this case had gone to trial?"

"Your Honor." The prosecutor remained standing. As he named witnesses according to expected testimony detailing both their own court-entered pleadings of drug trafficking and your dad's acquaintance and direct knowledge of stated trafficking, I couldn't keep from glancing over to your mom and realizing how helpless I was to understand your parents' shared world. Your mom held you in her lap, her copper-tanned arms and shoulders the only hint of her past week in Las Vegas, gaining custody of you.

"Is the State seeking to dispose of any charges?"

"As part of the defendant's agreement the State will no longer pursue the initial charges of trafficking or conspiracy."

"Your Honor," Tom began, "should this case proceed to trial a jury will not likely find the defendant guilty of conspiracy, much less trafficking. The investigation yielded no evidence of my client profiting from or remaining privy to any trafficking as it occurred on his business property. The agreed upon public-nuisance charge comes down to my client's misfortune of owning property where trafficking happened to take place, not whether he knew the specifics of what was going on between customers."

"I'm aware of the charge, Mr. Getty." The judge cut Tom off before directing questions to your dad. "Is it fair to assume that the four witnesses who've already plead guilty to trafficking and are willing to testify for the State are your buddies?"

"Yes, Your Honor."

"Were you aware of their motives to use your premises for drug trafficking?"

"I didn't usually know details until after the fact, but yes, Your Honor, I was aware of their motives."

"You therefore had reason to believe that the use and selling of drugs was common occurrence at your property?"

"Yes, Your Honor."

"And you understand allowing this to continue on your premises amounts to the felony of maintaining a public nuisance?"

"Yes, Your Honor."

Your mom was quietly panicking by now, and to give her space to compose herself I traded her a box of tissues for holding you in my lap. I held you as though guarding you against the reality of the courtroom. With trusting calmness, you fixed your large eyes on the orange prison suit worn by your dad and the silver chains linking his handcuffs as he stood alongside Tom and nodded his understanding of the charges and the State's evidence to the judge, who in turn announced his prison sentence according to his plea deal: three-and-a-half years with the six months of pretrial confinement credited as time served.

Your dad will be released from prison by the time you're six years old. You're small enough to avoid memories of most of his time behind bars, but it won't matter if there's no reuniting with

TO BIANCA   203

your mom once your dad is free, which, to quickly consider, is a possibility I have mixed feelings over. You deserve a loving father just as I like to believe your mom and I did, only to regret most of our growing up without, but I'm not sure reuniting is best for your mom or won't relegate her focus away from you, as I worry has been the case. It's time to move on from your dad, at least while during his prison term, as I've spent the past few months urging your mom, and likewise practicing what I've preached by moving on from Tom, but this only works when Tom is out of sight and consequently diminished from mind. To see Tom again, and for your mom in the same moment to see your dad turn from the judge to look his final goodbye our way before armed guards escorted him out, was to evoke our vulnerability of needing a man to love us. And who's to blame when we end up disappointed? Us for risking our hopes? Or their respective (ir)responsibility?

All over now, your mom kept her head lowered, and I cradled you nearer as we found our way outside. Tom surprised us on the steps of the courthouse, bringing sudden voice to the aftermath of silence overcoming us.

"You guys care for a drink?" he asked.

"Actually, my office is hosting my farewell party at Penn Social, and they're waiting for me."

"I need a drink," your mom said.

We followed Tom for the few blocks and turns past what became a winding personal history of bars where from the beginning of my DC working life I'd taken earlier refuge in their many happy hours. At Penn Social Tom held open the front door, ushering us inside. Three steps in the bar came alive with thunderous cheers from grinning friends—Edith, Tara, and the rest of the office, two dozen strong and on their feet, giddy on afternoon cocktails and applauding as one. Even Dustin was here, surprising me with an earlier flight. You were just as overwhelmed, dropping your Easter basket and crying in my grasp until your mom returned its handle to your determined hold. And the office crowd held their own surprise—who might be this toddler I was holding?—as they sized up our unfamiliar gang. But Tara had the most abrupt reaction, halting her applause because this was the first time since their breakup that she was face-to-face with Tom. Beyond her surprise, I didn't bother discerning if she was angry or pained or whatever because I was too busy thanking everybody for the "three wonderful years" of working with them and answering nearly every question with "to Arizona" and "for paralegal work" until my smile ached and the afternoon took on a gratifying endlessness. Edith especially made a point to thank me and express her best wishes. When she left after two glasses of wine, those avoiding her lead back to the office stayed to drink into the early evening. This included Tara and Tom, who, when I finally left with you, your mom, and Dustin, were seated essentially in the same moment where they'd first met, drinking together, their heads lowered in secluded conversation, the last we might see of them.

I looked up the specific public-nuisance indictment under which your father plead guilty. The law reads: A) *Any place of business, dwelling, building, or other structure which is resorted to for the purpose of possessing, transporting, or distributing controlled substance shall be deemed a public nuisance. B) The prosecuting attorney may, in addition to any criminal prosecutions, prosecute a suit issuing an injunction against the public nuisance. If the court finds that the owner of the building or structure knew or had reason to believe that the premises were used for the illegal use, keeping, or selling of controlled substances, the court may order that the premises shall not be occupied or used for such period as the court may determine, not to exceed one year. C) All persons, including owners, renters, or employees, aiding or facilitating such a nuisance may be made defendants in any suit to enjoin the nuisance.*

There you have it, the hundred and thirty-two words imprisoning your father, weighing heavily on the circumstances of your mother's persistent outlook and passing incomprehensibly over your head. I looked up the law during one of the few free moments I had over the busy weekend of readying for our trip. I'm sorry I can't make sense of all this to you as it happens.

I didn't bother following up with Tara about leaving her at the bar with Tom, nor did she mention much of it when she returned,

To Bianca   205

which was the point: she instead spent the weekend with us. Anyway, all hands were focused on preparing for our move. On Saturday morning, while Dustin and your mom went to the auto shop for an oil change and an annual inspection of the SUV, Tara and I spent the morning dividing my belongings into what couldn't be packed into the SUV and would be left with her or thrown away. Starting with my pile of textbooks, I saved only the editions of statistical analysis and practical legal writing. It was a safe bet Tara would throw the rest away, especially when seeing how much more excited she was to move on to my clothes. She was thrilled to be left with my winter garments.

"You don't have to be so nice." She held up my scarf.

"My scarves and mitts and thermal shirts won't be necessary in Phoenix."

"But I mean yesterday Tom and I talked about you. How good you are to Santana and Bianca. And how lucky I was to have you as a roommate. I felt bad about some of our fights. And now you're giving me your winter best."

"Thank you." I faced her anew, the air between us for once testing free of competition and posturing.

"I'm going to miss you, Nicole."

A headrush of gratitude was tempered by a sentiment of pity over our inability to earlier reach mutual terms of goodwill. As much as I can look back on how my years here haven't gone well in the ways I'd most hoped, to leave discards the unexpected work-related ways that give doubt to whether Washington is worth leaving.

"I'll miss you too," was all I could say.

By the time we sorted through the kitchenware, packing only silverware and a pot in favor of my coffee maker, Crock-Pot, and cutting boards, I wasn't sure how much room was left in the SUV for Dustin's duffle bag and my suitcases along with all the luggage your mom expected to bring on your behalf.

The good news, when your mom returned, was Dustin discovered a car-top carrier deserted beside a dumpster on their walk back from the metro, which he was hosing off in the back alley.

The bad news was why they had to return by metro. Upon inspection the SUV needed new radiator hoses, which would keep the vehicle garaged until Tuesday, delaying our departure.

That evening we all gathered around the coffee table to chart our path. Tara uncorked a bottle of red blend and dialed up one of her playlists while Dustin opened his atlas to West Virginia. Did we want to stay at Aunt Cindy's in Rainelle again? But at the moment Aunt Cindy was vacationing in Florida, and for as much as I wanted to stay overnight in Rainelle to show your mom the Kanawha River's rushing swell of snowmelt and spring rainfall, taking time along the backwaters of my family roots was too close for comfort.

Dustin pointed further downriver to the Kanawha's merging with the Ohio at the town of Point Pleasant, where one of our uncles lived. Plus, your mom advocated, staying with him put us closer to Chicago where on her prompting we all agreed to spend the next night.

"A fellow waitress in Vegas is a flight attendant now, and she always says there's nothing like the Strip, the Grand Canyon, or the skylines of New York and Chicago."

After Chicago Dustin wanted the adventure of leaving our overnight stopovers to chance. He turned to the first few pages of his atlas to space out the expected stopovers across the blue web of the nation's interstate system.

"Iowa and Nebraska will have a corn town every ten or so miles where we can crash for the night before spending the next few days dipping into western Kansas and eventually New Mexico. Then we'll be within a day's drive from Phoenix."

Tuesday was our last evening living on East Capitol Street. There are heroes here in Washington, but mostly in their own mind, and there are the longsuffering, by mostly their own doing, and on the eve of leaving, nothing promised a more fitting ride into the sunset than that of putting Washington behind us.

By then we'd together downed another bottle of Tara's wine and had the okay from Uncle Barry to spend the first night of our trip in Point Pleasant, which I couldn't believe was one night away. Of course, we also had the SUV returned roadworthy, and Dustin had the carrier strapped to its roof and filled with our luggage. For Squibbles I'd bought a brush and some cat treats in exchange for Tara's promise to give him hands-on attention whenever he peered through the windows of our back door, looking for you. With you upstairs with your mom, Squibbles purred next to me on that last night I spent on the couch.

It was dark when Dustin awoke us on the first day of our road trip. He sent me upstairs to wake you and your mom while he warmed up our vehicle. In the moments it took us girls to get dressed into our jeans and zip up the last of our luggage Tara stationed herself on the front doorstep to wave us off. In her pajamas she nestled Squibbles in her grasp, his shining black eyes widened by our flurry of predawn activity.

"Say goodbye," Tara urged on behalf of Squibbles.

Massaging our hands through his thick fur, it was then in the quiet immensity of your shared gaze between his nocturnally large eyes that in your limited understanding you surely sensed the parting change. Or at least I like to believe that you were able to appreciate Squibbles one last time, as wisps of fur collected between our fingers, hastening his shedding coat.

Your goodbye to Tara amounted to running your fingers through her long blonde hair, shining by streetlight, while we hugged and she kissed you. You were back asleep once buckled in your car seat. I exchanged with Tara a last wave through the open car windows as we coasted away in the dewy predawn quiet of the dozing residential streets. The Capitol Dome glowed through the blooming treetops, their nectary rustle of breath giving way to the stale exhausts of yesterday's traffic at the interstate, where remaining in view the enameled pallor of the Capitol shone like a low moon over the dark river into Virginia and along the George Washington Parkway until Dustin took the Arlington exit. Rocketing west on I-66, Dustin didn't let off the gas until our accelerated escape velocity broke through the tightening fist of Washington's early-forming gridlock. Beyond the suburbs you and your mom remained peacefully asleep to the lull of the open interstate, while I melted into the weary amazement of Washington exactly as it was at our backs: the night dissolving to gray dawn. Eventually Dustin exited onto the slower Shenandoah highways where the birds began chirping and across the fields the first touches of sunlight gleamed silver in the dew. Deer peered above the cornstalks. Morning joggers and dog walkers were out along the golf courses near the Blue Ridge mountain towns of Front Royal and Strasburg when the coming day fully materialized as clear skies and free highways of crooked miles over the Appalachians. Following Highway 48 into the wilderness, dark mountains huddling along the West Virginia border loomed as the defiant limit of westward visibility.

For as much as escaping into my mom's home state of West Virginia revives aching memory of her, the highways calm me in open-armed assurance across the rocking landscape that, as go my prayers and questions of her passing, abandon all direction.

I've talked with your mom about the loss of our mothers, and to speak of the emptier world they left us to, where does it all eventually go? I ask this most strongly over the loss of my mom and for the sake of prayer as well.

In the time since she left us, I'm often at a loss when it comes to praying. So persistent was my prayer for her healing that what did my prayers amount to if death went ahead and laid her to rest? If she's in a better place, and is she lifted up?

The narrowing highway raised into the mountains. The last of Washington's fading radio stations were replaced by the faint signals of even farther away AM broadcasts from Cleveland (1100), New York (880), Toronto (740), and Chicago (720) before emptying entirely from reception past the state border. The scanning dial returned dead silence. West Virginia was quiet until gospel hymns were picked up on approaching the little town of Moorefield where Dustin stopped to refuel.

Bible scriptures were engraved on most every headstone in the town's cemetery. Chisel me this: *Continue in prayer, and watch in the same with Thanksgiving.*

If our prayers are most effective as a matter of diversification, lending thankfulness for what pans out, I prayed all in and went broke on the same repeated plea for her health, the only stock invested now sunk under. With nothing else prayed for, nothing else answered.

The churches in Moorefield represent most every expected denomination.

Church changed for me in the wake of my mom's death. I made a point to return and keep steady attendance, but I couldn't hold at bay my doubt over whether Sunday mornings weren't any better spent in bed. Why attend? To foster the expectation of a world where my mom and the inevitable rest can reunite?

But please see that our doubt plays no bearing on the reality of our condition, which is the point—that what we believe can't merely be used as our assurance for shoring up the better of a few eternal options. It's simplistic reasoning to expect this to be the case, but it happens against our better judgment because whenever a starting point for faith must be found, heaven and hell and nonexistence are always ready motivations of fortitude in coming to terms with our life for the next. All the more when sunken by the privations of this one.

It was so quiet in the back seat that in Moorefield I expected to find you and your mom still asleep. Instead, to see you silently absorbed in the newness of scenery beyond your window returned my spirits to the dramatic backcountry. After Moorefield the roadways weaved through miles of shaded woodlands. Sudden switchbacks climbed the ridges of one river valley to the next. Sunlight poured with weightless calm through the tree tops in green and yellow rays as though illuminated through the stained-glass windows of nature's cathedral. Though serene, this stretch of Highway 48 was a less-forgiving speed dare of its own numbering than was Highway 60 paralleling the Kanawha's flooding last fall. There was no exceeding speeds of fifty until the land relaxed into smoothly farmed hillsides. The skies opened to wavy banners of sunlight draping through breaks in the few drifting clouds whose shadows floated without homeport on the seas of wild grass. Joining Highway 33 through a succession of towns with names like Elkins, Buckhannon, and Weston, my tanning arm rested pleasantly warm in the open passenger-side window. On through Glenville and Ripley to the banks of the Ohio River the drive was the sunny innocence of heavenly light forging the landscape as far as the hilltops could see. To this vastness of earth, we could only exhale.

When we reached the Ohio River upstream of Point Pleasant, Dustin had me call Uncle Barry.

"You're a few towns away. Watch for the two bridges over the confluence," he told us.

Pressed against the Ohio by unexpected stretches of cliffs, the small towns on both sides faced the rising river's spring surge with more than a few sagging porches, boarded windows, and blocks of crumbling riverfront sidewalks. Miller Lite posters crookedly hung by their last nail to smoke shacks and barbeque dives, places where frequenting for daily six-packs, cigarettes, and to-go lunches was to live an unhurried existence along the Ohio. Even with the vague acquaintance of these many stagnating river towns cradling our mom's roots, West Virginia's rivers felt to Dustin and me like exposed arteries, as though our visits were incisions deep into the nation's flesh. I could only imagine how much more rustic the sights were for your mom. But slowing for the school zones in Point Pleasant you found familiarity, pointing to the burger- and pizza-chain signs recognized from your shopping with your mom around the Beltway.

Down the town's busiest road, the bridges spanning both the Ohio and Kanawha arose as backdrop above the nearer rows of Main Street buildings when Dustin turned down the residential street where Uncle Barry stood waving in his driveway. Directing Dustin to park alongside his hay trailer, he apologized for appearing unready to host us once we stepped out to shake his hand.

"Was across the river all morning, delivering a load of bales," he greeted, looking very much to your unselfconscious fascination the farmer's part of working the day outdoors.   Gathered in my hold you studied his trucker hat, white beard, and grassy coveralls.

Your mom's matching interest followed with questions.

"Bales of hay?" She smiled.

To Bianca   211

"For our buyers in Ohio. Cattle breeders."

"Have you always worked as a farmer?"

"More so now that I'm retired. I was navy before becoming a trucker after the Vietnam War. I settled here and worked for the county until a few years ago."

"And you harvest hay?"

"Some hay but mostly corn a few miles upstream of the Kanawha on land from my wife's side. She grew up here. Whenever we're ready she's fixed us a late lunch or early dinner, however you want to call it. How about you?" His eyes lit up at you. "Is your little tummy ready for a big dinner?"

"Thanta." You removed your thumb to answer. "Santa *granjero.*"

"My baby is calling you Santa Farmer." Your mom shared a laugh with Uncle Barry.

Inside Aunt Rachel had the kitchen table laid out with green beans, potato salad, biscuits, and fried chicken. Her meal, once we were seated for our first helping, was more ready for us than her understanding of why we were stopping over.

"Tomorrow we head to Chicago," Dustin explained.

"And you didn't stick to the interstates?"

"We wanted to take the scenic route," Dustin said. "And visit you, of course."

"Ask your uncle where all the shortcuts and best stops for gas or lunch are," Aunt Rachel said. "He spent two decades trucking every which way between here and Chicago."

"It's been too long since my trucking days."

"We'll find our way into Chicago tomorrow," I added.

"Stay here too long and there's no going back to wherever you're passing to and from," Aunt Rachel warned. "Didn't you learn that the hard way, Barry?"

"I tell everybody I just followed the Kanawha and ended up in Point Pleasant," he joked. "Growing up with your mom in Rainelle we weren't but a hop and a skip from where the Kanawha begins as a tributary from the New River, and now I'm settled where the Kanawha finishes at the Ohio."

"Aging in the direction of the river," Dustin said.

"Small towns are the confessions of old age," Aunt Rachel said. "Unlike in the cities, small towns reflect your growing older. Your neighbors and coworkers and the people you attend church with or run into at the farmer's market or whose fields you drive by all started school with you and remember sharing your younger years."

"So you've always lived in West Virginia?" your mom asked.

"Never left."

"I can't imagine staying in one place." Your mom said what I thought too.

"I seen my outside share. Tagged along on many of Barry's truck routes back when we first married, even making it as far west as visiting your mom in Arizona," she said, turning to Dustin and me, "before either of you were born. I assumed she'd return one day like most West Virginians. Appalachian folk tend to start looking for their first chance back when they leave, but she's the only one I knew who never did."

After dinner I helped Aunt Rachel wash dishes while your mom settled you into their guest room.

"My mom loved to glory in the memories of her upbringing. Many times she told Dustin and me about the pumpkin harvests, school dances, and rafting trips. Whenever we asked her why she left she'd say she had to go at first chance."

"She left in the tiny window small towns allow right after high school. Usually by college or the military. If you don't take the jump or marry your way out you're probably never leaving."

From the wall bounding one end of the kitchen counter hung an aerial photo of a grain silo overlooking the river. Across its banks rolled the hills into distant mountains. The sky quoted Abraham Lincoln: *All the armies of Europe and Asia could not by force take a drink from the Ohio River or make a track on the Blue Ridge in the trial of a thousand years.*

"Did you ever wish to leave West Virginia?"

"Sure. Wanting out of your hometown is part of being young. I remember when I was a little girl playing outside in the summer evenings with my sisters and friends our daddy would walk us home just as it started to darken and the lights of the traffic over the bridges could be seen flickering between its beams. I asked him where everybody was driving so late, and he said the trucks were heading to Cincinnati, Indianapolis, and Chicago; bigger cities that made going West sound like an adventure. I was only five, and that's the first of many times I let the late traffic lead my imagination beyond the river."

"Now you know better." I spoke also for myself, hoping for similar hometown solace on my return to Arizona. "We've both seen enough of where the traffic goes. No need to watch the bridge."

"Growing up will do that, but as for the bridge," she hesitated, "it collapsed a few years later, in 1967."

"Oh." I didn't know what to say until spotting a large bag of cat food on my search through the cabinets for where to put oven trays away.

"We have two tabbies squatting under our front porch. Leave 'em some leftover chicken too."

I brought you outside, by now dressed in fresh pajamas. On the porch Dustin and Uncle Barry reclined in the soft twilight, an hour doubling as the cat's end of day-bird stalking. Both cats were patrolling the property line of bushes when they marched over at the metallic echo of their dish filling.

I was proud to see how carefully you approached the orange tabbies, in the light-footed way I'd showed you with Squibbles, and offered your hand for their noses before petting. But they wanted no part of our attention, retreating from their bowl with greasy wedges of chicken in their jaws.

"They ain't much friendly to humans," Uncle Barry said.

After several more round trips to their bowl the tabbies settled side by side in the grass, flicking their tails in lazy watch of the wrens and sparrows trafficking bird feeders in the trees.

Us grown-ups were on the porch, relaxing in the satisfaction of our first day on the road or of hosting said travelers, all watching you in wild scamper beneath the roll call of fireflies filling the falling darkness.

"Fireflies," I called.

"Lightning bugs," Uncle Barry said, turning to us. "Ever notice they're referred by our lightning storms, but go west and their name takes after fire, as in the forest fires?"

"I would've never correlated that," Dustin realized, "although Arizona sure see its share of lightning. Which sparks many of our wildfires."

I took the car keys in the gray morning, sipping coffee to the warming of the engine. When everybody was loaded half-awake in the vehicle we exchanged goodbyes with Uncle Barry and Aunt Rachel, waving from the porch as we eased from their driveway. Coasting the empty streets of Point Pleasant's few downtown blocks we passed by the chrome Mothman statue on our way to crossing the bridge. The river refused sight of its charcoal surface, delaying its waking until midmorning sunlight later melted its ghostly cloak of fog. From Point Pleasant we officially crossed the Ohio River and launched into the flat, more-space-than-place sameness of the Midwest. With the last of Appalachia's upheavals behind us, that was it for West Virginia—our drive through my mom's native Appalachia not even lasting a full twenty-four hours.

Ohio was four lanes of easy highway across the state's lower half. Due for Dayton by midmorning, the great leveling out of the midlands began, easing to a gradual roll of fenced pasturelands.

"Moo-moos," your mom said, pointing your attention to the herds of cattle socializing around the passing bales of hay.

"Imagine those bales sold from Uncle Barry's fields," I remarked.

"I liked your uncle and aunt," your mom said with a smile. "Kindly farmer folk."

Beyond the cattle and a few windmills and unpainted barns, there wasn't much else to interest you as the wider highway bypassed the small towns from view. Dustin, fixing his sight on the horizon's outpacing of the traffic, compared Ohio to the bottom of a dried-out ocean floor.

"And it was probably a prehistoric ocean," he continued, "and would still be if the Appalachia's weren't blocking the Atlantic."

"This empty ocean is about to fill," I warned ahead to the thunderheads shrouding the horizon and soon drenching the fields, the fatter raindrops smacking the windshield one at a time. Nearing Dayton the thunderstorm lightened to a drizzle.

Welcoming us into Dayton were garages for wheel realignments, brake-pad replacements, tire specials, and nothing else to keep us here as long as our vehicle held up.

"Cincinnati?" your mom asked from her back-seat nap.

"Dayton," Dustin corrected, "but what's the difference? Cincinnati, Cleveland, Columbus, Canton, pick your poison."

"The Rock and Roll Hall of Fame is in Cleveland," your mom remembered.

"Yes," Dustin answered, "and the Pro Football Hall of Fame is in Canton."

"How did Ohio get both?"

"So inductees could be remembered in a place where they'd never bother to step foot again."

Stopping at a corner gas station, Dustin refueled while your mom and I walked you inside for a potty break. When we returned, Dustin was seated behind the wheel, ready to take over the driving into Indiana.

"Chili," you smelled as I buckled you.

"You're not missing anything, Bianca," Dustin promised, testing a spoonful of chili from the convenience mart. Before starting the engine, he tossed its nearly full Styrofoam container into the trash bin beside the fuel pump. "That's what I'll have to remember Dayton by, yuck. How can you call it chili without peppers or garlic? It's just pure grease."

"We'll save lunch for Indianapolis."

"Meanwhile, Ohio: the only reason for stopping is to hit the restrooms," he said.

"Why is Ohio's license-plate slogan 'Birthplace of Aviation?'" Your mom looked the traffic over.

"The Wright Brothers were born in Ohio, and they invented airplanes to get out of it," Dustin joked.

From Dayton Dustin kept to the same highway that had brought us across Ohio, until turning off onto a farm-to-market road before the wider highway angled northwest to join I-70 toward Indiana. The crossing of the state border on the sparsely trafficked county roads was noticeable only by the renumbering of the roadway signs, which in turn slimmed from the shape of Ohio to Indiana; the lack of any welcoming billboard likened the informality of entering Indiana through a side door. As the sun leapt through the thinning overcast, the afterness of the fallen rain lifted as mild humidity from the soaked-dark cornfields. Acreages of cornfields spread across the land as flat and square as tiles, segmented by access roads progressing from county to county as a grid for tractors tending the planting and harvest seasons. Each passing county was centered by their single town large enough for a high school. Through Liberty, Connersville, Rushville, and Shelbyville, the embarking corn belt patterned provincial order, each farmland-centered town likewise centered by their county courthouses, their grandest building and point at which the highways from surrounding counties converged.

Just past Rushville a sizable grasshopper buzzed into our passenger window, crash landed onto your shoulder, and frightened you to tears. You fought the grasshopper off by a panicked flailing before your mom tried to flick it out the window. You wouldn't calm down, so to prove it was gone Dustin pulled the vehicle alongside another endless cornfield and searched the back. Perched on a suitcase, I grasped the grasshopper by its hindwings and brought it around to your window. "Grasshopper," I said as you quieted in amazement of its toy-like detail of compound eyes, jittery antenna, leafy green torso, and thrashing legs, until dancing away from my release into the fields, which were only in their first foot of growth, low enough to spot a scarecrow fallen from its post a dozen rows of cornstalks deep.

"Scarecrow." I pointed, prompting Dustin to drag its straw-stuffed bulk over from its facedown spot. Straw filling trailed from the scarecrow's stuffed flannel and torn jeans, but his face intact, you gave such an adorably serious study of his stitched grin and huge button eyes sewn onto his burlap skin that I, too, was filled by the suddenly wonderful world.

To Bianca 217

If you're a little too young for episodic memory, then I like to think of our scarecrow as lasting until then as part of your developing vocabulary, a bridge I cross with you, reliving and filling in for you the moments when the world stilled for your first scarecrow or grasshopper or firefly. May your own travels appreciate your first road trip with me. And may you someday know the affection I've had for you when your own two-year-old naps on your lap. Moments all the more wonderful by their unforeseen nature. In the cornfields of Indiana, who would've guessed?

From Shelbyville we caught I-74 to the 465 loop around Indianapolis and exited to I-65 north for Chicago. Miles of more farmland glided flatly by, while you napped to interstate speeds of eighty and ninety mph, missing nothing of the land as empty at ground level as seen from the sky on my cross-country flights.

Leaving Indiana, Chicago's immense skyline slowly solidified into lakefront-crowning view. We beheld the monument of its glinting throne above the anxious traffic of our approach. The density of its towers yielded our entry onto its shaded streets as though into the clouds breached by the height of its towers, which until today was from the only direction I'd cheated a glimpse of downtown, on descent into the airports.

"Good idea routing us through Chicago," Dustin said to your mom.

"I always wanted a trip here," she admired the skyline.

My thoughts nagged ahead to where we might sleep tonight. Without a bed or couch or floor in mind, and with Dustin promising us a happy hour with undergraduate friends, and your mom responding in the back seat by applying makeup, I defaulted to mothering you through however this Thursday night unfolded.

Dustin's college friend waited for us inside an Irish sports pub with another buddy, both wearing unbuttoned Cubs jerseys and lighting up at the sight of your mom and me putting you in a booster seat at our high table crowded with glasses of beer. Both were a few days unshaven, a look holding well under the pub's amber-lighted mahogany interior, proud to show us their tattoos when your mom asked for a translation of the Chinese characters on one of their wrists, and with names like Shane and Blair, they were exactly what I expected of Dustin's college friends. Shane turned to me, showing off the University of Arizona logo on his shoulder, and like a little wingman, you stole my burden to validate the shared familiarity, recognizing with audible admiration the block A's red-and-blue colors.

I laughed. "She recognizes the Arizona logo from my hoodies and keychains."

Shane explained he was from Naperville ("Naperthrill!" cheered Dustin and Blair) and was working downtown since graduating with Dustin in Tucson, a story true to the volume of Chicagoland kids recruited to the University of Arizona.

Shane pressed for what I'd studied and whether we'd had any of the same professors, but from a campus of over thirty thousand students it wasn't likely. The excited questions Shane and Blair had for your mom and me weren't much more sophisticated from how boys sought us in college. Instead of asking us to their Friday-night dorm party they wanted to proudly show us Chicago.

"Do you want to go with us to the Cubs game?"

Your mom and Dustin eagerly agreed. But there were no tickets to go around without both Blair and Shane giving up theirs, which I didn't realize was the point until Blair made a show of offering Dustin his ticket so he could remain with your mom and me, promising us a bar crawl once Dustin and Shane hurried out to catch the L train north.

Live music occupied your attention while Blair and your mom talked over another round, leaving me to finish a cider on his tab. We left for another bar as the outfield of the Cubs first inning glowed emerald across the bank of flat screens above the bar.

The rains picked up as Blair led us into the darkening evening, holding above us a black umbrella wide enough to include only your mom beside him. Glancing back at me, she pulled down the hood of her parka across her shoulders and gave me a nod, smiling, and checking by shared glance that this guy was okay. Our skirts from knee to hem were rain dampened to a ghostly translucence that faintly held the streetlight and outlined through the near weightless fabric our stride swiftly picking across the black sidewalk puddles that mirrored, window by glowing window skyward, the soaring towers.

The next bar refused us entry on account of your age. Blair's fallback plan sounded like his original intent. He promised us a thirtieth-floor view of the city if we allowed him to mix us drinks in the condo that him and Shane shared.

"Thirty floors up," your mom gushed.

"Well, we're already parked there." I wanted out of the rain. "The view must be fantastic."

Inside the lobby Blair vouched us past the welcome desk and in the elevator punched the button for his floor. The button's activating glow excited you into leaning from my arms to light more buttons, incrementing a stop-and-go rise for a dozen floors before our stop.

Inside his apartment Blair flipped on the Cubs game. Across the living room a full-length window faced the skyline. The view certainly was fantastic.

"So this is living it *up*," your mom said.

Chicago's impressive skyline gleamed in the rain-streaked window, thrilling our conversation and shimmering as a mirage of lights lifting into the brooding drift of clouds. For once, as Blair brought us drinks, I stood on the privileged side of the glass. These figures, us, in the glowing window that in past secluded moments of looking up from the streets I'd caught sight of mingling in the windows—here in the sky was me. We talked and sipped our drinks, which you understood as orange juice because your smaller pour wasn't infused with vodka. On the TV the infield was covered by a tarp, the Cubs game rained out. When the time came to retrieve another round of drinks Blair asked your mom if she'd join him on a booze run.

"And pick us up some dinner," I added as Blair handed your mom a raincoat.

"There's pizza in the fridge." Blair closed the door behind him.

I texted Dustin, asking if he was returning with Shane. Without response from Dustin or your mom's return with Blair, for the first time our togetherness didn't shield me from feeling alone and dismissed. I rummaged the kitchen, finding more options in the way of liquor and a stash of weed in the knife drawer, while you scampered between the open bedrooms. The cleaner of the two was Shane's, recognizable by the college flag hanging over his bed—Arizona as opposed to Blair's Michigan State. Other than leaving my luggage in our car, I had no reason to pass on a quick shower before redressing from my clammy clothes and giving you a bath.

Of their two beds one was neatly made, which settled the decision to sleep atop his pulled-tight covers. You fell asleep first, and until I followed, my gaze remained level with the skyline, too far from the bed to angle an overlook of the soaked streets and its reminder of your mom and Blair ditching me, a letdown weighing heavier on my sternum than you nestled in my hold. Sometimes what should remain inconsequential is what drags the last of your well-being under.

The disappointment ended as suddenly as your mom's return with Blair awoke us not much later with their commotion. Before I could muster a proper interruption, you called out, your little voice becoming very big: "Mama!" Which led her into our room. She collapsed onto our bed, her heavy breathing humid with beer as she fell asleep.

The next morning a 4AM text from a 630 area code awaited my response: *hey its shane. dustin is with me in napervil. take 88 on your way out of chicago and its right on the way.*

I texted for an exact address and waited out an hour of lying awake in the dull morning light. Evidently you and I were the only souls awake after skipping Chicago's long night of drinking. Your wide eyes reminded me of Squibbles's fully black nighttime eyes when I rolled over to find you yawning very sweetly between your mom and me, peacefully waiting our start to the day.

The digital alarm glowed 7:30 when I finally stepped out of bed and flipped on cartoons to occupy you while I tried to wake your mom.

"You can sleep it off in the back seat," I whispered.

By 8AM Blair was brewing coffee in the kitchen and "late for work," he groaned as an excuse for rushing off.

"He's gone," I stirred your mom again. She sat up.

Soon collecting ourselves into the vehicle, the parking garage was chilly from the cold front ushered in by last night's rainstorm. Driving the surface streets fresh air vented into the lowered windows as we followed Wacker Drive rounding south at the split of the canal, I opened the sunroof and drew your attention to how high the towers reached.

"What about Dustin?" your mom asked as I caught the nearest interstate onramp just south of the Willis Tower.

"We're picking him up in Naperville."

Your mom slept off the nearly hour of traffic, toll stops, and interstate exchanges. Along the way, as the skyline diminished behind us, the urban density of apartment towers and DC-like row housing gave way for the greener space of Chicago's vast suburbs. Hungry, and with still no word from Dustin, we waited in the red booth of a diner, ordering before the breakfast menus switched to lunch.

"I haven't eaten since lunch in Indianapolis yesterday," I said when our pancakes arrived.

"Did you see Blair this morning? I had him put the rest of our dinner into a to-go box for you last night, but he must've forgot it at the next bar."

"I saw Blair on his way out to work, but he didn't mention any leftovers. He looked like he wanted us gone."

"I'm sorry."

"For leaving the to-go box?"

"No, for leaving you with Bianca. Again." She sighed. "Blair assumed she was yours."

"Mine? He said that? He couldn't tell Bianca was your child? The brown eyes, the dark hair?" I fanned my fingers through my sandy hair.

"He noticed the way she's attached to you, kinda like how she's staying on your side of the booth; he probably figured you had her with a Latino guy."

"Did you tell him you were her mother?"

"I let him know when I wanted things to wind down. I let myself get excited by Chicago and a guy buying me drinks."

"Yeah, well." I wanted to lecture her. "Responsibilities, right?"

"I know."

You're twenty-five, I wanted to remind her; you're a mother, and Bianca needs to count on a stable mommy every night. I wanted to warn her against last night's sideshow becoming a regular occurrence once we're settled in Phoenix, but before I could face whether to follow through or let the moment die, Dustin called.

"Hey, where are you?"

"Naperville," he answered.

"Us too."

I gave him the name of the diner, and by the time we paid Shane had dropped Dustin off. Unshaven and unshowered, Dustin's hangover perspired through his wrinkled shirt, unchanged since West Virginia. I rolled the vehicle windows down once he took the passenger-side front seat.

"After the Cubs game rained out Shane got us a ride to Naperville," Dustin explained in the slow tone of an apology. "He wanted to show me around his hometown."

"I guess I'm doing the driving today?" I said.

"Thanks. You can probably tell I was out late."

So I drove the day's leg into Iowa. The delays of our morning roundup meant we weren't fully free of Chicago's sprawl until past noon. We could afford the lapse because Dustin's plan after Chicago was only to reach Des Moines—three hundred cruise-controlled miles of more farmland. The first half of the drive's flat approach of the Mississippi remained especially mindless without either Dustin or your mom awake. I had only you to talk to while they slept off their late night, and once we exhausted your vocabulary of birdies and animals and your reciting of our bedtime storybooks, the quiet miles distilled to flat highway, prairie winds, and the bleached glare of infinite sky. The heartlands mirrored my blank pages of thought, symbolic in both their open clearness and calm harbor between Washington's potential regrets and my worries over our Arizona

To Bianca

future. I hadn't once thought of Tom in the now three days away from Washington or overthought the uncertain details of starting over in Phoenix. But as our progress across America portended the real West as we neared the Mississippi River, the rugged peaks of the Rockies poised any day now to pierce the horizon as far as the greater plains could see, my worries similarly closed in. Your mom's indulgence of Chicago spooked my hopes of her willing responsibility toward the three of us living together.

It's a fair concern given how her most-profitable employment starts with bartending where I'm sure she'll face the invite to chase the night given how pretty she is. Maybe she and Dustin are a better fit as roommates, a reluctant thought just as quickly dismissed as I woke them both to see the Mississippi, the first time any of us had crossed the river by bridge.

The corn in Iowa was taller than we'd seen yesterday in Indiana. Dustin praised Iowa's soil as the world's best for growing corn, "fertile for a half-foot deep and never needs the intensive irrigation you see everywhere else." Hours more of cornfields happened by with barely the remotest interruption of small towns along the interstate. Past Iowa City the exits for Williamsburg, Brooklyn, Grinnell, and Newton yielded only gas stations marking the narrower county-road turnoffs for the few miles each town lay offset from the interstate, visible from passing view only by their grain silos.

In Des Moines it was dinnertime, or rather, by the chorus of small engines down every residential street, this was the great lawn-mowing hour to commence the weekend. After finding a hotel we ordered pizza and began our turns showering while you watched cartoons from one of the beds.

Saturday in Des Moines dawned with the dewy fragrance of fresh grass clippings. You awoke first, giving me a buddy for an early coffee run to the indie café sharing the plaza of our hotel. I loaded you into your stroller. Mucho Mocha was decidedly enlightened despite its silly name, promising fair-traded brews and listing the sources of its coffee beans in differing colors of chalk on the blackboard menu above the counter. The owner was more than pleased to introduce himself as such when I praised the customer copies of the *Chicago Tribune, Washington Post,* and *New York Times* he was scattering about. He recommended his Italian-roast special, and seeing your stroller, a detour down the adjacent residential street to check out his mom's yard sale. His girlfriend, he said, was already cruising with their toddler, combing the cluttered lawns and texting him when she paid for porch furniture needing pickup later. Asking where we were from, I told him about our move to Arizona.

"Well, welcome to Iowa. Saturdays are good days to see us at our most communal."

"Yard sales must be why everyone was mowing their lawn last night."

"I could promote our yard sales as a form of neighborhood revitalization, though I doubt anyone selling from their yards sees it that way. We've been at yard sales for so long it follows tradition more than trendy renewal. The call-in show you're hearing," he pointed to an overhead speaker, "has been airing on the AM dial ever since I can remember. Yard-sale hunters will drive around listening to callers announce their address and the big-ticket items."

Leaving a dollar in their tip jar, we walked the enclave of shaded residential streets, passing three yard sales, one for every speed bump, and pausing at the fourth when his mom recognized the Mucho Mocha cup in my hand. The driveway prices were refreshingly not much higher than what I remember from twenty years ago when my mom bargain hunted with Dustin and me in tow. A porch swing for thirty bucks. Barstools for fifteen apiece. A backpack for ten. Baseball gloves and fishing poles for five each. Pots and pans a dollar. A bottle opener for fifty cents.

Back at the hotel Dustin was unlatching the luggage carrier from the top of our vehicle. He wanted us to wait in our parking spot with the carrier while he ran the vehicle through the automatic carwash at the neighboring gas station. But on the instinct of your fascination I volunteered for the chore, buckling you beside me for a front-row seat. You sat straight up, your eyes peering over the dashboard and your sense of adventure revved for

To Bianca   225

your first experience of "giving the car a bath." The vehicle jerked
as its tires locked into the conveyor and steadied us into the misty
garage. Safe in the dry interior and relishing the omnidirectional
cascade of jet spray against the sunroof and windshield, you gave
the satisfied "aaaah" I was hoping for. Then to the spinning col-
umns of foamers darkening our windows with their soapy scrub
down, I guessed from your intense anticipation of their bright
colors and fluffy shapes a likening to the friendly monsters from
your cartoons. At the carwash exit, cannons of industrial blow-
ers dried the exterior from all angles, hastening the last beads of
water across our windshield, now cleared of bugs and the layers of
dust from five states.

Dustin raced us out of Iowa. Departing from Des Moines on
I-80 for Omaha, I found the same AM station that was airing in
the café. By now the call-ins for yard sales had turned to farmers
announcing cattle for sale, citing the previous year's drought for a
lack of feed. Others, selling tractors and combines, signed off with
a prayer for rain.

"What are we listening to?" Your mom and Dustin disapproved.

"It's Saturday in Iowa, where else are we ever going to hear
farm shows?"

"Anywhere across all the sameness between Ohio and the Rockies." Dustin had a point—the western half of Iowa was another
Ohio of gradually sloping fields. For as straight as the highways
and interstates proceeded, the sense of our progress amounted to
only a vagueness of going from one state to the next, as though
the roads moved through us in a circling repeat of endless plains
broken only by the next city, Chicago to Des Moines to Omaha; by
the next river, the Ohio to the Mississippi to the Missouri; and by
the shedding of one country-music signal for the next.

"What are we listening to now?" Dustin again disapproved.

"There's nothing but country stations."

Crossing the Missouri River into Nebraska, Dustin's critical
mood of Ohio resurfaced as the same negativity toward your
mom's billboard-prompted proposal for a steakhouse lunch.

226   RESPONSIBLE DISTRACTIONS

"Haven't you heard Omaha steaks are the best?"

"Because what else would Omaha be known for?"

"Corn?" I defended.

"Great steaks are the default claim of boring cities, except for Dayton, which doesn't have anything."

"I'm sure the people here are very nice," your mom said. But by the time Dustin pulled off the interstate at one of Omaha's suburban exits he'd changed his mind for margaritas and tacos.

"I didn't pass up barbeque to have tacos in Nebraska," your mom said. "There's better Mexican food in Phoenix."

Dustin counted aloud three cantinas as they passed by, the wide brims of neon margarita glasses outlined across their cloudy windows, before parking at the first barbeque joint.

Over an order of sticky ribs, Dustin lobbied we cut the day short and hotel in Lincoln for the night.

"It's already afternoon," he said, "and there's nothing past Lincoln. We have all day to go as far as we want tomorrow."

Dustin ordered another beer, free to indulge once I agreed to take the wheel. But, after Lincoln I kept driving, turning us off I-80 for Hastings and continuing on the state highways, the boundless farmlands gradually giving way from corn to wheat as the topsoil thinned. Between the small towns of Minden, Holdrege, Arapahoe, and Cambridge—all centered by grain elevators—ran the railways alongside the highways, the trains outpaced by flatbed traffic. AM radio hourly reported the Ag market's crop futures. We stopped for the night in McCook.

The next morning we continued headlong into what Dustin offhandedly meant by more of the "nothing past Lincoln." South from McCook, western Kansas opened into a stark nothingness, a spacious vastness every bit as imposing as Appalachia's mountains or Chicago's skyline. The morning sunrise simmered slower against our east-facing vehicle windows, as though the sun needed double the golden hour to rise over the land's furthering expanses; land that once we started the day's drive southward stretched tight as a tablecloth to the horizon. Once an afterthought at twelve or so miles ahead, now the horizon lay a dramatic twenty or thirty miles off, bordering the land from the equally constant sky. Across the wavier seas of wheat crops the dustier emptiness of the plains exiled the few passing towns, their Main Street centerpieces of grain silos hulking into view halfway to the next town in a sequence yielding more dust than bugs on our windshield. Through Oberlin, Oakley, Scott City, Garden City, and Cimarron, the larger towns were populated enough for a water tower, the smaller no more than picnic-table stops. After a town aptly named Plains we stopped in Liberal for refueling before Highway 54 dipped into the finger of Oklahoma.

"Looks like I can finally get a margarita." Dustin noted the billboard for a Mexican restaurant alongside another for the Wizard of Oz museum.

"Or tacos," your mom responded to the food truck parked at the gas station we pulled into.

The taco truck's long lunch line was comprised entirely of shift workers on break from the nearby beef-packing plant, its cow's-head logo imprinted on their shirts. All of them turned to take notice of us walking you inside the convenience mart for a bathroom break while Dustin manned the gas pump.

"Never mind stopping for lunch here," she said at the mirror of the bathroom sink, sizing up her minimal makeup.

"I'm in no condition to be seen today. Not with my hair like this." She combed out a strand of tangles. "And not in these sweats."

The next town of Hooker, Oklahoma, was too small for lunch options, and it was Sunday, so the sleepy burger stop that didn't appear open probably wasn't. Twenty more miles of Highway 54 foretold by road sign the usual fast-food stops in the larger town of Guymon.

In Guymon we joined the after-church rush for the lunch buffet at a pizzeria called Mazzios. I was finishing my second slice and picking off the bits of sausage from yours—"buggies," you refused—when my phone rang. The church was calling. I motioned you over to your mom's lap as Pastor Kraikmeyer's stony voice straightened my spine. He wanted to know why he hadn't seen me lately.

"I don't live in Washington anymore," I said.

Dustin and your mom's suddenly concerned attention drove me to the parking lot.

"Where did you move?"

"Phoenix."

"Were you planning on letting us know?"

"I need to find a job and apartment first."

"Yes. But as a point of wise counsel we advise everybody to meet with us beforehand about whether leaving us is really in their best interest."

"It didn't occur to me."

"If we'd met with you beforehand and agreed that leaving us was in good reason we would work with you to confirm a suitable church elsewhere, but in your case, we can allow you time to join a new church. Any longer and you're in violation of their signed covenant to continue church elsewhere."

At this point I was too pissed off to say anything beyond whatever it took to abort the call, blaming the disruptive wind and agreeing to their expectations, but if you were to read this conversation later, absent of any history or sense of tone, I wonder if it reads too matter-of-fact to sound as personally upsetting as I've internalized. I can hardly relive it now, and especially not then, in its hollowing aftermath of kneeling by our vehicle in the remote panhandle of Oklahoma to cry it all out, the word "excommunication" triggering tides of disappointment over Tom. Or the sense of failing to meet the endless burden of explaining myself, such as whether I knew Tom, whom they had excommunicated, or what I knew of your situation in the way of caring for you, whose questionable custody I hid under threat of a child-services investigation. I wanted credit to be left to my own responsibility, not more of their cornering questions, which instead assumed my irresponsibility and frustrated our only continuing basis of interaction.

"What happened?" Your mom appeared beside me, placing a hand on my shoulder.

"I'm not sure of anything anymore. I'm sorry."

"Who called?"

"Remember when Tom called you about Bianca's custody?"

"Tom called?"

"No, the pastors who'd originally raised questions about Bianca's guardianship—they called."

"About Bianca?"

"About all sorts of crap. Wanting to know why I left and what my plans are for Phoenix. It's too upsetting to explain, but I'm doubting everything now. It especially hurts because involving myself in church was meant in good faith and now with Bianca and you crossing the country on my promises for more stability, all my intentions fall under doubt. I don't know if moving was the right decision."

"Nicole, sometimes you won't know if a decision was good or bad until after you're forced to decide."

"But what if this move turns out to be a terrible idea?"

"It'll only get better once we get there. Moving is a decision I should've made long ago."

"Thank you." I stood to hug her. "I just feel so helpless over this failure regarding church, especially given how it works out for the good of so many others."

"You're the most responsible person I know." Your mom embraced me.

When lunch ended in Guymon, Dustin had you bring me a brownie from the dessert buffet, which was very sweet of you; thank you. Dustin withheld asking anything, avoiding my likely embarrassment and having learned since we were youngsters that there wasn't much to say to an upset sister. To fill the silent letdown in our vehicle, Dustin found a classic country station and let the lonesome voices of Hank Williams and Marty Robbins narrate our crossing into the Texas panhandle. Gone was the sage-green surface of Kansas for a sun-stricken paleness from one single grain-elevator town to the next, first through Stratford, with its Texas-state high school football banners rustling in the blowing dusts of its dryer basin, the potential for dust storms matched by my still-churning thoughts. Ahead, the larger town of Dalhart smelled like cattle. The railroads joining alongside the highways through Dalhart were occupied with stock cars packed with livestock, heading, we guessed, to the meat-packing facilities we'd passed back in Kansas. Just beyond Dalhart two large cattle feedlots spread out from either side of Highway 54, their muddy enclosures segmenting cattle by the hundreds. "Moo-moos," you proudly shouted. I'd never seen so many either.

Empty railroads paralleled the highway all the way into New Mexico, crossing the Dust Bowl barrenness of land save for the few vertical interruptions of seesawing oil derricks and rickety windmills marking the isolated ranches. Outside the lake town of Logan, the grass and farmlands, flat or gently rolling since the Ohio River, finally broke open into the jaggedness we knew of the desert Southwest. Over the Canadian River a dramatic stretch of trestle bridge crossed what was more of a canyon delineating the nearly dry river on its way to the Route 66 town of Tucumcari; our first appreciations of the Southwest continued at the sight of Tucumcari Mountain, more of a dark bluff, rising at Highway 54's joining of I-40.

By crossing into New Mexico and gaining an hour in the Mountain time zone, it was only 5PM, our hotel's earliest check-in time, where we planned to channel surf until we felt like dinner. The unexpected concern, as Dustin checked in at the front desk, were the bikers loitering along the hotel's second-floor railing, their twenty-some bikes at the edge of the lot giving them away, as did their black leather vests.

"The Bandidos," your mom said. "I recognize their vests from one of the casinos where I waitressed. They'd stop through on their rides, drunk and drugged as anything."

No way we stay here tonight, I determined, but I wasn't about to rush across the lot and pull Dustin away from the check-in desk because we were drawing notice.

"One of the bouncers I worked with was a hangaround for the Bandidos. You can spot them." Your mom looked at the bikes parked a few spots away. "They guard the bikes and pickups."

"What's taking Dustin so long?" I wanted to speed off, but he had the keys. Only a biker gang could find two girls and a toddler parked at a hotel suspicious enough to approach.

To Bianca   231

"Can we help you?" one of the bikers asked. Your mom, lowering her back-seat window, took over, thank goodness, because I tensed into a nervousness beyond the shudder of facing Tara at her worst. These bikers lurching at our windows were convicts, addicts, maybe gunrunners, and all the other unnerving degeneracies reeking more in my mind as smoke and alcohol and tattoos and leather through the open window.

"You wouldn't happen to have a cigarette?"

"Sure," they obliged. "You girls staying the night?"

"Should we stop by later?"

As they bantered my gaze drifted to the moody figure of Tucumcari Mountain beyond the hotel, as though to steady my racing thoughts above the worry of the attention gathering our way from the rest of the bikers along the second-floor railing.

When Dustin finally emerged he wasn't but a few steps outside before slowing at the sudden notice of the three bikers at our vehicle. His awareness of the rest was returned with glares. Dustin searched across the lot for my eye as to what to do. I placed my hand on the steering wheel to motion him back to the driver's seat, leaving a sweaty palm print on its rim.

Once Dustin was back behind the wheel he powered the engine to lower the windows.

"Good idea," I muttered.

"There wasn't anybody at the front desk to check us in. I say we go find dinner until somebody comes back."

"Can we grab a bite while refueling?" I said. "Then hit the interstate?"

"There's pretty much nothing until Albuquerque."

"We can't stay here," I insisted, before composing myself. "I'll drive."

From Tucumcari, its lone mountain withdrew in the plateaued distance. As for dinner, only the pit-stop towns of Santa Rosa and Moriarty offered anything more than a gas pump and payphone, so we headed on, the three hours toward Albuquerque darkening to the brink of dusk. Preceded only by a few stubbier mesas, the land at last lifted into the sight of our first mountain ranges, the southernmost reaches of the Rockies jaggedly contrasted by the deepening sunset, its long-awaited homeward colors bloodshot. The mountain range before Albuquerque approached like a dead end—there couldn't be an opening through its solid wall—but of course the interstate snaked its way through to the vast lights of Albuquerque blanketing the valley.

In Albuquerque we stopped for dinner at a cantina where Dustin finished his first margarita before our orders arrived. On your mom's advice I got a bowl of the regionally famed red chili while Dustin countered with the green chili and another margarita. For you your mom ordered guacamole.

"So now what?" Dustin asked. "Find a hotel down the road?"

"You want to just drive through the night? We're only one state away."

"Have you visited the Grand Canyon?" your mom asked.

We all had.

"What about Monument Valley?"

We shook our heads.

"We should do sunrise at Monument Valley!"

Monument Valley wasn't directly on the way to Flagstaff, the last turn in our final course to Phoenix; we'd need to detour north into the Four Corners of the Navajo lands.

"We've bought ourselves pretty much another day by skipping Tucumcari. You'll have to drive, Nicole."

"While you snooze off your drinks," I said, adding a coffee to go when the waitress returned.

Coffee kept me going as everyone else slept away the long drive toward New Mexico's far northwest towns of Farmington and Shiprock. After exiting the heavier traffic of the Denver-bound interstate past the last lights of Albuquerque, the big desert night rolled on as only land, stars, and cool air. I cracked open our windows to inhale the enlivening fullness of the high-desert breeze, its detoxing effects relaxing my body more than my mind until reduced to a blade's edge of consciousness sharpening against the harder rocks of the day's reliving.

I'd cried today, and nearly lost it again given those bikers, both

To Bianca

for about the only few times since you came into my life. This only after crying a few times in wake of my mom's death, once on the night of being jailed with your mom last summer and never when Edith was on my case or when Tara and I fought. It's not like me to fall apart, and it's not the Bandidos unsettling me—it's church, mile after mile. Of how I wish it didn't come across as a checklist I couldn't live up to. Do I doubt, do I confess, do I repent? Maybe that's my misinterpretation of church?

Nevertheless its impossibility forgets the peace that passes understanding, to remember the New Testament's wording. That is to say there is a transcendence church can speak for but never truly impart within the individual, and when church takes itself as arbiter of the Christian walk, there's no way I can answer any of their concerns for you by answering what a miracle you are to me—you, yourself, your very being.

I've mentioned margaritas and smoking weed, prison and whatever else you've been exposed to at so young an age, but when you're old enough to hear me out, please know that as church over and over emphasizes the harms of lust it's also our unforgiveness, indwelling anger, greedy personal competitions, envy, and drunkenness that also act as a blindness from being able to appreciate the world softened with innocence, as God surely sees it. Knowing this, I've come to reevaluate certain beatitudes—Blessed are the pure in heart, for they will see God—as also Blessed are the pure in heart, for they will see *as God sees*. Or as David's prayers in 2nd Samuel follow—to the pure you show yourself pure—as to the pure you show *your world as pure*. That essence of purity is a daily life lived apart from unforgiveness, anger, envious competition, and my past of drunkenness, a life of not grieving the Holy Spirit, to recall another verse. I never knew what it was to see the world as God does until I saw the world through your innocence. It's in that lived innocence when I most trust that my prayers are heard. The way through hours as dark as these is prayer, and there's plenty to pray for in anticipation of our beginning anew in Phoenix.

Starting tomorrow, I remind myself.

It was well past midnight when we stopped for refueling at the first open gas station we came across in Farmington. After bathroom breaks Dustin bought me another coffee and asked how many hours were left to sunrise at Monument Valley. With everybody soon lulled back asleep, I tried the radio at a soft volume, its scanner landing on one of those overnight paranormal call-ins, the first caller recounting a UFO sighting and the second questioning whether the government controls the weather. The next channel spoke another language, not your familiar Spanish, but Dine, the ancient Navajo dialect. We'd entered into the expansive Navajo reservation, and for the first time I caught sight of Shiprock Peak, its darker outline knifing the horizon in the starry distance, more jagged and imposing than Tucumcari's lone mountain. Even in the dark I wanted to wake everybody, and if it weren't for Monument Valley ahead, experience sunset under the shadow of Shiprock. Hoping to share the view, I quickly gave the passenger seats a glance, and to my surprise you were wide awake, chewing your pacifier. It was only the two of us again, like our many shared winter nights in Washington, and to see your nocturnally wide eyes absorbing the midnight world, I can't tell you how glad I was for our togetherness to continue in Phoenix.

"Drums." I turned the radio's Navajo instrumentals up. You clutched your blankie, happy and calm, reminding me of it being said how children are wonderful observers but terrible little interpreters, which exemplifies the innocence I'm attempting to point out: that as you come to age your wide-eyed vision narrows into the self-preserving work of interpretation. Yes, your mom and I have watched out for you in ways you cannot, passing by strangers whose faces you unselfconsciously study from your stroller but lost apart from your eyes is the world reborn.

And how can the world appear any more reborn than at dawn, the sunrise setting Monument Valley afire? The red rock and sandstone of its mesas, buttes, and chimney rocks burning with immense color as we spread blankets for seating on the dry desert floor. I watched with the amazed weariness of no sleep since Nebraska. All of our wonder for once matched what for you naturally flowers from of the simplest moments of fireflies along the Ohio River, the scarecrow overlooking Indiana's cornfields, the rains over Chicago's skyline, the automatic carwash in Iowa. I can try to detail Monument Valley for the sake of remembering together, but awe strains description and is better left to the majesty of its impact. You will remember the stillness as I do, and anyway, I was falling asleep even before Dustin and your mom were ready to leave. Back at the vehicle they left you and me to sleep in the back seat while they spent the morning hiking the red desert. They returned a few hours later, escorted by a Navajo guide on horseback, warning against further wandering the native lands. I awoke to your mom talking the guide out of calling the park service, her voice joining the cool air through the slightly open vehicle windows. It was nearly noon. The sun at full strength. Dustin, taking over our last day of driving, began a mile or so on the Utah side of Monument Valley, straddled by the state border, and soon we crossed into Arizona, your new home.

I could also detail our first hours together in Arizona, driving the bluffs and bare canyon ledges of Navajo Nation. Dustin pointed out sightings of eight-sided ceremonial lodges, "hogans." I briefly awoke to his explanation of the Navajo people's ancient corn cultivation using soil only an inch deep. Otherwise I half-slept off our drive, remembering what I remembered from the years before leaving Arizona. How nearing Flagstaff from the north the high desert gives way to the pine forests familiar from my childhood summer camps in northern Arizona.

After their morning of hiking, Dustin and your mom kept to easy enough terms to extend our late lunch of pizza into more than a few rounds of drinks that lasted into the early evening. By the time we departed Flagstaff on I-17, I was rested enough to take the wheel of our last leg to Phoenix, a one hundred and forty-mile stretch I'd driven before, and this time, our time, anticipating like never before the darker pine country lowering to hotter desert and the land holding the day's final heat when at long last the vast lights of Phoenix danced in the cooling night.

Without anything of pressing consequence to tell you, I've just taken a seat in a downtown bagel shop, not too far a walk from where we're renting in Phoenix. I'm so far the first and only customer, ordering a blonde roast before settling at the window facing the morning sun brimming in the downtown's glassy gathering of corporate towers. The day promises to be another late-July scorcher, as sunny as hot. Last night never fully cooled off, and it's why I'm up and about so early on a quiet Saturday. The heat shallowed my sleep, and all night I awoke to the overworked respiring of our window AC unit unable to sink me to the cooler bottom of uninterrupted rest. But as I swore by in Washington, give me the desert heat over the winters of the East and the sun over the icy months held fast by darkness, though with enough blankets sleep was never as fleeting as in last night's heat.

Three months have passed since that evening we coasted into a seasonably breezier Phoenix. Brad, a childhood acquaintance, allowed us to crash in the extra room of his house just off the light-rail north of downtown, while your mom and I started our searches for work and housing. Notice my referring to Brad as an *acquaintance*—he's much more than that. For starters, we're childhood friends on the basis of our moms being best friends. He's five years older than me, and though our moms teased us both about dating, they were never serious about encouraging us. Instead I once dated one of his friends, a coworker of his, during a summer internship that Brad had gotten me at his law firm, so you see, he continues to offer much help. An acquaintance, I refer to him out of teasing deference to his fiancé, whom I'm certain prefers the two of us to see ourselves as such and whom I'm more certain did not want your mom and me living with Brad for very long, if understandably not at all. But I'd months earlier given Brad a heads-up about hoping he could let us use his empty room, and more importantly his mom supported us staying there, as part of her looking out for Dustin and me in the wake of our mom's passing, even offering her place if

To Bianca

it wasn't too inconvenient to stay so far to the west of the metro area.

Thankfully it took us only three weeks to secure work and a place to rent. Each weekday of those three weeks started out like today, with me marching down to a coffee shop by the light-rail stop. After the first week of using the Wi-Fi to apply and send resumes over the usual job-posting sites, the interviews started lining up, first as initial phone screenings. On more than a few mornings after returning from the coffee shop I'd find you tiptoeing atop a chair at the bathroom mirror beside your mom, swimming in the adventure of dress up, the air clouded by foundation powder and the countertops taken over by the full gamut of her moisturizers, mascaras, concealers, blushes, lipsticks, and eyebrow pencils (which we stopped you from marking the walls with).

Your mom is always proud to style herself as though guest-listed for the very nightclubs where her first wave of interviews gave her reason to do so, and similarly I'm proud to tie my hair back and dress business formal as a few of my applications turned into formal interviews. Your mom is as proud to show off her Las Vegas experience in all ways of cocktail waitressing, bartending, and heading up bottle service as I am of my contract-auditing experience. I'm proud of my political science degree from the University of Arizona and telling my interviewers how glad I am to return home. And as of two months ago, I'm proud to be employed as a paralegal by a firm of trial attorneys that Brad's firm regularly sits opposite of during depositions.

My hiring was, in part, aided by glossy references from Edith and Brad.

Don't let me forget what's prompted me to update you on this bright morning. Today is the one-year anniversary of my arrest for DUI, an arrest resulting in the night I was jailed with your mom. As absurd as that sounds it speaks to how far she and I have responsibly moved on. I'll have to mention the anniversary to your mom later today. The three of us should celebrate with dinner somewhere. I'll be sure to ask you where we should go.

After all, you're owed much credit for activating within me a nurturing purpose that has served to restore me from the sinking unrest my life was becoming in wake of my mom's passing. I still mean to bring you to my mom's grave in Tucson, for her sake as much as yours. Forgive that last bit of sentiment, but my Mom's gravestone is where I spent July Fourth. You stayed with your mom, playing with the neighbor's little girl until fireworks arched over the skyline, which our backyard boasts clear view of over the railyard.

The neighbors, who also own the duplex, thankfully encourage our feeding and trapping of cats in the backyard we share. They're an older couple, raising their grandchild, a little girl only a few months your senior. They're glad to have you as the first real playmate for their toddler, the feeling of course mutual, your mom tells them. The grandfather is retired navy. His hats commemorate the ships he's sailed. The grandmother, retired from teaching, waters the backyard's palms and cactus of saguaro, prickly pear, and cholla while I'm readying for work in the mornings, a peaceful sight under watch of the Phoenix skyline. They're glad to rent to us. We pay $900/month for the two-bedroom, 1.5-bathroom layout.

Our neighborhood easily falls under the label of "working class" by most any account of the vehicles parked at the houses down our street: Phoenix PD and airport-parking security cruisers, utility trucks for pest control and satellite cable, a bread-delivery truck and a food truck emblazoned with "Carne Asada" across both sides. This is largely a bilingual neighborhood around the railyard, with more residences like ours filling the lots between a veteran's cemetery, warehouses, and a high-fenced storage lot supplying the railyard with cable spools, stacked piping, and pallets of sheet metal. There's a Catholic church and a Spanish gospel church where, for the past few Sundays, the three of us have attended. A few of the songs are sung in English, but the sermon, communion, offering, and the greetings at the door are all in Spanish. I explained this when my former pastors called. Hesitant regarding my choice when I attempted my new church's full name—"Iglesia Evangelica de Phoenix"—they encouraged me to find a church home among the evangelical options prevalent across such a large city.

Phoenix certainly is a large city. Over four million people reside in and around its commuting radius of Maricopa County. But for its growing and transient population it's not so uncommon to come across a few recognizable faces closer to where Dustin and I graduated high school on the north side. Just last week, while I was waiting in line at the Fry's grocery store where I worked in high school, I recognized the similarly aged red-haired cashier from my time there. Eight years ago—has it been that long? Had he worked here this whole time? Living with his parents while I'd gone to college in Tucson and started a career in Washington? Not that I wanted him to recognize me after nearly a decade, but him handing me the receipt provided a swell of perspective on staying safely put verses taking faraway risks.

I haven't yet detailed your mom's work. For a while she bartended weekends at a nightclub until a sports bar in Tempe hired her for double the evening shifts in the lead up to the fall return of both the weekend football crowds and the nightly student crowds when classes go back in session on the Arizona State campus. It's an arrangement that on most days covers caring for you because I can usually catch the light-rail from work in time to be home before your mom leaves for her evening shift. At first we used daycare to handle any overlap of mutual absence, but your mom is on friendly enough terms with the grandma next door to leave you in her care. She insists on supporting your stayovers as playtime with her granddaughter.

Your mom wakes with you in the morning and keeps you through the night after getting home from work. Either she puts you to bed or comes home to find you properly put to sleep after I've read you bedtime stories. Now and again she mentions your father. After her latest weekly call with him, she got to asking me about how power of attorney would work for your dad to sign over the Porsche to her name for Arizona registration. She speculates what his release in three years will mean for the two of you.

We'll see. Until then you're beside her through most every night, save the few you've braved the dark hallway to stay with me. Take last weekend, when the peak of Arizona's monsoon season rolled over the desert, serving the skies over Phoenix more lightning than rain, the midnight hours flashing like a welding shop right outside our windows before the brief rains raised the smell of earth. I heard your little steps right before your wide eyes peered into my half-opened doorway. Summoned by my open arms you scrambled into bed beside me. You were already falling asleep as I whispered, "Where will your mommy think Cupcake went *de la manana*?"

We'll see. Until then, and always, I am with you.

ABRAHAM TIMLER works as a Marine Engineer along the Pacific Coast. He is a graduate of the University of Arizona and resides in San Diego, CA. This is his first novel.

Made in the USA
Las Vegas, NV
07 September 2024

94894604R00134